African Myths

African Myths

General Editor: Jake Jackson

Associate Editor: Catherine Taylor

FLAME TREE
PUBLISHING

This is a FLAME TREE Book

FLAME TREE PUBLISHING
6 Melbray Mews
Fulham, London SW6 3NS
United Kingdom
www.flametreepublishing.com

First published 2019

19 21 23 22 20
1 3 5 7 9 8 6 4 2

ISBN: 978-1-78755-274-6

Contributors, authors, editors and sources for this series include: Loren Auerbach, Norman Bancroft-Hunt, George W. Bateman, E.M. Berens, Katharine Berry Judson, W.H.I. Bleek and L. C. Lloyd, Laura Bulbeck, Jeremiah Curtin, Elphinstone Dayrell, O.B. Duane, Dr Ray Dunning, W.W. Gibbings, H. A. Guerber, James A. Honey M.D., Jake Jackson, Joseph Jacobs, Judith John, J.W. Mackail, Donald Mackenzie, Chris McNab, Minnie Martin, Professor James Riordan, Sara Robson, Lewis Spence, Henry M. Stanley, Capt. C.H. Stigand, Rachel Storm, K.E. Sullivan, François-Marie Arouet a.k.a. Voltaire, E.A. Wallis Budge, Dr Roy Willis, Epiphanius Wilson, Alice Werner, E.T.C. Werner.

A copy of the CIP data for this book is available from the British Library.

Printed and bound by Clays Ltd, Elcograf S.p.A

Contents

Series Foreword 10

Introduction to African Myths 12
African Storytelling 13
A Diverse Mythology 14
Origins of the World 14
Witchcraft and Sorcery 16
Animal Myths 18
Sacrifice and Offerings 20
Death 22

Myths of Origin, Death & The Afterlife 25
The Creation of the Universe 26
Obatala Creates Mankind 28
Olokun's Revenge 30
Agemo Outwits Olokun 32
The Gods Descend from the Sky 34
God Abandons the Earth 35
The Coming of Darkness 37
The Sun and the Moon 38
Why the Sun and the Moon Live in the Sky 39
Why the Moon Waxes and Wanes 40
The Story of the Prince Who Insisted on Possessing the Moon 41
The Story of the Lightning and the Thunder 46
How Death First Entered the World 47
Wanjiru, Sacrificed by Her Family 50
The Chameleon (How Death Came into the World) 53
King Kitamba Kia Shiba (and the Kingdom of Death) 54
How Ngunza Defied Death 56

The Man Who Would Shoot Iruwa.......57
The Road to Heaven.......59
The Tale of Murile.......61
How a Girl Reached the Land of the Ghosts and Came Back.......65
Why Dead People Are Buried.......67
The King and the Ju Ju Tree.......68

Animal Stories & Fables.......72

How Anansi Became a Spider.......73
Anansi Obtains the Sky God's Stories.......75
Anansi and the Corn Cob.......79
Tortoise and the Wisdom of the World.......83
The Tortoise and the Baboon.......85
Tortoise and the Hot-water Test.......87
The Tortoise and the Elephant.......91
Tortoises Hunting Ostriches.......93
Why the Worms Live Underneath the Ground.......94
How the Leopard Got His Spots.......95
The Donkey Who Sinned.......96
The Two Suns.......98
Gihilihili: The Snake-man.......99
The Story of the Hunters and the Big Snake.......102
How Ra-Molo Became a Snake.......103
The Ape, the Snake and the Lion.......105
How the Dog Came to Live with Man.......110
The Truth About Cock's Comb.......113
Chameleon Wins a Wife.......115
The Chief and the Tigers.......119
The Lion of Manda.......121
The Hyena and the Moonbeam.......124
The Jackal and the Wolf.......124
Cloud Eating.......125
Cock and Jackal.......126

The Lion, the Hyena and the Hare 126
Why the Bat Flies by Night 127
The Fish and the Leopard's Wife; or, Why the Fish Lives in the Water 128
Why the Flies Bother the Cows 129
Why the Cat Kills Rats 130
Segu the Honey Guide 130
Why a Hawk Kills Chickens 131
The King and the Nsiat Bird 133
The Kites and the Crows 134
Tink-Tinkje 136
The Lost Message 138
The Monkey's Fiddle 139
The Lioness and the Ostrich 141
Crocodile's Treason 142
The Judgment of Baboon 146
The Zebra Stallion 148
When Lion Could Fly 148
Why Has Jackal a Long Black Stripe on His Back? 149
Horse Cursed by Sun 150
Lion's Defeat 150
The Monkey, the Shark and the Washerman's Donkey 151
A Hospitable Gorilla 155

Stories of Wit & Wisdom 159

The Rich Man and the Poor Man 160
How Walukaga Answered the King 163
The Young Man and the Skull 166
The Story of the Glutton 168
The Feast 173
The Three Tests 175
The Two Rogues 180

The Girls Who Wanted New Teeth 186
The Kinyamkela's Bananas 189
The Two Brothers 190
The Tale of Nyengebule 192
The Story of Takane 195
How Khosi Chose a Wife 200
Lelimo and the Magic Cap 203
The Famine 205
The Cat's Tail 206
The Young Thief 207
The Woodcutter and His Donkey 212
Kitangatanga of the Sea 215
The Story of the Fools 218
The Poor Man and his Wife of Wood 222
The Sultan's Daughter 225
The Woman with Two Skins 226
Ituen and the King's Wife 231
Of the Pretty Stranger Who Killed the King 234
Of the Fat Woman Who Melted Away 235
The Lucky Fisherman 237
Goso, the Teacher 238
The Magician and the Sultan's Son 242
King Gumbi and His Lost Daughter 245
Out of the Mouths of Babes 253

Series Foreword

STRETCHING BACK to the oral traditions of thousands of years ago, tales of heroes and disaster, creation and conquest have been told by many different civilizations in many different ways. Their impact sits deep within our culture even though the detail in the tales themselves are a loose mix of historical record, transformed narrative and the distortions of hundreds of storytellers.

Today the language of mythology lives with us: our mood is jovial, our countenance is saturnine, we are narcissistic and our modern life is hermetically sealed from others. The nuances of myths and legends form part of our daily routines and help us navigate the world around us, with its half truths and biased reported facts.

The nature of a myth is that its story is already known by most of those who hear it, or read it. Every generation brings a new emphasis, but the fundamentals remain the same: a desire to understand and describe the events and relationships of the world. Many of the great stories are archetypes that help us find our own place, equipping us with tools for self-understanding, both individually and as part of a broader culture.

For Western societies it is Greek mythology that speaks to us most clearly. It greatly influenced the mythological heritage of the ancient Roman civilization and is the lens through which we still see the Celts, the Norse and many of the other great peoples and religions. The Greeks themselves learned much from their neighbours, the Egyptians, an older culture that became weak with age and incestuous leadership.

It is important to understand that what we perceive now as mythology had its own origins in perceptions of the divine and the rituals of the sacred. The earliest civilizations, in the crucible of the Middle East, in the Sumer of the third millennium BC, are the source to which many of the mythic archetypes can be traced. As humankind collected together in cities for the first time, developed writing and industrial scale agriculture, started to irrigate the rivers and attempted to control rather than be at the mercy of its environment, humanity began to write down its tentative explanations of natural events, of floods and plagues, of disease.

Early stories tell of Gods (or god-like animals in the case of tribal societies such as African, Native American or Aboriginal cultures) who are crafty and use their wits to survive, and it is reasonable to suggest that these were the first rulers of the gathering peoples of the earth, later elevated to god-like status with the distance of time. Such tales became more political as cities vied with each other for supremacy, creating new Gods, new hierarchies for their pantheons. The older Gods took on primordial roles and became the preserve of creation and destruction, leaving the new gods to deal with more current, everyday affairs. Empires rose and fell, with Babylon assuming the mantle from Sumeria in the 1800s BC, then in turn to be swept away by the Assyrians of the 1200s BC; then the Assyrians and the Egyptians were subjugated by the Greeks, the Greeks by the Romans and so on, leading to the spread and assimilation of common themes, ideas and stories throughout the world.

The survival of history is dependent on the telling of good tales, but each one must have the 'feeling' of truth, otherwise it will be ignored. Around the firesides, or embedded in a book or a computer, the myths and legends of the past are still the living materials of retold myth, not restricted to an exploration of origins. Now we have devices and global communications that give us unparalleled access to a diversity of traditions. We can find out about Native American, Indian, Chinese and tribal African mythology in a way that was denied to our ancestors, we can find connections, match the archaeology, religion and the mythologies of the world to build a comprehensive image of the human experience that is endlessly fascinating.

The stories in this book provide an introduction to the themes and concerns of the myths and legends of their respective cultures, with a short introduction to provide a linguistic, geographic and political context. This is where the myths have arrived today, but undoubtedly over the next millennia, they will transform again whilst retaining their essential truths and signs.

Jake Jackson
General Editor

Introduction to African Myths

AFRICA IS A VAST CONTINENT, over three times the size of the United States of America, incorporating a huge expanse of desert and scrubland, mountains, valleys, rain forests, swamps, rivers and lakes. For much of its history, however, a large part of southern Africa has remained cut off from the outside world. The Sahara Desert, which divides the north from the south, covers nearly one third of the continent, presenting an almost impossible obstacle for even the most resilient traveller.

North Africa stretches from Morocco to Egypt, and down through the Nile valley as far as Ethiopia. This rich and fertile region nurtures a distinctly Mediterranean culture dominated by Muslim and Christian religions. Africa south of the Sahara – the area from which the myths and legends of this book derive – extends from the east and west Sudan, down through the savannas and central rain forests right into South Africa.

Sub-Saharan Africa is a land of colourful contrasts and diverse cultures, many of which have existed for hundreds and even thousands of years. Archaeological research has revealed that by about 1200 BC, rich and powerful civilizations, such as that of Ancient Egypt, had developed in the northern part of Africa. Nothing now remains of these impressive empires, but their customs and beliefs are well recorded. Relatively little is known, on the other hand, of the earliest history of the peoples living south of the Sahara. Geographical isolation dictated that these peoples developed largely by themselves. Written culture became widespread only in the nineteenth century; before that time, the art of writing was completely unknown to Africans in the equatorial forests and the south.

Europeans remained ignorant of the region's rich history until the fifteenth century when the Portuguese arrived on the west coast, landing at the Cape of Good Hope. Before long, they were transporting thousands of

African slaves to Europe and the Americas, a lucrative trade that continued until the mid-nineteenth century.

During the late nineteenth century, white settlers, among them the French, English and Dutch, began to explore further inland, and throughout the 1880s and 1890s they competed furiously for ownership of territories rich in natural resources, carving up the continent between them. By 1900, almost all of Africa was in European hands, remaining under European control until the 1950s, when the colonies began to demand their independence.

The radical changes forced on the African continent as a result of colonialism and the slave trade led to the destruction of many traditional societies which had evolved over the centuries. Much information on Africa's cultural heritage remains buried forever, since there are no ancient books or documents to enlighten us.

African Storytelling

But Africa has always had a powerful tradition of storytelling. Before a European way of life prevailed, the old religions, rules and customs provided the raw material for those tribesmen who first promoted this extremely colourful oral culture. African people have persevered with their storytelling and continue to leave records of their history in songs and stories they pass down from parent to child through the generations. Stories are commonly told in the evening when the day's work is done, accompanied by mime and frequently music. They are an important medium of entertainment and instruction woven out of the substance of human experience and are very often realistic and down-to-earth.

The first African stories to reach western ears were written down only at the turn of the century when a number of missionaries, anthropologists and colonial officials arrived in Africa and made a concerted effort to record descriptions of the rituals and ceremonies they witnessed, and to transcribe as faithfully as possible tales told to them by old and young Africans before they had disappeared altogether. Some of these committed scholars wrote down what the elders told them about their gods, while others transcribed narrative myths, fables, poems, proverbs, riddles and even magic spells. Most of the stories in this collection are from these original first-hand sources.

A Diverse Mythology

No real unified mythology exists in Africa, however. The migration of its peoples, the political fragmentation, and the sheer size of the continent have resulted in a huge diversity of lifestyles and traditions. Literally thousands of completely different languages are spoken, 2,000 in West Africa alone between the Senegal River and the headwaters of the Congo River. A complete collection of all myths of the African peoples would fill countless volumes, even if we were to ignore the fact that the collection is being added to all the time by modern-day enthusiasts.

To give a useful summary of the main characteristics of African mythology is therefore an extremely difficult task but, broadly speaking, a number of beliefs, ideas and themes are shared by African peoples, embellished by a creative spirit unique to a tribe, village or region. Nearly every tribe has its own set of cosmological myths – tales which attempt to explore the origin of the universe, the unseen forces of nature, the existence of God or a supreme being, the creation of mankind and the coming of mortality. Other stories, detailing the outrageous adventures and anti-social behaviour of one or another trickster figure are also common to nearly every tribe. Moral stories abound and animal fables, in particular, are some of the most popular of all African tales.

This book is divided into three sections containing only a cross-section of African tales. It is intended to provide an introduction to African mythology and is in no way a comprehensive study of its subject. A selection of creation stories, animal stories, and tales which amuse and teach has been made with the aim of providing as interesting and entertaining an overview as possible. But first, we will outline a little more about some key African mythological elements, beliefs and traditional practices.

Origins of the World

Supreme God

Despite its rich diversity, many African myths contain related themes, including gods and the origin of the world and humans. Most peoples in tropical and southern Africa share the hazy notion of a supreme sky god who originally lived on earth, but moved up to the sky by means of a spider's thread when humans started misbehaving. Earth and water are invariably goddesses. For the Yoruba, Ile is the goddess of earth and mother of all creatures; Yemoja is the goddess of water – her messengers are crocodile and hippopotamus and her daughter Aje is goddess of the Niger river from which Nigeria takes its name.

The Great Serpent

Given the prevalence of dangerous snakes in many parts of Africa, it is hardly surprising that several peoples talk of creation in terms of a huge serpent, usually a python, out of whose body the world and all creatures came. In northern areas, the sky god first made the cosmic serpent, whose head is in the sky and whose tail is in underground waters. In central and southern regions, the primordial serpent Chinawezi is identified with the rainbow. Whatever shape God's intermediary took, it is common for God to create sky and earth first, then fire and water, thunder and lightning. After these elements, the supreme being made the first living beings: a human, an elephant, a snake and a cow. In other legends, the supreme god first sent rain, lightning, locusts and then twins. Twins are often referred to as the 'children of heaven' and in some parts thought lucky, in others very unlucky and in the past have even been killed.

First Man and Woman

A widespread belief among the Zulus is that the first man and woman burst out of a reed; others say from a tree, yet others from a hole in the ground to the west of Lake Nyasa in Malawi. Many peoples do not speculate on the creation. The Masai of Kenya and Tanzania have a story about a time when meat hung down from the sky for people to eat. When it moved out of reach, people built a bamboo tower to the sky. To their surprise, sky messengers came down with three gifts: a bow to shoot the new wild animals in the bush, a plough with which to till the land in the new seasons of wind, rain and sun and a three-stringed fiddle to sing to in their leisure time. Other tales talk of earth and sky being connected by a rope by which gods sent down cattle.

In other creation stories, the world passed through three ages. First was an ideal or golden age when gods, humans and animals lived in harmony in a sort of celestial nirvana. Then came the age of creation in which the supreme god separated sky and earth, with the latter intended to mirror the harmony of the former age, and humans formed in the gods' image. But it did not work out, for humans were fallible and caused destruction, so introducing death: the Ashanti say humans set fire to the bush, so killing each other. The third age is the modern age where gods and humans live separately and people have lost their divine virtue of immortality completely. Through their myths and rituals, people are constantly trying to recreate the long-lost golden age.

Witchcraft and Sorcery

Sorcery has always played a big part in mythology all over Africa. Just as the difference between gods and spirits is blurred, so is the distinction between witchcraft and sorcery as conscious crafts. All that can be distinguished is the good or evil intent on the part of the person working the magic. The term 'doctor' (as in witch doctor) basically denotes a person skilled in any art or knowledge. So the doctor may be a diviner, herbalist, sage, storyteller, conjurer or dancer.

Some tribes claim that the 'doctor' is someone who develops special powers after a serious illness, during which time he communes with the spirits, having come close to death. Thereafter he is able to see spirits that are invisible to ordinary mortals. After apprenticeship to a professional and an initiation, he becomes skilled at dancing, singing and chanting, and is called upon to perform at funerals and other ceremonies.

The trance is a familiar phenomenon among many tribes. It is induced by doctors either spontaneously or by chewing certain hallucinatory herbs, inhaling their smoke or drinking a concoction which gives them superhuman strength and power to know and see things others cannot. The trance state may be caused, people believe, by a person's spirit leaving his body, travelling off into unknown regions and being possessed by spirits of the dead, so that when he returns he begins to speak in a strange way, telling of the wonderful things he has seen. It is the possessing spirits that enable him to cure an illness, bring rain or luck in hunting.

Such spiritual doctors have often had an exotic, even unkempt, appearance, letting their hair grow, smearing it with oil and ochre and adorning it with shells, feathers and charms – the insignia of their profession. They may have a magic wand in the form of a zebra tail on a stick which they wave about during exorcisms or other operations. The fly whisk carried by some African leaders is a remnant of this fusion of chieftainship and magic.

Sorcerers and Witches

Sorcerers and witches are naturally evil and perform black magic out of a hatred for people. Their tools are the spirits they control and they can enslave people by causing their death, before reviving them as the living dead – zombies (from the Congo word *zombi*, meaning 'enslaved spirit'). They also make fetishes possessed by servant spirits which fly through the air and attack victims. Often a victim dies of fright merely by seeing such a monster approaching.

Witches can change into animals at night or have animals as their familiars, especially baboons, hyenas, leopards or owls, and they can be seen flying through the air at night with fire coming out of their backsides. Their aim is to devour human bodies, dead or alive. But they can also change others into animals to be at their service. Mostly they brew poison, put it in the victim's food and enslave his or her spirit. The *muloyi* (or *mulaki*, *murozi*, *ndozi*, *ndoki* – all of which translate approximately to 'sorcerer') of Central Africa creates an *erirogho* (magic) mixture from the ashes of dead bodies, does a ritual dance around it and then mixes it with the victim's food or beer. Sometimes he adds the victim's fingernails, hair or earth from his footsteps to the *erirogho*, wrapping it in leaves or burying it beside the victim's house. The victim's spirit will be forced to go and live in the *erirogho* while his body decays. Often the *muloyi* can be heard laughing in the darkness.

The Forest

Other Central African peoples regard the forest as being the other or spirit world inhabited by dwarf-demons or imps, the *elokos*, who feed off human flesh. Anyone entering their world must perform certain rituals. Sorcerers carve a fetish or piece of wood taken from the spirit world (which therefore possesses magical properties) and use it to kill their enemies. Every tree has its spirit, which survives in the wood even after it has been chopped down and made into a hut, drum or boat. Without the spirit's goodwill, the carved item will bring only bad luck.

Foretelling the Arrival of Europeans

More than one witch doctor is said to have foretold the coming of Europeans to Africa. A certain prophet, Mulengo of Ilala (Zaire), foretold that, "There will come people who are white and shining with bodies like locusts". Another, Podile, a chief of the Bapedi (South Africa), prophesied the arrival of the Boers: "Red ants will come and destroy our land... . They will have baskets (hats) on their heads. Their feet will be like those of zebras (boots). Their sticks will give out fire. They will travel with houses drawn by oxen." Missionaries in the early nineteenth century left reports of seers who made their prophesies during a trance or illness. One missionary, Reverend E.W. White, referred to the prophet Mohlomi, who died in 1815, as "the greatest figure in Basuto history"; Mohlomi said he saw "a cloud of red dust coming out of the east, consuming our tribes".

Animal Myths

Animals play a key role in mythology – and not only in Africa. African slaves took their stories around the world, often as fables, and adapted them to their new environments. The Uncle Remus stories of America's southern states (Brer Rabbit was originally the hare; Brer Terrapin was originally the tortoise) came from West Africa, as did the Aunt Nancy (Kwaku Anansi) spider tales of the Caribbean, originally told by the Ashanti, Yoruba, lbo and Dahomey. It is believed that the Greek slave Aesop originally came from Ethiopia.

In the oldest versions of African myths, the characters are mostly animals, such as the serpent involved in the world's creation. At this stage they are deities of supernatural size and strength. Anansi the spider can climb up to the heavens to commune with Nyame, the sky god (Ashanti); Simba the lion is a potent god from whom several African chiefs traced their ancestry (such as Haile Selassie, the Lion of Judah). Similarly, some Zulu chiefs have claimed descent from the python. Some clans bow before a python and address it as "Your Majesty", offering it sacrifices of goats. In Mozambique there are traces of the worship of Sangu, the hippopotamus, a goddess who rules an underwater realm of lush, flowering meadows; she protects pregnant women and has to be sacrificed to by fishermen.

In the northwestern regions (Mali, Guinea), the sky god Faro sent down the antelope to teach the Bambara people farming skills; hence the many wooden carvings of the sacred antelope. According to the Bushmen of the Kalahari Desert, the mantis stole fire from the ostrich and passed it on to humans. The mantis is also credited among the Khosians of southwest Africa of inventing language through which animals and humans can converse.

Half-human Animals

As myths evolved, animals became half-human, half-animal characters who can be either good or evil, depending on their whim or veneration. They can take either form and foster human children, often coupling with human beings. Such children display both human and animal characteristics, so they can catch prey and speak animal languages. The human offspring of lions are particularly gifted: they can hunt at night and they know the bushlore and power of putting a spell on game (since no animal dies without the gods willing it). Ordinary mortals fear such half-human offspring, for they are brave, fierce warriors possessing magic and charms. Women love lion-men, who often become great rulers. As for lion-women, they grow up to be irresistibly attractive to men, who fall in love with them; the men, however, can end up being eaten by their wives. Lions are so potent that even a lion's eyelash can give a woman power over her husband, so that she can have children merely by instructing his mind to do so.

Tricksters

At the third stage of evolution of myths, animals lose their divine qualities and take their animal shape, but act as humans do, with their own characteristics. Two particular animals stand out as tricksters who use cunning to outwit more powerful beasts: the hare and the tortoise. In parts of Africa where there are no hares or tortoises (the Congo River basin), the trickster is the little water antelope, the jackal or the turtle. The lion, elephant and especially the hyena are the foils, their brute force and stupidity being no match for the nimble wits of the hare or the slow, patient wisdom of the tortoise. Even the hare (in the famous race) is overcome by the tortoise's quiet, dogged determination. A person of exceptional intelligence among the lbo is referred to as *Mbai* and among the Ibani is *Ekake*, both meaning 'tortoise'. Not only is the tortoise harmless, eating only fallen fruits of the forest, he is practically immune from attack and his silent nature implies mystery and veiled purpose – qualities valued in the human world.

Sacrifice and Offerings

All around people are spirits who have to be appeased and gods who have to be placated; in the past this could mean anything up to and including sacrifice. Since life is based on a balance in nature, there must be as much giving as receiving – someone has to die in order that others may live. If rain does not come, sacrifices and offerings must be made to induce the rain god to end a drought. Every tribe and region has its rituals and special doctors, priests and diviners who know exactly what offering must be made.

In many clans, it is the traditional duty of the eldest son to sacrifice to the clan spirits – those of his father and grandfather. Without such sacrifices the people could die and the sacrifice must be gladly offered, otherwise it is not acceptable. The common purpose of sacrifice is to create, celebrate or restore good relations with the deity of ancestral spirits. Usually the gods will be satisfied with nothing less than the slaughter of an animal (normally chicken, goat or lamb). The Dogon people of Mali, for example, have a special sacrificial rite called *bulu* (meaning 'to revive'), restoring the community's relations with the universe of life. The living sacrifice has a soul (*kikinu*) and vital force (*nyama*). As the victim's blood flows into the earth, it carries its *nyama*. The deity, thus nourished, has the will to give back into the sacrifice's liver, which is eaten by the priest in a ritual meal, thereby consuming the divine energy. These sacrificial rituals were transported with slaves to the Caribbean, especially Haiti, where the sacrifices (usually of chickens) come under the name voodoo/vodoun.

Mediums

Another sacrifice common to Mali is intended to induce the rainbow god, Sajara (a multicoloured serpent) to send rain. A white ram is sacrificed by a forked tree and has its blood sprinkled over the tree as dancers circle the tree. The sky gods take possession of some of the dancers and speak through their mouths. These oracles or mediums often become 'possessed' women who speak in a strange voice they do not understand and which has to be interpreted by a priest. Besides inducing rain, people consult them on sickness in the family or in domestic animals, sterility, floods or drought – even about marital problems.

Divination

When the deity does not speak through a medium, it may give signs or omens which can be read only by trained diviners who will make offerings or sacrifices to reveal knowledge that is concealed from ordinary mortals. That also includes advice on the best time for hunting, sowing, harvesting, fishing, migration or performing sacrificial rituals. For divining they may read the stars, throw lots, study lines in the soil or sand or examine the entrails of the sacrificed animal. Some diviners have a divining board on which they cast palm nuts or stones. The diviner also has to be consulted on sacrifice in the case of sickness and after a funeral to remove the contagion of death.

Another occasion for special offerings and sacrifices is when going hunting or gathering in the forest, which is inhabited by terrifying spirits, monsters and ghosts. Among the Ashanti of Ghana, the forest spirits are called the *mnoatia* and the forest ogre, Sasabonsam, is a hairy giant with large blood-red eyes and enormous feet that trip up unwary travellers. The hunter has to be on good terms with all these horrifying creatures. He needs special offerings for them all, as well as charms and fetishes to ward off evil.

In the past it was not unknown for soccer teams (notably in southern Africa) to offer sacrifices to the gods to let them win or to place fetishes in the goal of the opposing team, hoping their spirits would let goals in.

Ifa and Eshu

Among the Yoruba people of southern Nigeria, sacrifices are often made to two contradictory gods simultaneously: Ifa and Eshu. Ifa is the god of wisdom, knowledge and divination. At the time of the creation, he came down to earth with the other deities to establish order. He settled on earth, married and had eight sons, all of whom became chiefs of the provinces of Yorubaland. Eshu had been sent into the world by Olodumare, the supreme god, to test people and examine their real characters. One day Ifa felt insulted by his sons and went to live in heaven, so leaving the mischievous god Eshu to cause quarrels, make women barren and trick people into insulting the gods, for which they had to pay sacrifices. In despair, Ifa's sons went to heaven to beg their father's help. He refused to return, but he did give each son a divining board and set of 16 palm nuts as divination tools. It is through these palm nuts that Ifa conveys the will of the gods to people.

Death

Three vital questions concern all African cultures: how did death come into the world; why do people die and what happens after death? Despite the wide disparities in cultures, there is general agreement on the answers to these questions.

Death was not part of the original scheme of things in African myth: it came later, typically as a result of a blunder, a mistaken message or late delivery of a message. A common myth is that from southern Africa about the moon goddess who returns after dying; she originally decided on life and death, promising that people would be restored to life. The message is sent to earth with the chameleon or mantis, as well as the hare. The hare is first to arrive, but gives a garbled message, thus depriving humans of immortality, since gods can never revoke a message once delivered. The Ibo have a similar tale, with a message sent by the great spirit Chuku; here the dog dawdles and the sheep muddles the message.

Origin of Death

Some myths put the blame for the coming of death on women. The Baluba and Chaga say a girl disturbed her grandmother as she was discarding her old skin, so breaking a secret ritual. The Ganda people to the north of Lake Victoria blame the supreme god's daughter Nambi who married a mortal, but went back for grain to feed her chicken and was overtaken by her brother Walube (Death), who then accompanied her to earth. The Dinka, herders of southern Sudan, tell that the supreme god gave a grain of millet to an earthly couple, but the woman Abuk was too greedy and accidentally hit the god with the end of her hoe, after which he sent a bird to cut the rope of life linking heaven and earth.

Why People Die

In a continent where mortality is high, the cause of death, especially premature death, is often attributed to evil spells cast by agents of misfortune. The all-pervading fear of death provides work for diviners, witch doctors, shamans and makers of charms, amulets and fetishes. Dead ancestors, too, play an important role. Often when someone falls ill, it is supposed that an ancestral spirit has been offended and sent the sickness, or that some human enemy has put a spell on the victim. In either case, the result is more work (and remuneration) for the various doctors.

Afterlife

It is a commonly held belief that death is not the end of existence, but instead that it is merely the moment when a person can no longer dispose of his body, except as a ghost or spirit in someone or something else's body, whether animal, tree, plant, river or wind. The living sometimes see and talk to the dead in their dreams or receive messages through omens or mediums. The spirits of the dead usually remain near their funeral place for a time – whether under their hut (usually for chiefs), in forest or river, or even inside hyenas, who frequently devour corpses. After a while the spirits depart for the land of the dead.

It is the duty of the spirit's descendants to serve ancestors by erecting a shrine where they regularly place offerings of food and drink. If the rites are neglected, the ancestors will blight their descendants' lives for several generations. In Tanzania, family spirits (those of father, grandfather and maternal uncle) are called *makungu*. These spirits are venerated for three generations, after which time they merge with the host of spirits called *vinyyamkela* (*kinyamkela* singular).

The Underworld

Many peoples believe that the dead live in the bowels of the earth, very much as they did on earth, tending plentiful herds of speckled cattle. To the Ibo people, the earth goddess Aje is also goddess of the underworld, where she rules over many deities as well as the ancestors buried in her womb. Sometimes when she is angry, she moves forests, mountains and rivers if the relatives of the deceased have not made proper offerings to her when burying the corpse. In a Fon tale from West Africa, the rainbow serpent Aido-Hwedo, who supports the earth in the ocean, will one day run out of food; he will then chew on his tail and cause the whole earth to topple into the sea.

The Dahoman people believe that in the underworld social status remains unchanged: the chieftain continues to rule and the slave to serve forever. The Basutos believe that the dead wander silently and dully about their green valleys, called *mosima* ('the abyss'), with no emotions of joy or sorrow. The Swahili name for this spirit land is *kuzimu*. On the other hand, in the underworld there is no retribution for earthly sins, and no distinction between heaven and hell.

Paths to the Underworld

The land of the dead can be reached through caves or holes in the ground. The Bapedi of South Africa traditionally claim that the gateway to *mosima*, the underworld, lies on their land and can be entered by anyone sufficiently daring. Myths say that two people go together, holding hands as they enter the pass and shout, "Spirits, clear the way or we'll throw stones at you!", and they pass by without difficulty. Many are the adventures of living beings who accidentally stumble into the underworld. They often follow a porcupine or some other burrowing animal they are hunting into its hole. This happened to a hunter, Mpobe, in Uganda and to a Zulu hunter, Uncama. The hunters return unharmed to tell the tale, but never find their way back down again.

Myths of Origin, Death & The Afterlife

MOST AFRICAN PEOPLES RECOGNIZE some sort of all-powerful, omniscient god, but the sheer size of the African continent has not allowed a uniform system of beliefs to develop. Innumerable myths on the origin and evolution of the universe exist as a result. The Fon of Dahomey speak of a supreme God, Mawu-Lisa, the 'twins' from whom all the gods and demigods are descended. The Zulu of South Africa call their deity uKqili, the wise one, and believe he raised mankind out of "beds of grass". The Hottentots refer to their god as Utixo, a benevolent deity who inhabits the sky and speaks with the voice of thunder.

The creation myth retold at the beginning of this chapter comes from the Yoruba tribe in west Africa, whose pantheon alone contains over 1,700 deities. The most important Yoruban gods feature in the stories. Olorun, the supreme being, is capable of seeing both "the inside and the outside of man", while the other gods are depicted as sensitive to human problems and particularly receptive to human prayers.

Again, nearly every tribe has its own story on the creation of mankind, the origin of death and darkness, and its own unique descriptions of the Otherworld. Only a selection of these tales is retold here.

The Creation of the Universe
(From the Yoruba people, west Africa)

BEFORE THE UNIVERSE WAS CREATED, there existed only a vast expanse of sky above and an endless stretch of water and uninhabited marshland below. Olorun, the wisest of the gods, was supreme ruler of the sky, while Olokun, the most powerful goddess, ruled the seas and marshes. Both kingdoms were quite separate at that time and there was never any conflict between the two deities. Olorun was more than satisfied with his domain in the sky and hardly noticed what took place below him. Olokun was content with the kingdom she occupied, even though it contained neither living creatures nor vegetation of any kind.

But the young god Obatala was not entirely satisfied with this state of affairs, and one day, as he looked down from the sky upon the dull, grey terrain ruled by Olokun, he thought to himself:

"The kingdom below is a pitiful, barren place. Something must be done to improve its murky appearance. Now if only there were mountains and forests to brighten it up, it would make a perfect home for all sorts of living creatures."

Obatala decided that he must visit Olorun, who was always prepared to listen to him.

"It is a good scheme, but also a very ambitious one," Olorun said to Obatala. "I have no doubt that the hills and valleys you describe would be far better than grey ocean, but who will create this new world, and how will they go about it?"

"If you will give me your blessing," Obatala replied, "I myself will undertake to do this work."

"Then it is settled," said Olorun. "I cannot help you myself, but I will arrange for you to visit my son Orunmila. He will be able to guide you."

Next day, Obatala called upon Orunmila, the eldest son of Olorun, who had been given the power to read the future and to understand the secret of existence. Orunmila produced his divining tray, and when he had placed sixteen palm nuts on it, he shook the tray and cast its contents high into the air. As the nuts dropped to the ground, he read their meaning aloud:

"First, Obatala," he announced, "you must find a chain of gold long enough for you to climb down from the sky to the watery wastes below. Then, as you descend, take with you a snail shell filled with sand, a white hen, a black cat and a palm nut. This is how you should begin your quest."

Obatala listened attentively to his friend's advice and immediately set off to find a goldsmith who would make him the chain he needed to descend from the sky to the surface of the water below.

"I would be happy to make you the chain you ask for," said the goldsmith, "provided you can give me all the gold I need. But I doubt that you will find enough here for me to complete my task."

Obatala would not be dissuaded, however, and having instructed the goldsmith to go ahead with his work, he approached the other sky gods and one by one explained to them his purpose, requesting that they contribute whatever gold they possessed. The response was generous. Some of the gods gave gold dust, others gave rings, bracelets or pendants, and before long a huge, glittering mound had been collected. The goldsmith examined all the gold that was brought before him, but still he complained that there was not enough.

"It is the best I can do," Obatala told him. "I have asked all of the other gods to help out and there is no more gold left in the sky. Make the chain as long as you possibly can and fix a hook to one end. Even if it fails to reach the water below, I am determined to climb down on it."

The goldsmith worked hard to complete the chain and when it was finished, the hook was fastened to the edge of the sky and the chain lowered far below. Orunmila appeared and handed Obatala a bag containing the sand-filled snail's shell, the white hen, the black cat and the palm nut, and as soon as he had slung it over his shoulder, the young god began climbing down the golden chain, lower and lower until he saw that he was leaving the world of light and entering a world of twilight.

Before long, Obatala could feel the damp mists rising up off the surface of the water, but at the same time, he realized that he had just about reached the end of his golden chain.

"I cannot jump from here," he thought. "If I let go of the chain I will fall into the sea and almost certainly drown."

And while he looked around him rather helplessly, he suddenly heard a familiar voice calling to him from up above.

"Make use of the sand I gave you," Orunmila instructed him, "toss it into the water below."

Obatala obeyed, and after he had poured out the sand, he heard Orunmila calling to him a second time:

"Release the white hen," Orunmila cried.

Obatala reached into his bag and pulled out the white hen, dropping her on to the waters beneath where he had sprinkled the sand. As soon as she had landed, the hen began to scratch in the sand, scattering it in all directions. Wherever the grains fell, dry land instantly appeared. The larger heaps of sand became hills, while the smaller heaps became valleys.

Obatala let go of his chain and jumped on to the solid earth. As he walked he smiled with pleasure, for the land now extended a great many miles in all directions. But he was proudest of the spot where his feet had first landed, and decided to name this place Ife. Stooping to the ground, he began digging a hole, and buried his palm nut in the soil. Immediately, a palm tree sprang up from the earth, shedding its seeds as it stretched to its full height so that other trees soon shot up around it. Obatala felled some of these trees and built for himself a sturdy house thatched with palm leaves. And here, in this place, he settled down, separated from the other sky gods, with only his black cat for company.

Obatala Creates Mankind

(From the Yoruba people, west Africa)

OBATALA LIVED QUITE CONTENTEDLY in his new home beneath the skies, quite forgetting that Olorun might wish to know how his plans were progressing. The supreme god soon grew impatient for news and ordered Agemo, the chameleon, to go down the golden chain to investigate. The chameleon descended and when he arrived at Ife, he knocked timidly on Obatala's door.

"Olorun has sent me here," he said, "to discover whether or not you have been successful in your quest."

"Certainly I have," replied Obatala, "look around you and you will see the land I have created and the plants I have raised from the soil. Tell Olorun that it is now a far more pleasant kingdom than it was before, and that I would be more than willing to spend the rest of my time here, except that I am growing increasingly weary of the twilight and long to see brightness once more."

Agemo returned home and reported to Olorun all that he had seen and heard. Olorun smiled, for it pleased him greatly that Obatala had achieved what he had set out to do. The young god, who was among his favourites, had earned a special reward, and so Olorun fashioned with his own hands a dazzling golden orb and tossed it into the sky.

"For you, Obatala, I have created the sun," said Olorun, "it will shed warmth and light on the new world you have brought to life below."

Obatala very gladly received this gift, and as soon as he felt the first rays of the sun shining down on him, his restless spirit grew calmer. He remained quite satisfied for a time, but then, as the weeks turned to months, he became unsettled once more and began to dream of spending time in the company of other beings, not unlike himself, who could move and speak and with whom he could share his thoughts and feelings.

Obatala sat down and began to claw at the soil as he attempted to picture the little creatures who would keep him company. He found that the clay was soft and pliable, so he began to shape tiny figures in his own image. He laid the first of them in the sun to dry and worked on with great enthusiasm until he had produced several more.

He had been sitting for a long time in the hot sunshine before he realized how tired and thirsty he felt.

"What I need is some palm wine to revive me," he thought to himself, and he stood up and headed off towards the nearest palm tree.

He placed his bowl underneath it and drew off the palm juice, leaving it to ferment in the heat until it had turned to wine. When the wine was ready, Obatala helped himself to a very long drink, and as he gulped down bowl after bowl of the refreshing liquid, he failed to realize that the wine was making him quite drunk.

Obatala had swallowed so much of the wine that his fingers grew clumsy, but he continued to work energetically, too drunk to notice that the clay figures he now produced were no longer perfectly formed. Some had crooked backs or crooked limbs, others had arms and legs of uneven length. Obatala was so pleased with himself he raised his head and called out jubilantly to the skies:

"I have created beings from the soil, but only you, Olorun, can breathe life into them. Grant me this request so that I will always have human beings to keep me company here in Ife."

Olorun heard Obatala's plea and did not hesitate to breathe life into the clay figures, watching with interest as they rose up from the ground and began to obey the commands of their creator. Soon they had built wooden shelters for themselves next to the god's own house, creating the first Yoruba village in Ife where before only one solitary house had stood. Obatala was filled with admiration and pride, but now, as the effects of the palm wine started to wear off, he began to notice that some of the humans he had created were contorted and misshapen. The sight of the little creatures struggling as they went about their chores filled him with sadness and remorse.

"My drunkenness has caused these people to suffer," he proclaimed solemnly, "and I swear that I will never drink palm wine again. From this day forward, I will be the special protector of all humans who are born with deformities."

Obatala remained faithful to his pledge and dedicated himself to the welfare of the human beings he had created, making sure that he always had a moment to spare for the lame and the blind. He saw to it that the people prospered and, before long, the Yoruba village of Ife had grown into an impressive city. Obatala also made certain that his people had all the tools they needed to clear and cultivate the land. He presented each man with a copper bush knife and a wooden hoe and taught them to grow millet, yams and a whole variety of other crops, ensuring that mankind had a plentiful supply of food for its survival.

Olokun's Revenge

(From the Yoruba people, west Africa)

AFTER HE HAD LIVED among the human race for a long period of time, Obatala came to the decision that he had done all he could for his people. The day had arrived for him to retire,

he believed, and so he climbed up the golden chain and returned to his home in the sky once more, promising to visit the earth as frequently as possible. The other gods never tired of hearing Obatala describe the kingdom he had created below. Many were so captivated by the image he presented of the newly created human beings, that they decided to depart from the sky and go down to live among them. And as they prepared to leave, Olorun took them aside and counselled them:

"Each of you shall have a special role while you are down there, and I ask that you never forget your duty to the human race. Always listen to the prayers of the people and offer help when they are in need."

One deity, however, was not at all pleased with Obatala's work or the praise he had received from Olorun. The goddess Olokun, ruler of the sea, watched with increasing fury as, one by one, the other gods arrived in her domain and began dividing up the land amongst themselves.

"Obatala has never once consulted me about any of this," she announced angrily, "but he shall pay for the insult to my honour."

The goddess commanded the great waves of her ocean to rise up, for it was her intention to destroy the land Obatala had created and replace it with water once more. The terrible flood began, and soon the fields were completely submerged. Crops were destroyed and thousands of people were swept away by the roaring tide.

Those who survived the deluge fled to the hills and called to Obatala for help, but he could not hear them from his home high above in the sky.

In desperation, the people turned to Eshu, one of the gods recently descended to earth.

"Please return to the sky," they begged, "and tell the great gods of the flood that threatens to destroy everything."

"First you must show that you revere the gods," replied Eshu. "You must offer up a sacrifice and pray hard that you will be saved."

The people went away and returned with a goat which they sacrificed as food for Obatala. But still Eshu refused to carry the message.

"You ask me to perform this great service," he told them, "and yet you do not offer to reward me. If I am to be your messenger, I too deserve a gift."

The people offered up more sacrifices to Eshu and only when he was content that they had shown him appropriate respect did he begin to climb the golden chain back to the sky to deliver his message.

Obatala was deeply upset by the news and extremely anxious for the safety of his people, for he was uncertain how best to deal with so powerful a goddess as Olokun. Once more, he approached Orunmila and asked for advice. Orunmila consulted his divining nuts, and at last he said to Obatala:

"Rest here in the sky while I descend below. I will use my gifts to turn back the water and make the land rise again."

Orunmila went down and, using his special powers, brought the waves under control so that the marshes began to dry up and land became visible again. But although the people greeted the god as their saviour and pleaded with him to act as their protector, Orunmila confessed that he had no desire to remain among them. Before he departed, however, he passed on a great many of his gifts to the people, teaching them how to divine the future and to control the unseen forces of nature. What he taught the people was never lost and it was passed on like a precious heirloom from one generation to another.

Agemo Outwits Olokun
(From the Yoruba people, west Africa)

BUT EVEN AFTER Orunmila had returned to his home in the sky, all was not yet settled between Olokun and the other sky gods. More embittered than ever before by her defeat, Olokun began to consider ways in which she might humiliate Olorun, the god who had allowed Obatala to usurp her kingdom.

Now the goddess was a highly skilled weaver, but she was also expert in dyeing the cloths she had woven. And knowing that no other sky god possessed greater knowledge of cloth making, she sent a message to

Olorun challenging him to a weaving contest. Olorun received her message rather worriedly and said to himself:

"Olokun knows far more about making cloth that I will ever know, but I cannot allow her to think that she is superior to me in anything. Somehow I must appear to meet her challenge and yet avoid taking part in the contest. But how can I possibly do this?"

He pondered the problem a very long time until, at last, he was struck by a worthwhile thought. Smiling broadly, he summoned Agemo, the chameleon, to his side, and instructed him to carry an important message to Olokun.

Agemo climbed down the golden chain and went in search of Olokun's dwelling.

"The ruler of the sky, Olorun, greets you," he announced. "He says that if your cloth is as magnificent as you say it is, then the ruler of the sky will be happy to compete with you in the contest you have suggested. But he thinks it only fair to see some of your cloth in advance, and has asked me to examine it on his behalf so that I may report to him on its quality."

Olokun was happy to accommodate Olorun's request. She retired to a backroom and having put on a skirt of radiant green cloth, she stood confidently before the chameleon. But as the chameleon looked at the garment, his skin began to change colour until it was exactly the same brilliant shade as the skirt. Next Olokun put on an orange-hued cloth. But again, to her astonishment, the chameleon turned a beautiful shade of bright orange. One by one, the goddess put on skirts of various bright colours, but on each occasion the chameleon perfectly matched the colour of her robe. Finally the goddess thought to herself:

"This person is only a messenger, and if Olorun's servants can reproduce the exact colours of my very finest cloth, what hope will I have in a contest against the supreme god himself?"

The goddess conceded defeat and spoke earnestly to the chameleon:

"Tell your master that the ruler of the seas sends her greetings to the ruler of the sky. Say to him that I acknowledge his supremacy in weaving and in all other things as well."

And so it came to pass that Olorun and Olokun resumed their friendship and that peace was restored to the whole of the universe once more.

The Gods Descend from the Sky
(From the Dahomean people, west Africa)

NANA BALUKU, the mother of all creation, fell pregnant before she finally retired from the universe. Her offspring was androgynous, a being with one body and two faces. The face that resembled a woman was called Mawu and her eyes were the moon. She took control of the night and all territories to the west. The male face was called Lisa and his eyes were the sun. Lisa controlled the east and took charge of the daylight.

At the beginning of the present world, Mawu-Lisa was the only being in existence, but eventually the moon was eclipsed by the sun and many children were conceived. The first fruits of the union were a pair of twins, a male called Da Zodji and a female called Nyohwè Ananu. Another child followed shortly afterwards, a male and female form joined in one body, and this child was named Sogbo. The third birth again produced twins, a male, Agbè, and a female, Naètè. The fourth and fifth children were both male and were named Agè and Gu. Gu's torso was made of stone and a giant sword protruded from the hole in his neck where his head would otherwise have been. The sixth offspring was not made of flesh and blood. He was given the name Djo, meaning air, or atmosphere. Finally, the seventh child born was named Legba, and because he was the youngest, he became Mawu-Lisa's particular favourite.

When these children had grown to adulthood and the appropriate time had arrived to divide up the kingdoms of the universe among them, Mawu-Lisa gathered them together. To their first-born, the twins Da Zodji and Nyohwè Ananu, the parents gave the earth below and sent them, laden with heavenly riches, down from the sky to inhabit their new home. To Sogbo, who was both man and woman, they gave the sky, commanding him to rule over thunder and lightning. The twins Agbè and Naètè were sent to take command of the waters and the creatures of the deep, while Agè was ordered to live in the bush as a hunter where he could take control of all the birds and beasts of the earth.

To Gu, whom Mawu-Lisa considered their strength, they gave the forests and vast stretches of fertile soil, supplying him also with the tools and weapons mankind would need to cultivate the land. Mawu-Lisa ordered Djo to occupy the space between the earth and the sky and entrusted him with the life-span of human beings. It was also Djo's role to clothe the other sky gods, making them invisible to man.

To each of their offspring, Mawu-Lisa then gave a special language. These are the languages still spoken by the priests and mediums of the gods in their songs and oracles. To Da Zodji and Nyohwè Ananu, Mawu-Lisa gave the language of the earth and took from them all memory of the sky language. They gave to Sogbo, Agbè and Naètè, Agè and Gu the languages they would speak. But to Djo, they gave the language of men.

Then Mawu-Lisa said to Legba: "Because you are my youngest child, I will keep you with me always. Your work will be to visit all the kingdoms ruled over by your brothers and sisters and report to me on their progress."

And that is why Legba knows all the languages of his siblings, and he alone knows the language of Mawu-Lisa. You will find Legba everywhere, because all beings, human and gods, must first approach Legba before Mawu-Lisa, the supreme deity, will answer their prayers.

God Abandons the Earth
(From Ghana, west Africa)

IN THE BEGINNING, God was very proud of the human beings he had created and wanted to live as close as possible to them. So he made certain that the sky was low enough for the people to touch and built for himself a home directly above their heads. God was so near that everyone on earth became familiar with his face and every day he would stop to make conversation with the people, offering a helping hand if they were ever in trouble.

This arrangement worked very well at first, but soon God observed that the people had started to take advantage of his closeness. Children began to wipe their greasy hands on the sky when they had finished their meals and often, if a woman was in search of an extra ingredient for dinner, she would simply reach up, tear a piece off the sky and add it to her cooking pot. God remained tolerant through all of this, but he knew his patience would not last forever and hoped that his people would not test its limit much further.

Then one afternoon, just as he had lain down to rest, a group of women gathered underneath the sky to pound the corn they had harvested. One old woman among them had a particularly large wooden bowl and a very long pestle, and as she thumped down on the grains, she knocked violently against the sky. God arose indignantly from his bed and descended below, but as he approached the woman to chastise her, she suddenly jerked back her arm and hit him in the eye with her very long pestle.

God gave a great shout, his voice booming like thunder through the air, and as he shouted, he raised his powerful arms above his head and pushed upwards against the sky with all his strength, flinging it far into the distance.

As soon as they realized that the earth and the sky were separated, the people became angry with the old woman who had injured God and pestered her day and night to bring him back to them. The woman went away and although she was not very clever, she thought long and hard about the problem until she believed she had found the solution. Returning to her village, she ordered her children to collect all the wooden mortars that they could find. These she piled one on top of the other until they had almost bridged the gap between the earth and the heavens. Only one more mortar was needed to complete the job, but although her children searched high and low, they could not find the missing object. In desperation, the old woman told them to remove the lowest mortar from the bottom of the pile and place it on the top. But as soon as they did this, all the mortars came crashing down, killing the old woman, her children and the crowd who had gathered to admire the towering structure.

Ever since that day, God has remained in the heavens where mankind can no longer approach him as easily as before. There are some, however, who say they have caught a glimpse of him and others who offer up sacrifices calling for his forgiveness and asking him to make his home among them once more.

The Coming of Darkness
(From the Kono people, Sierra Leone)

WHEN GOD FIRST MADE THE WORLD, there was never any darkness or cold. The sun always shone brightly during the day, and at night, the moon bathed the earth in a softer light, ensuring that everything could still be seen quite clearly.

But one day God sent for the Bat and handed him a mysterious parcel to take to the moon. He told the Bat it contained darkness, but as he did not have the time to explain precisely what darkness was, the Bat went on his way without fully realizing the importance of his mission.

He flew at a leisurely pace with the parcel strapped on his back until he began to feel rather tired and hungry. He was in no great hurry he decided, and so he put down his load by the roadside and wandered off in search of something to eat.

But while he was away, a group of mischievous animals approached the spot where he had paused to rest and, seeing the parcel, began to open it, thinking there might be something of value inside of it. The Bat returned just as they were untying the last piece of string and rushed forward to stop them. But too late! The darkness forced its way through the opening and rose up into the sky before anyone had a chance to catch it.

Quickly the Bat gave chase, flying about everywhere, trying to grab hold of the darkness and return it to the parcel before God discovered what had happened. But the harder he tried, the more the darkness eluded him, so that eventually he fell into an exhausted sleep lasting several hours.

When the Bat awoke, he found himself in a strange twilight world and once again, he began chasing about in every direction, hoping he would succeed where he had failed before.

But the Bat has never managed to catch the darkness, although you will see him every evening just after the sun has set, trying to trap it and deliver it safely to the moon as God first commanded him.

The Sun and the Moon
(From the Krachi people, west Africa)

THE SUN AND THE MOON fell in love and decided to marry. For a time they were very happy together and produced many children whom they christened 'stars'. But it was not long before the moon grew weary of her husband and decided to take a lover, refusing to conceal the fact that she greatly enjoyed the variety.

Of course, the sun soon came to hear of his wife's brazen infidelity and the news made him extremely unhappy. He attempted to reason with the moon, but when he saw that his efforts were entirely fruitless, he decided to drive his wife out of his house. Some of the children sided with their mother, while others supported their father. But the sun was never too hard on his wife, in spite of their differences, and saw to it that their possessions were equally divided up.

The moon was always too proud to accept her husband's kindness, however, and even to this day, she continues to make a habit of trespassing on his lands, often taking her children with her and encouraging them to fight the siblings who remain behind with their father.

The constant battles between the star-children of the sun and the star-children of the moon produce great storms of thunder and lightning and it is only when she becomes bored of these confrontations that the moon sends her messenger, the rainbow, into the field, instructing him to wave a cloth of many colours as a signal for her children to retreat.

Sometimes the moon herself is caught by the sun attempting to steal crops from his fields. Whenever this happens, he chases after his estranged wife and if he catches her he begins to flog her or even tries to eat her.

So whenever a man sees an eclipse, he knows that things have come to blows once again between husband and wife up above. At this time, he must be certain to beat his drum and threaten the sun very loudly, for if he does not, the sun might finish the job, and we should certainly lose the moon forever.

Why the Sun and the Moon Live in the Sky
(From southern Nigeria)

MANY YEARS AGO, the sun and water were great friends, and both lived on the earth together. The sun very often used to visit the water, but the water never returned his visits. At last the sun asked the water why it was that he never came to see him in his house, the water replied that the sun's house was not big enough, and that if he came with his people he would drive the sun out.

He then said, "If you wish me to visit you, you must build a very large compound; but I warn you that it will have to be a tremendous place, as my people are very numerous, and take up a lot of room."

The sun promised to build a very big compound, and soon afterwards he returned home to his wife, the moon, who greeted him with a broad smile when he opened the door. The sun told the moon what he had promised the water, and the next day commenced building a huge compound in which to entertain his friend.

When it was completed, he asked the water to come and visit him the next day. When the water arrived, he called out to the sun, and asked him whether it would be safe for him to enter, and the sun answered, "Yes, come in, my friend." The water then began to flow in, accompanied by the fish and all the water animals.

Very soon the water was knee-deep, so he asked the sun if it was still safe, and the sun again said, "Yes," so more water came in.

When the water was level with the top of a man's head, the water said to the sun, "Do you want more of my people to come?" and the sun and moon both answered, "Yes," not knowing any better, so the water flowed on, until the sun and moon had to perch themselves on the top of the roof.

Again the water addressed the sun, but receiving the same answer, and more of his people rushing in, the water very soon overflowed the top of the roof, and the sun and moon were forced to go up into the sky, where they have remained ever since.

Why the Moon Waxes and Wanes
(From southern Nigeria)

THERE WAS ONCE AN OLD WOMAN who was very poor, and lived in a small mud hut thatched with mats made from the leaves of the tombo palm in the bush. She was often very hungry, as there was no one to look after her.

In the olden days, the moon used often to come down to the earth, although she lived most of the time in the sky. The moon was a fat woman with a skin of hide, and she was full of fat meat. She was quite round, and in the night used to give plenty of light. The moon was sorry for the poor starving old woman, so she came to her and said, "You may cut some of my meat away for your food." This the old woman did every evening, and the moon got smaller and smaller until you could scarcely see her at all. Of course this made her give very little light, and all the people began to grumble in consequence, and to ask why it was that the moon was getting so thin.

At last the people went to the old woman's house where there happened to be a little girl sleeping. She had been there for some little time, and had seen the moon come down every evening, and the old woman go out with her knife and carve her daily supply of meat out of the moon. As she was very frightened, she told the people all about it, so they determined to set a watch on the movements of the old woman.

That very night the moon came down as usual, and the old woman went out with her knife and basket to get her food; but before she could carve any meat all the people rushed out shouting, and the moon was so frightened that she went back again into the sky, and never came down again to the earth. The old woman was left to starve in the bush.

Ever since that time the moon has hidden herself most of the day, as she was so frightened, and she still gets very thin once a month, but later on she gets fat again, and when she is quite fat she gives plenty of light all the night; but this does not last very long, and she begins to get thinner and thinner, in the same way as she did when the old woman was carving her meat from her.

The Story of the Prince who Insisted on Possessing the Moon
(From the Congo and central Africa)

THE COUNTRY NOW INHABITED BY THE BASOKO TRIBE was formerly known as Bandimba. A king called Bahanga was its sole ruler. He possessed a houseful of wives, but all his children were unfortunately of the female sex, which he considered to be a great grievance, and of which he frequently complained. His subjects, on the other hand, were blessed with more sons than daughters, and this fact increased the king's grief, and made him envy the meanest of his subjects.

One day, however, he married Bamana, the youngest daughter of his principal chief, and finally he became the father of a male child, and was very happy, and his people rejoiced in his happiness.

The prince grew up to be a marvel of strength and beauty, and his father doted on him so much, that he shared his power with the boy in a curious manner. The king reserved authority over all the married people, while the prince's subjects consisted of those not yet mated. It thus happened that the prince ruled over more people than his father, for the children were, of course, more numerous than the parents. But with all the honour conferred upon him the prince was not happy. The more he obtained, the more he wished to possess. His eyes had but to see a thing to make him desire its exclusive possession. Each day he preferred one or more requests to his father, and because of his great love for him, the king had not the heart to refuse anything to him. Indeed, he was persuaded to bestow so many gifts upon his son that he reserved scarcely anything for himself.

One day the prince was playing with the youth of his court, and after the sport retired to the shade of a tree to rest, and his companions sat down in a circle at a respectful distance from him. He then felt a gush of pride stealing over him as he thought of his great power, at the number and variety of his treasures, and he cried out boastfully that there never was a boy so great, so rich and so favoured by his father, as he had become. "My father," said he, "can deny me nothing. I have only to ask, and it is given unto me."

Then one little slender boy with a thin voice said, "It is true, prince. Your father has been very good to you. He is a mighty king, and he is as generous as he is great. Still, I know of one thing that he cannot give you – and it is certain that you will never possess it."

"What thing is that which I may not call my own, when I see it – and what is it that is not in the king's power to give me?" asked the prince, in a tone of annoyance.

"It is the moon," answered the little boy; "and you must confess yourself that it is beyond the king's power to give that to you."

"Do you doubt it?" asked the prince. "I say to you that I shall possess it, and I will go now and claim it from my father. I will not give him any peace until he gives it to me."

Now it so happens that such treasures as are already ours, we do not value so much as those which we have not yet got. So it was with this spoiled prince. The memory of the many gifts of his father faded from his mind, and their value was not to be compared with this new toy – the moon – which he had never thought of before and which he now so ardently coveted.

He found the king discussing important matters with the old men.

"Father," said he, "just now, while I was with my companions I was taunted because I did not have the moon among my toys, and it was said that it was beyond your power to give it to me. Now, prove this boy a liar, and procure the moon for me, that I may be able to show it to them, and glory in your gift."

"What is it you say, my son, you want the moon?" asked the astonished king.

"Yes. Do get it for me at once, won't you?"

"But, my child, the moon is a long way up. How shall we be ever able to reach it?"

"I don't know; but you have always been good to me, and you surely would not refuse me this favour, father?"

"I fear, my own, that we will not be able to give you the moon."

"But, father, I must have it; my life will not be worth living without it. How may I dare to again face my companions after my proud boast before them of your might and goodness? There was but one thing that yonder pert boy said I might not have, and that was the moon. Now my soul is bent upon possessing this moon, and you must obtain it for me or I shall die."

"Nay, my son, speak not of death. It is an ugly word, especially when connected with my prince and heir. Do you not know yet that I live only for your sake? Let your mind be at rest. I will collect all the wise men of the land together, and ask them to advise me. If they say that the moon can be reached and brought down to us, you shall have it."

Accordingly the great state drum was sounded for the general palaver, and a score of criers went through the towns beating their little drums as they went, and the messengers hastened all the wise men and elders to the presence of the king.

When all were assembled, the king announced his desire to know how the moon could be reached, and whether it could be shifted from its place in the sky and brought down to the earth, in order that he might give it to his only son the prince. If there was any wise man present who could inform him how this could be done, and would undertake to bring it to him, he would give the choicest of his daughters in marriage to him and endow him with great riches.

When the wise men heard this strange proposal, they were speechless with astonishment, as no one in the Basoko Land had ever heard of anybody mounting into the air higher than a tree, and to suppose that a person could ascend as high as the moon was, they thought, simple madness. Respect for the king, however, held them mute, though what their glances meant was very clear.

But while each man was yet looking at his neighbour in wonder, one of the wise men, who appeared to be about the youngest present, rose to his feet and said:

"Long life to the prince and to his father, the king! We have heard the words of our king, Bahanga, and they are good. I – even I – his slave, am able to reach the moon, and to do the king's pleasure, if the king's authority will assist me."

The confident air of the man, and the ring of assurance in his voice made the other wise men, who had been so ready to believe the king and prince mad, feel shame, and they turned their faces to him curiously, more than half willing to believe that after all the thing was possible. The king also lost his puzzled look, and appeared relieved.

"Say on. How may you be able to perform what you promise?"

"If it please the king," answered the man, boldly, "I will ascend from the top of the high mountain near the Cataract of Panga. But I shall first build a high scaffold on it, the base of which shall be as broad as the mountain top, and on that scaffold I will build another, and on the second I shall build a third, and so on and so on until my shoulder touches the moon."

"But is it possible to reach the moon in this manner?" asked the king doubtingly.

"Most certainly, if I were to erect a sufficient number of scaffolds, one above another, but it will require a vast quantity of timber, and a great army of workmen. If the king commands it, the work will be done."

"Be it so, then," said the king. "I place at your service every able-bodied man in the kingdom."

"Ah, but all the men in your kingdom are not sufficient, O king. All the grown-up men will be wanted to fell the trees, square the timber and bear it to the works; and every grown-up woman will be required to prepare the food for the workmen; and every boy must carry water to satisfy their thirst, and bark rope for the binding of the timbers; and every girl, big and little, must be sent to till the fields to raise cassava for food. Only in this manner can the prince obtain the moon as his toy."

"I say, then, let it be done as you think it ought to be done. All the men, women, and children in the kingdom I devote to this service, that my only son may enjoy what he desires."

Then it was proclaimed throughout the wide lands of the Bandimba that all the people should be gathered together to proceed at once with the work of obtaining the moon for the king's son. And the forest was cut down, and while some of the workmen squared the trees, others cut deep holes in the ground, to make a broad and sure base for the lower scaffold; and the boys made thousands of rope coils to lash the timbers together, out of bark, fibre of palm, and tough grass; and the girls, big and little, hoed up the ground and planted the cassava shrubs and cuttings from the banana and the plantain, and sowed the corn; and the women kneaded the bread and cooked the greens, and roasted green bananas for food for the workmen. And all the Bandimba people were made to slave hard every day in order that a spoiled boy might have the moon for his toy.

In a few days the first scaffolding stood up as high as the tallest trees, in a few weeks the structure had grown until it was many arrow-flights in height, in two months it was so lofty that the top could not be seen with the naked eye. The fame of the wonderful wooden tower that the Bandimba were building was carried far and wide; and the friendly nations round about sent messengers to see and report to them what mad thing the Bandimba were about, for rumour had spread so many contrary stories among people that strangers did not know what to believe. Some said it was true that all the Bandimba had become mad; but some of those who came to see with their own eyes, laughed, while others began to feel anxious. All, however, admired the bigness, and wondered at the height of the tower.

In the sixth month the top of the highest scaffold was so high that on the clearest day people could not see half-way up; and it was said to be so tall that the chief engineer could tell the day he would be able to touch the moon.

The work went on, and at last the engineer passed the word down that in a few days more it would be finished. Everybody believed him, and the nations round about sent more people to be present to witness the completion of the great tower, and to observe what would happen. In all the land, and the countries adjoining it, there was found only one wise man who foresaw, if the moon was shifted out of its place what damage would happen, and that probably all those foolish people in the vicinity of the tower would be destroyed. Fearing some terrible calamity, he proposed to depart from among the Bandimba before it should be too late. He then placed his family in a canoe, and, after storing it with sufficient provisions, he embarked, and in the night he floated down the river Aruwimi and into the big river, and continued his journey night and day as fast as the current would take him – far, far below any lands known to the Bandimba. A week later, after the flight of the wise man and his family, the chief engineer sent down word to the king that he was ready to take the moon down.

"It is well," replied the king from below. "I will ascend, that I may see how you set about it."

Within twenty days the king reached the summit of the tower, and, standing at last by the side of the engineer, he laid his hand upon the moon, and it felt exceedingly hot. Then he commanded the engineer to proceed to take it down. The man put a number of cool bark coils over his shoulder and tried to dislodge it; but, as it was firmly fixed, he used such a deal of force that he cracked it, and there was an explosion, the fire and sparks from which scorched him. The timber on which the king and his chiefs were standing began to burn, and many more bursting sounds were heard, and fire and melted rock ran down through the scaffolding in a steady stream, until all the woodwork was ablaze, and the flames soared upward among the uprights and trestles of the wood in one vast pile of fire; and every man, woman, and child was utterly consumed in a moment. And the heat was so great that it affected the moon, and a large portion of it tumbled to the earth, and its glowing hot materials ran over the ground like a great river of fire, so that most of the country of the Bandimba was burnt to ashes. On those who were not smothered by the smoke, nor burnt by the fire, and who fled from before the burning river, the effect was very wonderful. Such of them as were grown up, male and female, were converted into gorillas, and all the children into different kinds of long-tailed monkeys. After the engineer of the works, the first who died were the king and the prince whose folly had brought ruin on the land.

If you look at the moon when it is full, you may then see on a clear night a curious dark portion on its face, which often appears as though there were peaky mountains in it, and often the dark spots are like some kind of horned animals; and then again, you will often fancy that on the moon you see the outlines of a man's face, but those dark spots are only the holes made in the moon by the man who forced his shoulders through it. Now ever since that dreadful day when the moon burst and the Bandimba country was consumed, parents are not in the habit of granting children all they ask for, but only such things as their age and experience warn them are good for their little ones. And when little children will not be satisfied by such things, but fret and pester their parents to give them what they know will be harmful to them, then it is a custom with all wise people to take the rod to them, to drive out of their heads the wicked thoughts.

The Story of the Lightning and the Thunder

(From southern Nigeria)

IN THE OLDEN DAYS the thunder and lightning lived on the earth amongst all the other people, but the king made them live at the far end of the town, as far as possible from other people's houses.

The thunder was an old mother sheep, and the lightning was her son, a ram. Whenever the ram got angry he used to go about and burn houses and knock down trees; he even did damage on the farms, and sometimes killed people. Whenever the lightning did these things, his mother used to call out to him in a very loud voice to stop and not to do any more damage; but the lightning did not care in the least for what his mother said, and when he was in a bad temper used to do a very large amount of damage. At last the people could not stand it any longer, and complained to the king.

So the king made a special order that the sheep (Thunder) and her son, the ram (Lightning), should leave the town and live in the far bush. This did not do much good, as when the ram got angry he still burnt the forest, and the flames sometimes spread to the farms and consumed them.

So the people complained again, and the king banished both the lightning and the thunder from the earth and made them live in the sky, where they could not cause so much destruction. Ever since, when the lightning is angry, he commits damage as before, but you can hear his mother, the thunder, rebuking him and telling him to stop. Sometimes, however, when the mother has gone away some distance from her naughty son, you can still see that he is angry and is doing damage, but his mother's voice cannot be heard.

How Death First Entered the World

(From the Krachi people, west Africa)

MANY YEARS AGO, a great famine spread throughout the land, and at that time, the eldest son of every household was sent out in search of food and instructed not to return until he had found something for the family to eat and drink.

There was a certain young man among the Krachi whose responsibility it was to provide for the family, and so he wandered off in search of food, moving deeper and deeper into the bush every day until he finally came to a spot he did not recognize. Just up ahead of him, he noticed a large form lying on the ground. He approached it cautiously, hoping that if the creature were dead, it might be a good source of food, but he had taken only a few steps forward when the mound began to stir, revealing that it was not an animal at all, but a ferocious-looking giant with flowing white hair stretched out for miles on the ground around him, all the way from Krachi to Salaga.

The giant opened one eye and shouted at the young man to explain his presence. The boy stood absolutely terrified, yet after some minutes, he managed to blurt out that he had never intended to disturb the giant's rest, but had come a great distance in search of food.

"I am Owuo," said the giant, "but people also call me Death. You, my friend, have caught me in a good mood and so I will give you some food and water if you will fetch and carry for me in return."

The young man could scarcely believe his luck, and readily agreed to serve the giant in exchange for a few regular meals. Owuo arose and walked towards his cave where he began roasting some meat on a spit over the fire. Never before had the boy tasted such a fine meal, and after he had washed it down with a bowl of fresh water, he sat back and smiled, well pleased that he had made the acquaintance of the giant.

For a long time afterwards, the young man happily served Owuo, and every evening, in return for his work, he was presented with a plate of the most delicious meat for his supper.

But one day the boy awoke feeling terribly homesick and begged his master to allow him to visit his family, if only for a few days.

"You may visit your family for as long as you wish," said the giant, "on the condition that you bring another boy to replace you."

So the young man returned to his village where he told his family the whole story of his meeting with the giant. Eventually he managed to persuade his younger brother to go with him into the bush and here he handed him over to Owuo, promising that he would himself return before too long.

Several months had passed, and soon the young man grew hungry again and began to yearn for a taste of the meat the giant had cooked for him. Finally, he made up his mind to return to his master, and leaving his family behind, he returned to Owuo's hut and knocked boldly on the door.

The giant himself answered, and asked the young man what he wanted.

"I would like some more of the good meat you were once so generous to share with me," said the boy, hoping the giant would remember his face.

"Very well," replied Owuo, "you can have as much of it as you want, but you will have to work hard for me, as you did before."

The young man consented, and after he had eaten as much as he could, he went about his chores enthusiastically. The work lasted many weeks and every day the boy ate his fill of roasted meat. But to his surprise he never saw anything of his brother, and whenever he asked about him, the giant told him, rather aloofly, that the lad had simply gone away on business.

Once more, however, the young man grew homesick and asked Owuo for permission to visit his village. The giant agreed on condition that this time, he bring back a girl to carry out his duties while he was away. The young man hurried home and there he pleaded with his sister to go into the bush and keep the giant company for a few months. The girl agreed, and after she had waved goodbye to her brother, she entered the giant's cave quite merrily, accompanied by a slave companion her own age.

Only a short time had passed before the boy began to dream of the meat again, longing for even a small morsel of it. So he followed the familiar path through the bush until he found Owuo's cave. The giant did not seem particularly pleased to see him and grumbled loudly at the disturbance. But he pointed the way to a room at the back and told the boy to help himself to as much meat as he wanted.

The young man took up a juicy bone which he began to devour. But to his horror, he recognized it at once as his sister's thigh and as he looked more closely at all the rest of the meat, he was appalled to discover that he had been sitting there, happily chewing on the body of his sister and her slave girl.

As fast as his legs could carry him, he raced back to the village and immediately confessed to the elders what he had done and the awful things he had seen. At once, the alarm was sounded and all the people hurried out into the bush to investigate the giant's dwelling for themselves. But as they drew nearer, they became fearful of what he might do to them and scurried back to the village to consult among themselves what steps should be taken. Eventually, it was agreed to go to Salaga, where they knew the giant's long hair came to an end, and set it alight. The chief of the village carried the torch, and when they were certain that the giant's hair was burning well, they returned to the bush, hid themselves in the undergrowth, and awaited the giant's reaction.

Presently, Owuo began to sweat and toss about inside his cave. The closer the flames moved towards him, the more he thrashed about and grumbled until, at last, he rushed outside, his head on fire, and fell down screaming in agony.

The villagers approached him warily and only the young man had the courage to venture close enough to see whether the giant was still breathing. And as he bent over the huge form, he noticed a bundle of medicine concealed in the roots of Owuo's hair. Quickly he seized it and called to the others to come and see what he had found.

The chief of the village examined the bundle, but no one could say what power the peculiar medicine might have. Then one old man among the crowd suggested that no harm could be done if they took some of the medicine and sprinkled it on the bones and meat in the giant's hut. This was done, and to the delight of everyone gathered, the slave girl, her mistress and the boy's brother returned to life at once.

A small quantity of the medicine-dust remained, but when the young man proposed that he should put it on the giant and restore him to life, there was a great uproar among the people. Yet the boy insisted that he should help the giant who had once helped him, and so the chief, by way of compromise, allowed him to sprinkle the left-over dust into the eye of the dead giant.

The young man had no sooner done this when the giant's eye opened wide, causing the people to flee in great terror.

But it is from this eye that death comes. For every time that Owuo shuts that eye, a man dies, and unfortunately for mankind, he is forever blinking and winking, trying to clear the dust from his eye.

Wanjiru, Sacrificed by Her Family
(From the Kikuyu people, Kenya)

THE SUN BEAT DOWN MERCILESSLY and there was no sign of any rain. This happened one year, and it happened again a second year, and even a third year, so that the crops died and the men, women and children found themselves close to starvation.

Finally, the elders of the village called all the people together, and they assembled on the scorched grass at the foot of the hill where they had sung and danced in happier times.

Sick and weary of their miserable plight, they turned to each other and asked helplessly:

"Why is it that the rains do not come?"

Not one among them could find an answer, and so they went to the house of the witch-doctor and put to him the same question:

"Tell us why there is no rain," they wept. "Our crops have failed for a third season and we shall soon die of hunger if things do not change."

The witch-doctor took hold of his gourd, shook it hard, and poured its contents on the ground. After he had done this three times, he spoke gravely:

"There is a young maiden called Wanjiru living among you. If you want the rain to fall, she must be bought by the people of the village. In two days' time you should all return to this place, and every one of you, from the eldest to the youngest, must bring with him a goat for the purchase of the maiden."

And so, on the appointed day, the people gathered together again, each one of them leading a goat to the foot of the hill where the witch-doctor waited to receive them. He ordered the crowd to form a circle and called for Wanjiru to come forward and stand in the middle with her relations to one side of her.

One by one, the people began to move towards Wanjiru's family, leading the goats in payment, and as they approached, the feet of the young girl began to sink into the ground. In an instant, she had sunk up to her knees and she screamed in terror as the soil tugged at her limbs, pulling her closer towards the earth.

Her father and mother saw what was happening and they, too, cried out in fear:

"Our daughter is lost! Our daughter is lost! We must do something to save her."

But the villagers continued to close in around them, each of them handing over their goat until Wanjiru sank deeper to her waist.

"I am lost!" the girl called out, "but much rain will come."

She sank to her breast, and as she did so, heavy black clouds began to gather overhead. She sank even lower, up to her neck, and now the rain started to fall from above in huge drops.

Again, Wanjiru's family attempted to move forward to save her, but yet more people came towards them, pressing them to take goats in payment, and so they stood still, watching as the girl wailed:

"My people have forsaken me! I am undone."

Soon she had vanished from sight. The earth closed over her, the rain poured down in a great deluge and the villagers ran to their huts for shelter without pausing to look back.

Now there was a particular young warrior of fearless reputation among the people who had been in love with Wanjiru ever since childhood. Several weeks had passed since her disappearance, but still he could not reconcile himself to her loss and repeated continually to himself:

"Wanjiru is gone from me and her own people have done this thing to her. But I will find her. I will go to the same place and bring her back."

Taking up his shield and his spear, the young warrior departed his home in search of the girl he loved. For almost a year, he roamed the countryside, but still he could find no trace of her. Weary and dejected, he returned home to the village and stood on the spot where Wanjiru had vanished, allowing his tears to flow freely for the first time.

Suddenly, his feet began to sink into the soil and he sank lower and lower until the ground closed over him and he found himself standing in the middle of a long, winding road beneath the earth's surface. He did not hesitate to follow this road, and after a time, he spotted a figure up ahead of him. He ran towards the figure and saw that it was Wanjiru, even though she was scarcely recognizable in her filthy, tattered clothing.

"You were sacrificed to bring the rain," he spoke tenderly to her, "but now that the rain has come, I shall take you back where you belong."

And he lifted Wanjiru carefully onto his back and carried her, as if she were his own beloved child, along the road he had come by, until they rose together to the open air and their feet touched the ground once more.

"You shall not return to the house of your people," the warrior told Wanjiru, "they have treated you shamefully. I will look after you instead."

So they waited until nightfall, and under cover of darkness, the young warrior took Wanjiru to his mother's house, instructing the old woman to tell no one that the girl had returned.

The months passed by, and Wanjiru lived happily with mother and son. Every day a goat was slaughtered and the meat served to her. The old woman made clothes from the skins and hung beads in the girl's hair so that soon she had regained the healthy glow she once had.

Harvest time was now fast approaching, and a great feast was to be held among the people of the village. The young warrior was one of the first to arrive but Wanjiru waited until the rest of the guests had assembled before she came out of the house to join the festivities. At first, she was not recognized by anyone, but after a time, one of her brothers approached her and cried out:

"Surely that is Wanjiru, the sister we lost when the rains came."

The girl hung her head and gave no answer.

"You sold Wanjiru shamefully," the young warrior intervened, "you do not deserve to have her back."

And he beat off her relatives and took Wanjiru back to his mother's house.

But the next day, her family knocked on his door asking to see the young girl. The warrior refused them once more, but still they came, again and again, until, on the fourth day, the young man relented and said to himself:

"Those are real tears her family shed. Surely now they have proven that they care."

So he invited her father and her mother and her brothers into his home and sat down to fix the bride-price for Wanjiru. And when he had paid it, the young warrior married Wanjiru who had returned to him from the land of shadows beneath the earth.

The Chameleon (How Death Came into the World)

(From the Zulu people, southern Africa)

IT IS SAID UNKULUNKULU (the Supreme Creator) sent a chameleon; he said to it, "Go, chameleon (*lunwaba*), go and say, "Let not men die!" The chameleon set out; it went slowly, it loitered in the way; and as it went it ate of the fruit of a bush which is called Ubukwebezane.

At length Unkulunkulu sent a lizard – *intulo,* the blue-headed gecko – after the chameleon, when it had already set out for some time. The lizard went; it ran and made great haste, for Unkulunkulu had said, "Lizard, when you have arrived say, 'Let men die!'"

So the lizard went, and said, "I tell you, it is said, 'Let men die!'" The lizard came back again to Unkulunkulu before the chameleon had reached his destination; the chameleon, which was sent first – which was sent and told to go and say, "Let not men die!" – at length it arrived and shouted, saying, "It is said, 'Let not men die!'" But men answered, "Oh, we have accepted the word of the lizard; it has told us the word, "It is said 'Let men die.' We cannot hear your word. Through the word of the lizard men will die."

King Kitamba Kia Shiba (and the Kingdom of Death)

(From the Mbundu people, Angola)

KITAMBA WAS A CHIEF who lived at Kasanji. He lost his head-wife, Queen Muhongo, and mourned for her many days. Not only did he mourn himself, but he insisted on his people sharing his grief. "My village, too, no man shall do anything therein. The young people shall not shout; the women shall not pound; no one shall speak in the village."

His headmen remonstrated with him, but Kitamba was obdurate, and declared that he would neither speak nor eat nor allow anyone else to do so till his queen was restored to him. The headmen consulted together, and called in a 'doctor' (*kimbanda*). Having received his fee (first a gun, and then a cow) and heard their statement of the case, he said, "All right," and set off to gather herbs. These he pounded in a 'medicine-mortar', and, having prepared some sort of decoction, ordered the king and all the people to wash themselves with it. He next directed some men to "dig a grave in my guest-hut at the fireplace," which they did, and he entered it with his little boy, giving two last instructions to his wife: to leave off her girdle (i.e., to dress negligently, as if in mourning) and to pour water every day on the fireplace. Then the men filled in the grave. The doctor saw a road open before him; he walked along it with his boy till he came to a village, where he found Queen Muhongo sitting, sewing a basket, She saw him approaching, and asked, "Whence comest thou?" He answered, in the usual form demanded by native politeness, "Thou thyself, I have sought thee. Since thou art dead King Kitamba will not eat, will not drink, will not speak. In the village they pound not; they speak not; he says, 'If I shall talk, if I eat, go ye and fetch my head-wife.' That is what brought me here. I have spoken."

The queen then pointed out a man seated a little way off, and asked the doctor who he was. As he could not say, she told him, "He is Lord Kalunga-ngombe; he is always consuming us, us all." Directing his attention to another man, who was chained, she asked if he knew him, and he answered, "He looks like King Kitamba, whom I left where I came from." It was indeed Kitamba, and the queen further informed the messenger that her husband had not many years to live, and also that "Here in Kalunga never comes one here to return again." She gave him the armlet which had been buried with her, to show to Kitamba as a proof that he had really visited the abode of the dead, but enjoined on him not to tell the king that he had seen him there. And he must not eat anything in Kalunga; otherwise he would never be permitted to return to earth.

Meanwhile the doctor's wife had kept pouring water on the grave. One day she saw the earth beginning to crack; the cracks opened wider, and, finally, her husband's head appeared. He gradually made his way out, and pulled his small son up after him. The child fainted when he came out into the sunlight, but his father washed him with some 'herb-medicine', and soon brought him to.

Next day the doctor went to the headmen, presented his report, was repaid with two slaves, and returned to his home. The headmen told Kitamba what he had said, and produced the token. The only comment he is recorded to have made, on looking at the armlet, is "Truth, it is the same." We do not hear whether he countermanded the official mourning, but it is to be presumed he did so, for he made no further difficulty about eating or drinking. Then, after a few years, he died, and the story concludes, "They wailed the funeral; they scattered."

How Ngunza Defied Death
(From the Mbundu people, Angola)

NGUNZA KILUNDU WAS AWAY FROM HOME when a dream warned him that his younger brother Maka was dead. On his return he asked his mother, "What death was it that killed Maka?" She could only say that it was Lord Kalunga-ngombe who had killed him. "Then," said Ngunza, "I will go out and fight Kalunga-ngombe."

He went at once to a blacksmith and ordered a strong iron trap. When it was ready he took it out into the bush and set it, hiding nearby with his gun. Soon he heard a cry, as of some creature in distress, and, listening, made out words of human speech: "I am dying, dying." It was Kalunga-ngombe who was caught in the trap, and Ngunza took his gun and prepared to shoot. The voice cried out, "Do not shoot me! Come to free me!" Ngunza asked, "Who are you, that I should set you free?" The answer came: "I am Kalunga-ngombe." "Oh, you are Kalunga-ngombe, who killed my younger brother Maka!" Kalunga-ngombe understood the threat which was left unspoken, and went on to explain himself. "You accuse *me* of killing people. I do not do it wantonly, or for my own satisfaction; people are brought to me by their fellow-men, or through their own fault. You shall see this for yourself. Go away now and wait four days: on the fifth you may go and fetch your brother in my country."

Ngunza did as he was told, and went to Kalunga. There he was received by Kalunga-ngombe, who invited him to take his place beside him. The new arrivals began to come in. Kalunga-ngombe asked the first man, "What killed you?" The man answered that on earth he had been very rich; his neighbours were envious and bewitched him, so that he died. The next to arrive was a woman, who admitted that "vanity" had been the cause of her death – that is, she had been greedy of finery and admiration, had coquetted with men, and had in the end been killed by a Jealous husband. So it went on: one after another came with more or less the same story, and at last Kalunga-Ngombe said, "You see how it is – I do not kill people; they are brought to me for one cause or another. It is very unfair to blame me. Now you may go to Milunga and fetch your brother Maka."

Ngunza went as directed, and was overjoyed at finding Maka just as he had left him at their home, and, apparently, leading much the same sort of life as he had on earth. They greeted each other warmly, and then Ngunza said, "Now let us be off, for I have come to fetch you home." But, to his surprise, Maka did not want to go. "I won't go back; I am much better off here than I ever was while I lived. If I come with you, shall I have as good a time?" Ngunza did not know how to answer this, and, very unwillingly, had to leave his brother where he was. He turned away sadly, and went to take leave of Kalunga, who gave him, as a parting present, the seeds of all the useful plants now cultivated in Angola, and ended by saying, "In eight days I shall come to visit you at your home."

Kalunga came to Ngunza's home on the eighth day, and found that he had fled eastward – that is, inland. He pursued him from place to place, and finally came up with him. Ngunza asked why Kalunga should have followed him, adding, "You cannot kill me, for I have done you no wrong. You have been insisting that you do not kill anyone – that people are brought to you through some fault of theirs." Kalunga, for all answer, threw his hatchet at Ngunza, and Ngunza turned into a *kituta* spirit (or *kianda* – a spirit or demon who rules over the water and is fond of great trees and of hill-tops).

The Man Who Would Shoot Iruwa
(From the Chaga people, Tanzania)

A POOR MAN, living somewhere in the Chaga country, on Kilimanjaro mountain, had a number of sons born to him, but lost them all, one after another. He sat down in his desolate house, brooding over his troubles, and at last burst out in wild wrath: "Who has been putting it into Iruwa's head to kill all my boys? I will go and shoot an arrow at Iruwa." So he rose up and went to the smith's forge, and got him to make some iron arrow-heads. When they were ready he put them into his quiver, took up his bow,

and said, "Now I am going to the farthest edge of the world, to the place where the sun comes up. The very moment I see it I will loose this arrow against it – *tichi*!", imitating the sound of the arrow.

So he set out and walked on and on till he came to a wide meadow, where he saw a gateway and many paths, some leading up towards the sky, some downward to. the earth. And he stood still, waiting till the sun should rise, and keeping very quiet. After a while he heard a great noise, and the earth seemed to shake with the trampling of many feet, as if a great procession were approaching. And he heard people shouting one to another: "Quick! Quick! Open the gate for the King to pass through!" Presently he saw many men coming towards him, all goodly to look on and shining like fire. Then he was afraid, and hid himself in the bushes. Again he heard these men crying: "Clear the way where the King is going to pass!" They came on, a mighty host, and all at once, in the midst of them, he was aware of the Shining One, bright as flaming fire, and after him followed another long procession. But suddenly those in front stopped and began asking each other, "What is this horrible smell here, as if an earth-man had passed?" They hunted all about till they found the man, and seized him and brought him before the King, who asked, "Where do you come from, and what brings you to us?" And the man answered, "Nay, my lord, it was nothing – only sorrow – which drove me from home, so that I said to myself, let me go and die in the bush." Then said the King, "But how about your saying you wanted to shoot me? Go on! Shoot away!" The man said, "Oh my lord, I dare not – not now!" "What do you want of me?" "You know that without my telling you, Oh chief!" "So you want me to give you your children back?" The King pointed behind him, saying, "There they are. Take them home with you!" The man looked up and saw all his sons gathered in front of him; but they were so beautiful and radiant that he scarcely knew them, and he said, "No, Oh chief, I cannot take them now. They are yours, and you must keep them." So Iruwa told him to go home and look out carefully on the way, for he should find something that would greatly please him. And he should have other sons in place of those he had lost.

And so it came to pass, for in due time other sons were born to him, who all lived to grow up. And what he found on the road was a great store of elephants' tusks, so that when his neighbours had helped him to carry them home he was made rich for life.

The Road to Heaven

(From the Ronga-speaking people, Mozambique)

THERE WAS ONCE A GIRL who was sent by her mother to fetch water from the river. On the way, talking and laughing with her companions, she dropped her earthen jar and broke it. "Oh, what shall I do now?" she cried, in great distress, for these large jars are not so easily replaced, and she knew there would be trouble awaiting her on her return. She exclaimed, "*Bukali bwa ngoti!* Oh, that I had a rope!" and, looking up, sure enough she saw a rope uncoiling itself from a cloud. She seized it and climbed, and soon found herself in the country above the sky, which appeared to be not unlike the one she had left.

There was what looked like a ruined village not far off, and an old woman sitting among the ruins called to her, "Come here, child! Where are you going?" Being well brought up and accustomed to treat her elders with politeness, she answered at once, and told her story. The old woman told her to go on, and if she found an ant creeping into her ear to let it alone. "It will not hurt you, and will tell you what you have to do in this strange country, and how to answer the chiefs when they question you."

The girl walked on, and in a little while found a black ant crawling up her leg, which went on till it reached her ear. She checked the instinctive impulse to take it out, and went on till she saw the pointed roofs of a village, surrounded by the usual thorn hedge. As she drew near she heard a tiny whisper: "Do not go in; sit down here." She sat down near the gateway. Presently some grave old men, dressed in white, shining bark-cloth, came out and asked her where she had come from and what she wanted. She answered modestly and respectfully, and told them she had come to look for a baby. The elders said, "Very good; come this way." They took her to a hut where some women were at work. One of them gave her a *shirondo* basket, and told her to go to the garden and get some of the new season's mealies. She showed no surprise at this unexpected request, but obeyed at once, and (following the directions of the ant in her ear) pulled up only one stalk at a time, and arranged the cobs carefully in the basket, so as not to waste any space.

When she returned the women praised her for performing her task so quickly and well, and then told her first to grind the corn and then to make porridge. Again instructed by the ant, she put aside a few grains before grinding, and, when she was stirring the porridge, threw these grains in whole, which, it seems, is a peculiar fashion in the cooking of the Heaven-dwellers. They were quite satisfied with the way in which the girl had done her work, and gave her a place to sleep in. Next morning the elders came to fetch her, and conducted her to a handsome house, within which a number of infants were laid out on the ground, those on one side wrapped in red cloth, on the other in white. Being told to choose, she was about to pick up one of the red bundles, when the ant whispered, "Take a white one," and she did so. The old men gave her a quantity of fine cloth and beads, as much as she could carry in addition to the baby, and sent her on her way home. She reached her village without difficulty, and found that everyone was out, as her mother and the other women were at work in the gardens. She went into the hut, and hid herself and the baby in the inner enclosure. When the others returned from the fields, towards evening, the mother sent her younger daughter on ahead to put on the cooking-pots. The girl went in and stirred the fire; as the flames leapt up she saw the treasures her sister had brought home, and, not knowing how they had come there, she was frightened, and ran back to tell her mother and aunts. They all hurried in, and found the girl they had thought lost, with a beautiful baby and a stock of cloth to last a lifetime. They listened to her story in great astonishment; but the younger sister was seized with envy, and wanted to set off at once for that fortunate spot. She was a rude, wilful creature, and her sister, knowing her character, tried to dissuade her, or, at any rate, to give her some guidance for the road. But she refused to listen. "You went off without being told anything by anybody, and I shall go without listening to anyone's advice."

Accordingly when called by the old woman she refused to stop, and even spoke insultingly; whereupon the crone said, "Go on, then! When you return this way you will be dead!" "Who will kill me, then?" retorted the girl, and went on her way. When the ant tried to get into her ear she shook her head and screamed with impatience, refusing to listen when it tried to persuade her. So the ant took itself off in dudgeon.

In the same way she gave a rude answer to the village elders when they asked her why she had come, and when requested to gather mealies she pulled up the stalks right and left, and simply ravaged the garden. Having refused to profit by the ant's warnings, she did not know the right way to prepare the meal or make the porridge, and, in any case, did the work carelessly. When taken to the house where the babies were stored she at once stretched out her hand to seize a red-wrapped one; but immediately there was a tremendous explosion, and she was struck dead. "Heaven," we are told, gathered up her bones, made them into a bundle, and sent a man with them to her home. As he passed the place where she had met with the ant that insect called out, "Are you not coming back dead? You would be alive now if you had listened to advice!" Coming to the old woman's place among the ruins, the carrier heard her cry, "My daughter, haven't you died on account of your wicked heart?" So the man went on, and at last he dropped the bones just above her mother's hut. And her sister said, "She had a wicked heart, and that is why Heaven was angry with her."

The Tale of Murile
(From the Chaga people, Tanzania)

A man and his wife living in the Chaga country had three sons, of whom Murile was the eldest. One day he went out with his mother to dig up *maduma*, and, noticing a particularly fine tuber among those which were to be put by for seed, he said, "Why, this one is as beautiful as my little brother!" His mother laughed at the notion of comparing a *taro* tuber with a baby; but he hid the root, and, later, when no one was looking, put it away in a hollow tree and sang a magic song over it.

Next day he went to look, and found that the root had turned into a child. After that at every meal he secretly kept back some food, and, when he could do so without being seen, carried it to the tree and fed the baby, which grew and flourished from day to day. But Murile's mother became very anxious when she saw how thin the boy was growing, and she questioned him, but could get no satisfaction. Then one day his younger brothers noticed that when his portion of food was handed to him, instead of eating it at once, he put it aside. They told their mother, and she bade them follow him when he went away after dinner, and see what he did with it. They did so, and saw him feeding the baby in the hollow tree, and came back and told her. She went at once to the spot and strangled the child which was 'starving her son'.

When Murile came back next day and found the child dead he was overcome with grief. He went home and sat down in the hut, crying bitterly. His mother asked him why he was crying, and he said it was because the smoke hurt his eyes. So she told him to go and sit on the other side of the fireplace. But, as he still wept and complained of the smoke when questioned, they said he had better take his father's stool and sit outside. He picked up the stool, went out into the courtyard, and sat down. Then he said, "Stool, go up on high, as my father's rope does when he hangs up his beehive in the forest!" And the stool rose up with him into the air and stuck fast in the branches of a tree. He repeated the words a second time, and again the stool moved upward. Just then his brothers happened to come out of the hut, and when they saw him they ran back and said to their mother, "Murile is going up into the sky!" She would not believe them. "Why do you tell me your eldest brother has gone up into the sky? Is there any road for him to go up by?" They told her to come and look, and when she saw him in the air she sang:

"Murile, come back hither!
Come back hither, my child!
Come back hither!"

But Murile answered, "I shall never come back, Mother! I shall never come back!"

Then his brothers called him, and received the same answer; his father called him – then his boy-friends, and, last of all, his uncle (*washidu*, his mother's brother, the nearest relation of all). They could just hear his answer, "I am not coming back, Uncle! I am never coming back!" Then he passed up out of sight.

The stool carried him up till he felt solid ground beneath his feet, and then he looked round and found himself in the Heaven country. He walked on till he came to some people gathering wood. He asked them the way to the Moon-chief's kraal, and they said, "Just pick up some sticks for us, and then we will tell you." He collected a bundle of sticks, and they directed him to go on till he should come to some people cutting grass. He did so, and greeted the grass-cutters when he came to them. They answered his greeting, and when he asked them the way said they would show him if he would help them for a while with their work.

So he cut some grass, and they pointed out the road, telling hill: to go on ill he came to some women hoeing. These, again, asked him to help them before they would show him the way, and, in succession, he met with some herd-boys, some women gathering beans, some people reaping millet, others gathering banana-leaves, and girls fetching water – all of them sending him forward with almost the same words. The water-carriers said, "Just go on in this direction till you come to a house where the people are eating." He found the house, and said, "Greeting, house-owners! Please show me the way to the Moon's kraal." They promised to do so if he would sit down and eat with them, which he did.

At last by following their instructions he reached his destination, and found the people there eating their food raw. He asked them why they did not use fire to cook with, and found that they did not know what fire was. So he said, "If I prepare nice food for you by means of fire what will you give me?" The Moon-chief said, "We will give you cattle and goats and sheep." Murile told them to bring plenty of wood, and when they came with it he and the chief went behind the house, where the other people could not see them. Murile took his knife and cut two pieces of wood, one flat and the other pointed, and twirled the pointed stick till he got some sparks, with which he lit a bunch of dry grass and so kindled a fire. When it burned up he got the chief to send for some green plantains, which he roasted and offered to him. Then he cooked some meat and various other foods. The Moon-chief was delighted when he tasted them, and at once called all the people together, and said to them, "Here is a wonderful doctor come from a far country! We shall have to repay him for his fire." The people asked, "What must be paid to him?" He answered, "Let one man bring a cow, another a goat, another whatever he may have in his storehouse." So they went to fetch all these things. And Murile became a rich man. For he stayed some years at the Moon's great kraal and married wives and had children born to him, and his flocks and herds increased greatly. But in the end a longing for his home came over him.

And he thought within himself: "How shall I go home again, unless I send a messenger before me? For I told them I was never coming back, and they must think that I am dead."

He called all the birds together and asked them one by one, "If I send you to my home what will you say?" The raven answered, "I shall say, *Kuruu! Kuruu!*" and was rejected. So, in turn, were the hornbill, the hawk, the buzzard, and all the rest, till he came to Njorovi, the mocking-bird, who sang:

"Murile is coming the day after tomorrow,
Missing out tomorrow.
Murile is coming the day after tomorrow.
Keep some fat in the ladle for him!"

Murile was pleased with this, and told her to go. So she flew down to earth and perched on the gate-post of his father's courtyard and sang her song. His father came out and said, "What thing is crying out there, saying that Murile is coming the day after tomorrow? Why, Murile was lost long ago, and will never come back!" And he drove the bird away. She flew back and told Murile where she had been. But he would not believe her; he told her to go again and bring back his father's stick as a token that she had really gone to his home. So she flew down again, came to the house, and picked up the stick, which was leaning in the doorway. The children in the house saw her, and tried to snatch it from her, but she was too quick for them, and took it back to Murile. Then he said, "Now I will start for home." He took leave of his friends and of his wives, who were to stay with their own people, but his cattle and his boys came with him. It was a long march to the place of descent, and Murile began to grow very tired. There was a very fine bull in the herd, who walked beside Murile all the way. Suddenly he spoke and said, "As you are so weary, what will you do for me if I let you ride me? If I take you on my back will you eat my flesh when they kill me?" Murile answered, "No! I will never eat you!" So the bull let him get on his back and carried him home. And Murile sang, as he rode along:

"Not a hoof nor a horn is wanting!
Mine are the cattle – hey!
Nought of the goods is wanting; Mine are the bairns today.

Not a kid of the goats is wanting; My flocks are on the way.
Nothing of mine is wanting; Murile comes today
With his bairns and his cattle – hey!"

So he came home. And his father and mother ran out to meet him and anointed him with mutton-fat, as is the custom when a loved one comes home from distant parts. And his brothers and everyone rejoiced and wondered greatly when they saw the cattle. But he showed his father the great bull that had carried him, and said, "This bull must be fed and cared for till he is old. And even if you kill him when he is old I will never eat of his flesh." So they lived quite happily for a time.

But when the bull had become very old Murile's father slaughtered him. The mother foolishly thought it such a pity that her son, who had always taken so much trouble over the beast, should have none of the beef when everyone else was eating it. So she took a piece of fat and hid it in a pot. When she knew that all the meat was finished she ground some grain and cooked the fat with the meal and gave it to her son. As soon as he had tasted it the fat spoke and said to him, "Do you dare to eat me, who carried you on my back? You shall be eaten, as you are eating me!"

Then Murile sang: "Oh my mother, I said to you, 'Do not give me to eat of the bull's flesh!'" He took a second taste, and his foot sank into the ground. He sang the same words again, and then ate up the food his mother had given him. As soon as he had swallowed it he sank down and disappeared.

How a Girl Reached the Land of the Ghosts and Came Back

(From the Chaga people, Tanzania)

MARWE AND HER BROTHER were ordered by their parents to watch the bean-field and drive away the monkeys. They kept at their post for the greater part of the day, but as their mother had not given them any food to take with them they grew very hungry.

They dug up the burrows of the field-rats, caught some, made a fire, roasted their game, and ate it. Then, being thirsty, they went to a pool and drank. It was some distance off, and when they came back they found that the monkeys had descended on the bean-patch and stripped it bare. They were terribly frightened, and Marwe said, "Let's go and jump into the pool." But her brother thought it would be better to go home without being seen and listen to what their parents were saying. So they stole up to the hut and listened through a gap in the banana leaves of the thatch. Father and mother were both very angry. "What are we to do with such good-for-nothing creatures? Shall we beat them? Or shall we strangle them?" The children did not wait to hear any more, but rushed off to the pool. Marwe threw herself in, but her brother's courage failed him, and he ran back home and told the parents: "Marwe has gone into the pool." They went down at once, quite forgetting the hasty words provoked by the sudden discovery of their loss, and called again and again, "Marwe, come home! Never mind about the beans; we can plant the patch again!" But there was no answer. Day after day the father went down to the pool and called her – always in vain. Marwe had gone into the country of the ghosts.

You entered it at the bottom of the pool. Before she had gone very far she came to a hut, where an old woman lived, with a number of children. This old woman called her in and told her she might stay with her. Next day she sent her out with the others to gather firewood, but said, "You need not do anything. Let the others do the work." Marwe, however, did her part with the rest, and the same when they were sent out to cut grass or perform any other tasks. She was offered food from time to time, but always made some excuse for refusing it. (The living who reach the land of the dead can never leave it again if they eat while there.) So time went on, till one day she began to weary, and said to the other girls, "I should like to go home." The girls advised her to go and tell the old woman, which she did, and the old body had no objection, but asked her, "Shall I hit you with the cold or with the hot?" and Marwe asked to be hit with the cold. The woman told her to dip her arms into a pot she had standing beside her. She did so, and drew them out covered with shining bangles. She was then told to dip her feet, and found her ankles adorned with fine brass and copper chains. Then the woman gave her a skin petticoat worked with beads, and said, "Your future husband is called Sawoye. It is he who will carry you home."

She went with her to the pool, rose to the surface and left her sitting on the bank. It happened that there was a famine in the land just then. Someone saw Marwe and ran to the village saying that there was a girl seated by the pool richly dressed and wearing the most beautiful ornaments, which no one else in the countryside could afford, the people having parted with all their valuables to the coast-traders in the time of scarcity. So the whole population turned out, with the chief at their head. They were filled with admiration of her beauty. They all greeted her most respectfully, and the chief wanted to carry her home; but she refused. Others offered, but she would listen to none till a certain man came along, who was known as Sawoye. Now Sawoye was disfigured by a disease from which he had suffered called *woye*, whence his name. As soon as she saw him Marwe said, "That is my husband." So he picked her up and carried her home and married her.

Sawoye soon lost his disfiguring skin disease and appeared as the handsomest man in the clan. With the old lady's bangles they bought a fine herd of cattle and built themselves the best house in the village. And they would have lived happy ever after if some of his neighbours had not envied him and plotted to kill him. They succeeded, but his faithful wife found means to revive him, and hid him in the inner compartment of the hut. Then, when the enemies came to divide the spoil and carry Marwe off to be given to the chief as his wife, Sawoye came out, fully armed, and killed them all. After which he and Marwe were left in peace.

Why Dead People are Buried

(From southern Nigeria)

IN THE BEGINNING OF THE WORLD when the Creator had made men and women and the animals, they all lived together in the creation land. The Creator was a big chief, past all men, and being very kind-hearted, was very sorry whenever anyone died. So one day he sent for the dog, who was his head messenger, and told him to go out into the world and give his word to all people that for the future

whenever anyone died the body was to be placed in the compound, and wood ashes were to be thrown over it; that the dead body was to be left on the ground, and in twenty-four hours it would become alive again.

When the dog had travelled for half a day he began to get tired; so as he was near an old woman's house he looked in, and seeing a bone with some meat on it he made a meal off it, and then went to sleep, entirely forgetting the message which had been given him to deliver.

After a time, when the dog did not return, the Creator called for a sheep, and sent him out with the same message. But the sheep was a very foolish one, and being hungry, began eating the sweet grasses by the wayside. After a time, however, he remembered that he had a message to deliver, but forgot what it was exactly; so as he went about among the people he told them that the message the Creator had given him to tell the people, was that whenever anyone died they should be buried underneath the ground.

A little time afterwards the dog remembered his message, so he ran into the town and told the people that they were to place wood ashes on the dead bodies and leave them in the compound, and that they would come to life again after twenty-four hours. But the people would not believe him, and said, "We have already received the word from the Creator by the sheep, that all dead bodies should be buried." In consequence of this the dead bodies are now always buried, and the dog is much disliked and not trusted as a messenger, as if he had not found the bone in the old woman's house and forgotten his message, the dead people might still be alive.

The King and the Ju Ju Tree

(From southern Nigeria)

UDO UBOK UDOM was a famous king who lived at Itam, which is an inland town, and does not possess a river. The king and his wife therefore used to wash at the spring just behind their house.

King Udo had a daughter, of whom he was very fond, and looked after her most carefully, and she grew up into a beautiful woman.

For some time the king had been absent from his house, and had not been to the spring for two years. When he went to his old place to wash, he found that the Idem Ju Ju tree had grown up all round the place, and it was impossible for him to use the spring as he had done formerly. He therefore called fifty of his young men to bring their matchets and cut down the tree. They started cutting the tree, but it had no effect, as, directly they made a cut in the tree, it closed up again; so, after working all day, they found they had made no impression on it.

When they returned at night, they told the king that they had been unable to destroy the tree. He was very angry when he heard this, and went to the spring the following morning, taking his own matchet with him.

When the Ju Ju tree saw that the king had come himself and was starting to try to cut his branches, he caused a small splinter of wood to go into the king's eye. This gave the king great pain, so he threw down his matchet and went back to his house. The pain, however, got worse, and he could not eat or sleep for three days.

He therefore sent for his witch men, and told them to cast lots to find out why he was in such pain. When they had cast lots, they decided that the reason was that the Ju Ju tree was angry with the king because he wanted to wash at the spring, and had tried to destroy the tree.

They then told the king that he must take seven baskets of flies, a white goat, a white chicken, and a piece of white cloth, and make a sacrifice of them in order to satisfy the Ju Ju.

The king did this, and the witch men tried their lotions on the king's eye, but it got worse and worse.

He then dismissed these witches and got another lot. When they arrived they told the king that, although they could do nothing themselves to relieve his pain, they knew one man who lived in the spirit land who could cure him; so the king told them to send for him at once, and he arrived the next day.

Then the spirit man said, "Before I do anything to your eye, what will you give me?" So King Udo said, "I will give you half my town with the people in it, also seven cows and some money." But the spirit man refused to accept the king's offer. As the king was in such pain, he said, "Name your own price, and I will pay you." So the spirit man said the only thing he was willing to accept as payment was the king's daughter. At this the king cried very much, and told the man to go away, as he would rather die than let him have his daughter.

That night the pain was worse than ever, and some of his subjects pleaded with the king to send for the spirit man again and give him his daughter, and told him that when he got well he could no doubt have another daughter but that if he died now he would lose everything.

The king then sent for the spirit man again, who came very quickly, and in great grief the king handed his daughter to the spirit.

The spirit man then went out into the bush, and collected some leaves, which he soaked in water and beat up. The juice he poured into the king's eye, and told him that when he washed his face in the morning he would be able to see what was troubling him in the eye.

The king tried to persuade him to stay the night, but the spirit man refused, and departed that same night for the spirit land, taking the king's daughter with him.

Before it was light the king rose up and washed his face, and found that the small splinter from the Ju Ju tree, which had been troubling him so much, dropped out of his eye, the pain disappeared, and he was quite well again.

When he came to his proper senses he realised that he had sacrificed his daughter for one of his eyes, so he made an order that there should be general mourning throughout his kingdom for three years.

For the first two years of the mourning the king's daughter was put in the fatting house by the spirit man, and was given food; but a skull, who was in the house, told her not to eat, as they were fatting her up, not for marriage, but so that they could eat her. She therefore gave all the food which was brought to her to the skull, and lived on chalk herself.

Towards the end of the third year the spirit man brought some of his friends to see the king's daughter, and told them he would kill her the next day, and they would have a good feast off her.

When she woke up in the morning the spirit man brought her food as usual; but the skull, who wanted to preserve her life, and who had heard what the spirit man had said, called her into the room and told her what was going to happen later in the day. She handed the food to the skull, and he said, "When the spirit man goes to the wood with his friends to prepare for the feast, you must run back to your father."

He then gave her some medicine which would make her strong for the journey, and also gave her directions as to the road, telling her that there were two roads but that when she came to the parting of the ways she was to drop some of the medicine on the ground and the two roads would become one.

He then told her to leave by the back door, and go through the wood until she came to the end of the town; she would then find the road. If she met people on the road she was to pass them in silence, as if she saluted them they would know that she was a stranger in the spirit land, and might kill her. She was also not to turn round if anyone called to her, but was to go straight on till she reached her father's house.

Having thanked the skull for his kind advice, the king's daughter started off, and when she reached the end of the town and found the road, she ran for three hours, and at last arrived at the branch roads. There she dropped the medicine, as she had been instructed, and the two roads immediately became one; so she went straight on and never saluted anyone or turned back, although several people called to her.

About this time the spirit man had returned from the wood, and went to the house, only to find the king's daughter was absent. He asked the skull where she was, and he replied that she had gone out by the back door, but he did not know where she had gone to. Being a spirit, however, he very soon guessed that she had gone home; so he followed as quickly as possible, shouting out all the time.

When the girl heard his voice she ran as fast as she could, and at last arrived at her father's house, and told him to take at once a cow, a pig, a sheep, a goat, a dog, a chicken, and seven eggs, and cut them into seven parts as a sacrifice, and leave them on the road, so that when the spirit man saw these things he would stop and not enter the town. This the king did immediately, and made the sacrifice as his daughter had told him.

When the spirit man saw the sacrifice on the road, he sat down and at once began to eat.

When he had satisfied his appetite, he packed up the remainder and returned to the spirit land, not troubling any more about the king's daughter.

When the king saw that the danger was over, he beat his drum, and declared that for the future, when people died and went to the spirit land, they should not come to earth again as spirits to cure sick people.

Animal Stories & Fables

A FABLE IS A SHORT MORAL STORY, and the African storyteller has shown a particular fondness for this sort of tale in which the actions and escapades of the characters are described not merely for our entertainment, but also for us to reflect on and from which to learn lessons.

Many African fables revolve entirely around animals, and the stories which follow are a selection of some of the most well-known. In all of the fables, animals have the ability to speak and they generally behave like humans. Some, like the chameleon in one story, even marry human beings.

Two of the most outstanding characters of the animal fables are the spider and the tortoise. The first three stories of this section centre on the adventures of the shrewd and designing spider Anansi, who usually manages to outwit all of his opponents, yet whose behaviour is not always intended to reflect the correct moral course. Equally shrewd and clever, despite his slow-moving body and wrinkled skin, is the tortoise who, again and again, triumphs over his adversaries. In the tales which follow, it is his uncanny wisdom that shines through, ensuring that he is never defeated, even by those who are much larger and stronger.

Of course, not all stories involving animals teach a clear lesson – they may instead have been told simply to entertain, through the telling of various trickster animals' exploits, or indeed they may be origin stories, told in order to explain how one creature animal came to have its spots, for instance, or why others live in the water. This section contains a wide range of such fascinating tales.

How Anansi Became a Spider
(From the Dagomba people, west Africa)

A VERY LONG TIME AGO, there lived a king who had amongst his possessions a very magnificent ram, larger and taller than any other specimen in the entire country. The ram was more precious to him than anything else he owned and he made it quite clear to his subjects that the animal must be allowed to roam wherever it chose, and be allowed to eat as much food as it desired, even if the people themselves were forced to go hungry. If anyone should ever hit or injure the king's ram, that man should certainly die.

Every citizen of the kingdom obeyed the king's orders without a great deal of complaint, but there was one among them, a wealthy farmer named Anansi, who was particularly proud of the crops he raised. Everyone suspected that he would not tolerate a visit from the king's ram and they prayed amongst themselves that such an event might never happen.

One day, however, when the rains had begun to fall, and his crops were already as tall as his waist, Anansi went out to make a final inspection of his fields. He was very pleased with what he saw and was just about to return to his farmhouse when he noticed in the distance an area of land where the corn had been trampled underfoot and the young shoots eaten away. There in the middle of the field, still munching away quite happily, stood the king's ram. Anansi was so furious he hurled a large pebble at the animal intending only to frighten him away. But the stone hit the ram right between the eyes and before he had quite realized what he had done, the animal lay dead at his feet.

Anansi did not know what he should do. Like everybody else in the village, he was only too familiar with the king's orders and knew he would face certain death if his crime was discovered. He leaned back against a shea-butter tree wondering how to resolve the dreadful mess. Suddenly a nut fell on his head from one of the branches above. Anansi picked it up and ate it. He liked the taste of it very much and so he shook the tree until several more nuts fell to the ground. Then the most fantastic idea entered his head. He picked up the nuts and put them in his pocket. He quickly lifted the ram and climbed the tree with him. As soon as he had tied the animal to a strong bough he descended once more and headed off towards the house of his friend, Kusumbuli, the spider.

Anansi found his friend at home and the two sat down and began to chat. After a few moments, Anansi took one of the shea-nuts from his pocket and handed it to his friend.

"This nut has an excellent flavour," said Kusumbuli, as he sat chomping on the ripe flesh, "tell me, where did you come across such a fine crop?"

Anansi promised to show the spider the exact spot and led him to the tree where the nuts were growing in large clusters.

"You'll have to shake quite hard to loosen them," Anansi advised Kusumbuli, "don't be afraid, the trunk is a strong one."

So the spider began shaking the tree violently and as he did so, the dead ram fell to the ground.

"Oh, my friend," cried Anansi at once, "what have you done? Look, the king's ram is lying at your feet and you have killed him."

Kusumbuli turned pale as a wave of panic swept over him.

"There is only one thing you can do now," Anansi urged the spider, "go and unburden your conscience at once. Tell the king precisely what has happened and with any luck he will understand that the whole affair was a most unfortunate accident."

Kusumbuli thought that this was good advice, so he picked up the dead ram and set off to confess his crime, hoping the king would be in a good mood.

The road towards the king's palace brought him past his own home and the spider went indoors to bid a sad farewell to his wife and children, believing that he might never set eyes on them again. Anansi stood at the entrance while Kusumbuli went into the back room and told his wife everything that had happened. She listened attentively to what he said and immediately saw that there was some trick involved.

"I have never seen a ram climb a tree before, Kusumbuli," she said to him. "Use your head. Anansi has something to do with this and you are taking the blame for him. Hear me now and do exactly as I say."

So she advised her husband that he must leave Anansi behind and pretend to go alone in search of the king. After he had gone some distance, she told him, he was to rest and then return home and announce that all had turned out well in the end. The spider agreed to do this and asked Anansi if he would be so good as to look after his wife and children. His friend promised to watch over them faithfully and the spider set off on his travels winking at his wife as he moved away.

Several hours later, Kusumbuli returned to his home, smiling from ear to ear as he embraced his family.

"Come and celebrate with us, Anansi," he cried excitedly, "I have been to see the king and he was not at all angry with me. In fact, he said he had no use for a dead ram and insisted that I help myself to as much of the meat as I wanted."

At this, Anansi became enraged and shouted out:

"What! You have been given all that meat when it was I who took the trouble to kill that ram. I should have been given my fair share, you deserved none of it."

Kusumbuli and his wife now leaped upon Anansi and bound his hands and legs. Then they dragged him to the king's palace and reported to their ruler the whole unpleasant affair.

Anansi squirmed on the floor and begged for the king's mercy. But the king could not control his fury and he raised his foot to kick Anansi as he lay on the ground. The king kicked so hard that Anansi broke into a thousand pieces that scattered themselves all over the room.

And that is how Anansi came to be such a small spider. And that is why you will find him in every corner of the house, awaiting the day when someone will put all the pieces together again.

Anansi Obtains the Sky God's Stories
(From the Ashanti people, west Africa)

KWAKU ANANSI had one great wish. He longed to be the owner of all the stories known in the world, but these were kept by the Sky God, Nyame [The Ashanti refer to God as 'Nyame'. The Dagomba call him 'Wuni', while the Krachi refer to him as 'Wulbari'.], in a safe hiding-place high above the clouds.

One day, Anansi decided to pay the Sky God a visit to see if he could persuade Nyame to sell him the stories.

"I am flattered you have come so far, little creature," the Sky God told Anansi, "but many rich and powerful men have preceded you and none has been able to purchase what they came here for. I am willing to part with my stories, but the price is very high. What makes you think that you can succeed where they have all failed?"

"I feel sure I will be able to buy them," answered Anansi bravely, "if you will only tell me what the price is."

"You are very determined, I see," replied Nyame, "but I must warn you that the price is no ordinary one. Listen carefully now to what I demand of you.

"First of all, you must capture Onini, the wise old python, and present him to me. When you have done this, you must go in search of the Mmoboro, the largest nest of hornets in the forest, and bring them here also. Finally, look for Osebo, the fastest of all leopards and set a suitable trap for him. Bring him to me either dead or alive.

"When you have delivered me these three things, all the stories of the world will be handed over to you."

"I shall bring you everything you ask for," Anansi declared firmly, and he hastened towards his home where he began making plans for the tasks ahead.

That afternoon, he sat down with his wife, Aso, and told her all about his visit to the Sky God.

"How will I go about trapping the great python, Onini?" he asked her.

His wife, who was a very clever woman, instructed her husband to make a special trip to the centre of the woods:

"Go and cut yourself a long bamboo pole," she ordered him, "and gather some strong creeper-vines as well. As soon as you have done this, return here to me and I will tell you what to do with these things."

Anansi gathered these objects as his wife had commanded and after they had spent some hours consulting further, he set off enthusiastically towards the house of Onini.

As he approached closer, he suddenly began arguing with himself in a loud and angry voice:

"My wife is a stupid woman," he pronounced, "she says it is longer and stronger. I say it is shorter and weaker. She has no respect. I have a great deal.

She is stupid. I am right."

"What's all this about?" asked the python, suddenly appearing at the door of his hut. "Why are you having this angry conversation with yourself?"

"Oh! Please ignore me," answered the spider. "It's just that my wife has put me in such a bad mood. For she says this bamboo pole is longer and stronger than you are, and I say she is a liar."

"There is no need for the two of you to argue so bitterly on my account," replied the python, "bring that pole over here and we will soon find out who is right."

So Anansi laid the bamboo pole on the earth and the python stretched himself out alongside it.

"I'm still not certain about this," said Anansi after a few moments. "When you stretch at one end, you appear to shrink at the other end. Perhaps if I tied you to the pole I would have a clearer idea of your size."

"Very well," answered the python, "just so long as we can sort this out properly."

Anansi then took the creeper-vine and wrapped it round and round the length of the python's body until the great creature was unable to move.

"Onini," said Anansi, "it appears my wife was right. You are shorter and weaker than this pole and more foolish into the bargain. Now you are my prisoner and I must take you to the Sky God, as I have promised."

The great python lowered his head in defeat as Anansi tugged on the pole, dragging him along towards the home of Nyame.

"You have done well, spider," said the god, "but remember, there are two more, equally difficult quests ahead. You have much to accomplish yet, and it would not be wise to delay here any longer."

So Anansi returned home once more and sat down to discuss the next task with his wife.

"There are still hornets to catch," he told her, "and I cannot think of a way to capture an entire swarm all at once."

"Look for a gourd," his wife suggested, "and after you have filled it with water, go out in search of the hornets."

Anansi found a suitable gourd and filled it to the brim. Fortunately, he knew exactly the tree where the hornets had built their nest. But before he approached too close, he poured some of the water from the gourd over himself so that his clothes were dripping wet. Then, he began sprinkling the nest with the remaining water while shouting out to the hornets:

"Why do you remain in such a flimsy shelter Mmoboro, when the great rains have already begun? You will soon be swept away, you foolish people. Here, take cover in this dry gourd of mine and it will protect you from the storms."

The hornets thanked the spider for this most timely warning and disappeared one by one into the gourd. As soon as the last of them had entered, Anansi plugged the mouth of the vessel with some grass and chuckled to himself:

"Fools! I have outwitted you as well. Now you can join Onini, the python. I'm certain Nyame will be very pleased to see you."

Anansi was delighted with himself. It had not escaped his notice that even the Sky God appeared rather astonished by his success and it filled him with great excitement to think that very soon he would own all the stories of the world.

Only Osebo, the leopard, stood between the spider and his great wish, but Anansi was confident that with the help of his wife he could easily ensnare the creature as he had done all the others.

"You must go and look for the leopard's tracks," his wife told him, "and then dig a hole where you know he is certain to walk."

Anansi went away and dug a very deep pit in the earth, covering it with branches and leaves so that it was well-hidden from the naked eye. Night-time closed in around him and soon afterwards, Osebo came prowling as usual and fell right into the deep hole, snarling furiously as he hit the bottom.

At dawn on the following morning, Anansi approached the giant pit and called to the leopard:

"What has happened here? Have you been drinking, leopard? How on earth will you manage to escape from this great hole?"

"I have fallen into a silly man-trap," said the leopard impatiently. "Help me out at once. I am almost starving to death in this wretched place."

"And if I help you out, how can I be sure you won't eat me?" asked Anansi. "You say you are very hungry, after all."

"I wouldn't do a thing like that," Osebo reassured him. "I beg you, just this once, to trust me. Nothing bad will happen to you, I promise."

Anansi hurried away from the opening of the pit and soon returned with a long, thick rope. Glancing around him, he spotted a tall green tree and bent it towards the ground, securing it with a length of the rope so that the top branches hung over the pit. Then he tied another piece of rope to these branches, dropping the loose end into the pit for the leopard to tie to his tail.

"As soon as you have tied a large knot, let me know and I will haul you up," shouted Anansi.

Osebo obeyed the spider's every word, and as soon as he gave the signal that he was ready, Anansi cut the rope pinning the tree to the ground. It sprung upright at once, pulling the leopard out of the hole in one swift motion. Osebo hung upside down, wriggling and twisting helplessly, trying with every ounce of his strength to loosen his tail from the rope. But Anansi was not about to take any chances and he plunged his knife deep into the leopard's chest, killing him instantly. Then he lifted the leopard's body from the earth and carried it all the way to the Sky God.

Nyame now called together all the elders of the skies, among them the Adonten, the Oyoko, the Kontire and Akwam chiefs, and informed them of the great exploits of Anansi, the spider:

"Many great warriors and chiefs have tried before," the Sky God told the congregation, "but none has been able to pay the price I have asked of them. Kwaku Anansi has brought me Onini the python, the Mmoboro nest and the body of the mighty Osebo. The time has come to repay him as he deserves. He has won the right to tell my stories. From today, they will no longer be called stories of the Sky God, but stories of Anansi, the spider."

And so, with Nyame's blessing, Anansi became the treasurer of all the stories that have ever been told. And even now, whenever a man wishes to tell a story for the entertainment of his people, he must acknowledge first of all that the tale is a great gift, given to him by Anansi, the spider.

Anansi and the Corn Cob
(From the Krachi people, west Africa)

ANANSI WAS BY FAR THE CLEVEREST of Wulbari's heavenly creatures. He was also the most ambitious among them and was always on the look-out for an opportunity to impress the supreme god with his intelligence and cunning.

One day he appeared before Wulbari and asked if he might borrow from him a corn cob.

"Certainly," said Wulbari, "but what a strange thing to ask for! Why do you wish to borrow a corn cob?"

"I know it is an unusual request," replied Anansi, "but Master, if you will give me the corn cob I will bring you a hundred slaves in exchange for it."

Wulbari laughed aloud at this response, but he handed Anansi the cob and declared that he looked forward to the day when the spider might deliver such a prize. Anansi meant every word he had spoken, however, and without further delay he set off on the road leading down from the sky to the earth.

It was nightfall by the time he completed his long journey and because he felt very weary, he went straightaway in search of a night's lodging. He soon happened upon the home of the village chief and having requested a bed, he was shown to a comfortable mattress in the corner of the room. But before he lay down to sleep he asked the chief where he might put the corn cob for safe-keeping:

"It is the corn of Wulbari," Anansi explained. "Our great Creator has instructed me to carry it to the people of Yendi, and I must not lose it along the way."

The chief pointed to a hiding place in the roof and Anansi climbed up and placed the cob amongst the straw. Then he retired to his bed and pretended to be asleep. But as soon as the sound of the chief's snoring filled the room, Anansi arose again and removed the corn from its hiding place. He crept quickly out of doors and threw the corn to the fowls, making certain that the greedy birds helped themselves to every last kernel.

On the following morning, when Anansi asked for his corn, the chief climbed to the roof, but could not find any trace of it. Anansi stared at his host accusingly and began to create the most appalling scene, screaming and shouting and stamping his feet until, at last, each of the villagers was ordered to present him with a whole basket of corn each. This appeared to pacify Anansi only slightly, and very soon afterwards he took his leave of the chief declaring that he would never again visit such dishonest people.

He continued on his journey, carrying with him the great sack of corn he had collected. After a time he sat down by the roadside to rest and soon he spotted a man heading towards him carrying a chicken. Anansi greeted the man warmly and before long they had struck up a lively conversation.

"That's a nice, plump bird you have there," Anansi said to the man. "Nothing would please me more right now than to exchange my sack of corn for your fowl, for I am sick and weary of carrying my load from place to place."

The man could scarcely believe his luck. There was enough corn in the bag to feed his entire family for several months and he very readily agreed to the exchange. The two shook hands and then went their separate ways, Anansi carrying the chicken under one arm, the man dragging the heavy sack behind him.

Later that day, Anansi arrived at the next village, and having asked the way to the chief's house, he knocked upon the door to beg a night's lodging. As before, the chief of the village welcomed him with open arms, and when Anansi showed him the fowl of Wulbari he had his people prepare a nice, quiet out-house where the bird could be placed out of harm's way overnight. But again, Anansi arose when he was certain everyone else had fallen asleep and killed the fowl, leaving the corpse in the bush and smearing some of the blood and feathers on the chief's own doorstep.

The next morning Anansi awoke and began shouting and thrashing about wildly.

"You have killed my precious fowl," he shrieked as he pointed to the blood and the feathers. "Wulbari will never forgive such a crime."

The chief and all his people begged Anansi to forgive them and tried desperately to think of something that might appease him. At long last Anansi announced that perhaps there was something they could give him to take to the people of Yendi instead, and he pointed to a flock of sheep grazing in a nearby field.

"We will give you any number of these sheep if you will only pardon us," said the chief.

So Anansi accepted the ten best sheep from the flock and went on his way once more.

It was not long before he reached the outskirts of Yendi, but before he entered the village he decided to allow his sheep to graze for a few minutes. And while he was seated on the grass watching them eat, he noticed a group of people approach, weeping and wailing as they returned home to their village bearing the body of a young man.

"Where are you taking the corpse?" Anansi asked them.

"We have a long way to go yet," they told him, "beyond those mountains to the west towards the dead boy's home."

"But you look worn out," said Anansi, "I would be only too delighted to help you in any way. Here, take my sheep and lead them to your village and I will follow behind with the body on my shoulders."

But Anansi allowed himself to fall further and further behind the men until finally they drifted out of sight. Then he retraced his steps and walked into the village of Yendi carrying with him the corpse. There he knocked on the door of the chief's house, explaining that he had with him the favourite son of Wulbari who was very weary from travelling and in desperate need of a bed for the night.

The chief and his people were delighted to have such an important guest among them and a comfortable hut was soon made ready for the favourite son of Wulbari. Anansi laid the body down inside the hut, covering it with a cloth before joining the chief for a splendid celebratory feast.

"I'm so sorry that our guest of honour is unable to join us," said Anansi to the chief, "but we have journeyed so far today, he has collapsed with exhaustion."

The chief insisted that some of the best food be set aside for the son of Wulbari, and at the end of the evening he presented it to Anansi who promised to feed it to his companion as soon as he awoke. But Anansi finished the entire meal himself and sat cross-legged on the floor of the hut, chortling away to himself in the darkness.

At dawn, he called to the chief's own children to go in and wake the son of Wulbari.

"If he does not stir," Anansi told them, "you will have to flog him, for nothing else appears to wake him when he has slept so soundly."

So the children did as they were instructed, but Wulbari's son did not wake.

"Beat him harder, beat him harder," Anansi encouraged them, and the children did as he told them. But still Wulbari's son did not wake. So Anansi announced that he would go and wake the boy himself.

Soon there was a great wailing from inside the hut as Anansi cried out that the children of the chief had beaten to death the favourite son of Wulbari. The chief himself rushed forward and examined all the evidence. He was convinced that Anansi had spoken the truth and immediately offered to have his children sacrificed to the supreme god for what they had done to the unfortunate boy. But Anansi continued to wail aloud. Then the chief offered to kill himself, but still Anansi refused and said that nothing he could think of would ever undo such a great loss.

"Please just bury the body, I can't bear to look upon him any longer" he told the people. "Perhaps when my mind is clearer I will think of some plan to appease Wulbari's anger."

It was much later that same evening when Anansi reappeared, his eyes red and puffy from squeezing out the tears, his body stooped in mock-anguish.

"I have been thinking long and hard," he said to the chief, "and I have decided that I will take all the blame on myself for this dreadful deed, for I know you would never survive the wrath of Wulbari. I will say that his son's death was a terrible accident, but you must allow one hundred of your men to accompany me, for I will need them to support my testimony."

The chief, who was more than pleased with this solution, immediately chose a hundred of the best young men and ordered them to prepare themselves for the long journey back to the kingdom of Wulbari. By midday they had departed the village and were well on the road leading upwards from the earth to the heavens.

Wulbari observed the crowd of youths approach and came out to greet them personally, anxious to discover their business, for he had forgotten all about Anansi and the bold promise he had made many weeks before.

"I told you it was possible, Master," Anansi piped up from amongst the crowd. "Do you not remember giving me that single corn cob? Now you have a hundred excellent slaves in exchange. They are yours to keep and I have kept my promise."

Wulbari smiled broadly and was so pleased with Anansi he confirmed his appointment as Chief of his Host there and then, ordering him to change his name from Anyankon to Anansi, which is the name he has kept to the present day.

Tortoise and the Wisdom of the World
(From Nigeria, west Africa)

TORTOISE WAS VERY ANGRY when he awoke one day to discover that other people around him had started to behave just as wisely as himself. He was angry because he was an ambitious fellow and wanted to keep all the wisdom of the world for his own personal use. If he succeeded in his ambition, he felt

he would be so wise that everyone, including the great chiefs and elders of the people, would have to seek his advice before making any decision, no matter how small. He intended to charge a great deal of money for the privilege, and was adamant that nothing would upset his great plan.

And so he set out to collect all the wisdom of the world before anyone else decided to help himself to it. He hollowed out an enormous gourd for the purpose and began crawling along on his stomach through the bush, collecting the wisdom piece by piece and dropping it carefully into the large vessel. After several hours, when he was happy he had gathered every last scrap, he plugged the gourd with a roll of leaves and made his way slowly homewards.

But now that he had all the wisdom of the world in his possession, he grew fearful that it might be stolen from him. So he decided straight away that it would be best to hide the gourd in a safe place at the centre of the forest. He soon found a very tall palm tree which seemed suitable enough and prepared himself to climb to the top. First of all he took a rope and made a loop around the neck of the gourd. When he had done this, he hung the vessel from his neck so that it rested on his stomach. Then he took a very deep breath and began to climb the tree.

But he found that after several minutes he had not made any progress, for the gourd was so large it kept getting in his way. He slung it to one side and tried again. Still he could not move forward even an inch. He slung the gourd impatiently to the other side, but the same thing happened. Finally, he tried to stretch past it, but all these efforts came to nothing and he beat the tree with his fists in exasperation.

Suddenly he heard someone sniggering behind him. He turned around and came face to face with a hunter who had been watching him with great amusement for some time.

"Tortoise," said the hunter eventually, "why don't you hang the gourd over your back if you insist on climbing that tree?"

"What a good idea," replied the tortoise, "I'd never have thought of that on my own."

But he had no sooner spoken these words when it dawned on him that the hunter must have helped himself to some of the precious wisdom.

Tortoise now grew even more angry and frustrated and began scuttling up the tree to get away from the thieving hunter. He moved so fast, however, that the rope holding the gourd slipped from around his neck causing the vessel to drop to the ground where it broke into hundreds of little pieces.

All the wisdom of the world was now scattered everywhere. And ever since that time nobody else has attempted to gather it all together in one place.

But whenever he feels the need, Tortoise makes a special journey to the palm tree at the centre of the forest, for he knows that the little pieces are still there on the ground, waiting to be discovered by anyone who cares to search hard enough.

The Tortoise and the Baboon

(From the Swahili-speaking peoples, east Africa)

THE TORTOISE AND THE BABOON had been friends for a very long time and so it was only natural that they should invite each other to their wedding feasts when they both decided to get married.

The Baboon was the first to celebrate his wedding and he insisted that the feast be as elaborate as possible. The most delicious food was prepared by a team of twelve cooks, and the finest palm wine was provided for every guest.

Tortoise arrived punctually on the day and was most impressed by what he saw. He was extremely hungry after his very long journey, and more than anything he looked forward to tucking into the food in the company of the other guests.

At last the dinner gong was sounded and all the baboons began climbing the trees where they sat waiting to be served. Tortoise, of course, could not climb at all well and struggled very hard to make it even to the lowest branch. By the time he eventually reached the party, the first half of the meal had been served and cleared and he found that he was ignored by the other guests who chatted loudly among themselves.

Finally, he thought it best to mention to his friend the slight problem he was having keeping his balance on the branch.

"But you must sit like the rest of us," the baboon told Tortoise, "it is our custom. When my people eat, they always sit this way. It would be so rude to lie on the ground when everyone else is upright."

And so Tortoise tried a little harder to make himself comfortable, but as soon as he reached forward to grab hold of some food, he fell flat on his belly. All the baboons roared with laughter at the sight of him and he hung his head in shame, feeling hungry and frustrated, knowing that he would never get to eat any of the delicious food.

When the day arrived for the Tortoise to marry, he had no wish to provide a lavish banquet for his guests, but prepared a small dinner-party for his closest friends. Before any of the guests was due to arrive, however, Tortoise went outdoors and lit a torch. Holding the flame to the earth, he began to burn the dry grass around his house and all the scrubland nearby.

Baboon and his new wife soon appeared in the distance and Tortoise slipped indoors again to resume the preparations. He embraced the couple warmly when they arrived and made sure that they were given one of the best seats at his table. The food was set down before them, and all were about to tuck in when Tortoise suddenly stood up and raised both arms in the air:

"Let's just make sure that we all have clean hands," he said. "Nothing upsets me more than people who eat their food with dirty hands."

One by one his guests began to examine their hands, quite confident that they were clean. But when Baboon stared at his, he was shocked to see that they were a filthy black colour.

"But I scrubbed them before I left my house," he protested.

"None the less," replied Tortoise, "they are very dirty indeed and it would be offensive to my people if you did not make an effort to clean them one more time. Go back to the river across the bush and try again. We promise to eat slowly so that you do not miss the meal."

Baboon set off to do as his host suggested, walking on all fours through the charred grass and soot until he reached the river. Here he washed his hands thoroughly and returned by the same path to Tortoise's house.

"But there is no improvement. You must go again," said Tortoise, munching on a delicious yam. "What a shame! We will have eaten everything if this keeps up."

Again the Baboon returned and again the Tortoise sent him away, a third and a fourth and a fifth time, until all the splendid dishes had been gobbled up.

So in the end, Tortoise had his revenge, and for many years afterwards he took great delight in telling his friends the story of how he managed to outwit Baboon on his wedding day.

Tortoise and the Hot-water Test

(From the Yoruba people, west Africa)

EVERY YEAR AT HARVEST TIME, the chief called upon his people to help him gather in the crops. And every year, just as the work was about to commence, Tortoise disappeared to the country for a few weeks, for he was never very interested in lending a hand.

But there came a season when his own crops failed him and he began to worry about how he might survive the harsh winter ahead. Looking out through the window of his hut, he saw that the chief's fields were full of sweet yams and decided he would have to get his hands on enough of them to fill his empty storehouse.

Finally he came up with a plan. In the middle of the night, when nobody was looking, he took a large shovel and made his way to the chief's fields. He began to dig a very deep hole, broad at the base and narrow at the top. Then he scattered leaves and branches over the hole to hide it and crept back to his bed.

Early the next morning, Tortoise knocked upon the door of the chief's house.

"I have come to help you in the fields," he told the chief, "and I am prepared to stay as long as it takes, until every single yam has been harvested."

Although very surprised, the chief was delighted with the extra pair of hands and sent Tortoise to join the others already hard at work filling their baskets. Opolo the frog had come to do his share, as had Ekun the leopard, Ekute the bush rat, Ewure the goat, and a great many more of the chief's people.

Tortoise watched for a few moments as each dug a yam, placed it in his basket and carried it to the chief's storehouse. He stooped and did the same for a while, making sure that his digging brought him closer and closer to the large hole he had made the night before. Then for every yam he placed in his basket, he began dropping one into the opening of the hole, slowly building a stockpile for himself and mopping his brow from time to time as if he were quite exhausted.

But some of the workers began to notice how little progress he was actually making and challenged Tortoise to increase his speed.

"Unlike the rest of you," he answered them shortly, "I have the greatest respect for the chief's yams and believe in handling them very gently so as not to bruise them."

And so the work continued until at last all the yams were harvested and the people drifted home wearily to their supper.

That night, as soon as darkness fell, Tortoise led his wife and children to the spot where he had buried the yams. They tiptoed back and forth across the field many times, each carrying an armful of yams, until the hole was empty and the family storehouse was full. Tortoise was very pleased with himself. Everything had been taken care of, and he felt certain that he had more than enough food to last him through the winter months.

But when morning came, a group of the chief's servants, who had been touring the empty fields, stumbled upon the large hole Tortoise had dug. They also found footprints made by Tortoise and his family as they scurried to and fro during the night, and followed the footprints to Tortoise's storehouse. Carefully, they opened the door so as not to disturb the sleeping household, and there, piled high to the ceiling, they came face to face with an impressive mound of freshly harvested yams.

The servants immediately rushed back to the chief's house and reported to him their discovery. The chief was enraged to have been deceived in such a manner and ordered Tortoise to be brought before him at once.

"It has been reported to me that you have stolen yams from my field," he challenged Tortoise, "what have you got to say for yourself?"

"It really saddens me to think you have such a poor opinion of me," replied Tortoise innocently, "when I have gone out of my way to be of service to you. I went to your fields to work for you, I stooped and sweated and carried yams to your storehouse all day long. Now you reproach me and call me a thief."

"Tortoise, your shrewd character is well known to me," replied the chief, "and you cannot argue your way out of this one as easily as you think. I have been told about the footprints leading from my fields to your storehouse."

"Yes, I'm sure you have," answered Tortoise confidently, "but I could easily have made them when I returned home from my work. And besides, there were a lot of other people in the fields as well as myself."

"There are no paths leading from my fields to their houses," continued the chief, "only to your house. But if you still insist you are innocent, I know of a way to prove it. Tomorrow you will take the hot-water test. Then we can put the matter to rest once and for all."

The next day, the people gathered together in front of the chief's house where a large cauldron of water stood heating over a fire. As soon as the water had come to the boil, the chief appeared and began to address the crowd:

"You are assembled here to witness Tortoise take the hot-water test. He denies that he is guilty of theft. Therefore, he must drink a bowl of the boiling water. If he is innocent, he will feel nothing at all. But if he is guilty, the water will burn his throat and cause him great pain. Let us begin at once."

But before the servants had ladled the water into the bowl, Tortoise spoke up:

"Sir, this test will only prove how faithful I have been to you and you will still be at a loss to know who has taken your yams. Don't you agree that it makes sense for everyone who worked alongside me in the fields to be tested as well?"

The chief considered this proposal a moment.

"Very well," he said. "Let everyone else who was in the fields come forward. I am sure they have nothing to hide and absolutely nothing to fear."

And now Tortoise became very helpful, behaving as though he were the chief's special assistant. He ordered the pot to be removed from the fire and placed it in a spot where the chief would have a better view of the proceedings. Then he insisted, that because he was the youngest, he should respectfully serve the others before himself.

The chief agreed, and Tortoise took the bowl, filled it with boiling water and served it first of all to Opolo the frog. Opolo cried out in pain as the hot water burned his insides. Next came the bush rat and he too cried out in agony as the liquid scorched his throat.

Tortoise refilled the bowl and handed it to Ewure the goat. Tears came to his eyes also and he writhed on the ground as the pain consumed his entire body. Last of all, Ekun the leopard came forward and let out a piercing scream as he swallowed and suffered the same dreadful pain.

"You disappoint me, my friends," said the chief, "for I see that you all share a portion of the blame. But let us turn now to the Tortoise and see whether he is guilty or innocent."

And so Tortoise stepped forward and filled his bowl to the brim. But before he held it to his lips he pushed it towards the chief:

"See how full it is, Sir," he announced, "I have taken more than anyone else."

"I see it," replied the chief, "the amount is a good one."

Tortoise carried the bowl towards the chief's wife.

"I see it also," she cried, "you have acted more than fairly, Tortoise."

Tortoise walked slowly into the crowd and tilted the bowl so the men of the village could see it more clearly.

"We see it," they said, "the bowl is very full."

He showed it to the women of the village.

"We see it," they chanted, "you are very brave indeed, Tortoise."

He turned and called to all the children of the village.

"We see it," they answered him, "you do well, Tortoise."

And as Tortoise presented the bowl for inspection to each group in turn, the water grew cooler and cooler until, at last, the chief called for him to get on with the drinking.

So Tortoise gulped down the water, but because it had grown so cool as he passed it around, it did not cause him any pain as it slid down his throat.

"You have seen it," shouted Tortoise triumphantly, "I did not cry out as the others did. How can I possibly be guilty?"

And as additional proof of his innocence, he poured the water over his entire body and rubbed it into his skin without showing any sign of discomfort.

"You can see it was not I who committed the crime," he added. "It must have been Opolo, Ekute, Ewure and Ekun. They should be taken away and punished severely."

The chief nodded in agreement and sentenced the other animals to two years' hard labour on his farm for having stolen his yams.

But although Tortoise was victorious, there were some among the crowd who still held him in suspicion and ever since that day, whenever a person tries to point the finger at others for a crime he has committed himself, you will hear the people say:

"When Tortoise accuses the whole community,
He himself must have a great deal to hide."

The Tortoise and the Elephant
(From the Akamba people, Kenya)

ONE DAY THE ELEPHANT WAS BOASTING as usual about his great size and strength. "Have you ever come across a more impressive figure in the whole of the land?" he asked Tortoise, as he stared admiringly at his reflection in the lake. "There is not one creature I know of that could outshine me. It wouldn't matter what sort of contest we were engaged in."

"You can't be absolutely certain of that," replied the Tortoise. "Size isn't everything you know, and I'm sure there is someone out there who would put you in your place given half a chance."

"I suppose you consider yourself worthy of that role," mocked the Elephant. "Come on then, prove to me that you are a greater athlete than myself."

"That won't be so difficult," answered the Tortoise defiantly. "I bet I could jump as high as your trunk and land twenty feet beyond it without putting in too much effort."

"Then meet me here later this afternoon," the Elephant chuckled, "and in the meantime go and work on your muscles! I can hardly wait to see you make a fool of yourself."

So the Tortoise went home where he found his wife preparing their midday meal.

"The Elephant has challenged me to a trial of strength," he told her, "and I think it's time somebody taught him a lesson, but I will need your help."

Leading his wife to the lakeside, Tortoise hid her among the bushes at exactly the spot where he judged he would land after making his miraculous leap. Soon afterwards, the Elephant arrived, still smirking to himself, and stood as he was instructed in the middle of a clear space where tortoise could get a good run at him.

"Jump high now, Tortoise," cried the Elephant sarcastically, "give it your best shot."

"I'm coming now, hold your trunk up high," called the Tortoise, pretending he was almost ready for his high jump.

The Elephant lifted his head towards the sky, and as he did so, the tortoise slipped into the grass, shouting "Hi-i!" as he went. "Eh-e!" came the reply from his wife who suddenly appeared on the other side of the grass, exactly twenty feet from the Elephant.

The Elephant now glanced to his right and found the Tortoise on the far side of his trunk. He was utterly astonished to see him there and suspected nothing, believing that the leap had been so masterfully executed, his eyes had not been quick enough to take it in.

"You have beaten me, Tortoise," he said, shaking his head in bewilderment, "I still can't quite believe it, however. Do you think you could convince me one more time, for I feel certain that you would never be able to outrun me in a foot-race."

"If you insist then," answered the Tortoise quite casually, "but not today. I need my rest after all that exertion. I will meet you tomorrow morning by the great tree in the forest, and to make things easier, I suggest we run a circular course through the woods, finishing up in the same place where we started from."

"That sounds ideal," replied the Elephant and he tramped his way homewards, confident that he would achieve his victory on the following day.

Before the sun had risen the next morning, Tortoise had gathered together his wife and children and spent several hours placing them along the course, instructing them what to do once the race had started. Shortly afterwards, he spotted the Elephant pushing his way through the thick undergrowth as he headed towards the appointed tree. Tortoise went forward to greet him and without further delay the two took up their starting positions, anxious to begin the race.

Smiling happily to himself, the Elephant trotted off at an easy pace and was soon well ahead of the Tortoise who began to puff and pant under the strain. The Elephant laughed loudly at the sight of him, well pleased with himself for having chosen such a punishing contest.

When he had been running for quite some time he shouted back, "Tortoise!", believing he had left his opponent far behind. But to his horror he heard a voice saying:

"Why are you looking behind you? I am here in front of you. Can't you move any faster?"

Shocked by the sight of Tortoise, the Elephant broke into a gallop, putting as much energy into his stride as he could possibly manage. But he had only moved on a short distance when he spotted Tortoise up ahead of him once more. This happened again and again, all the way along the course, until the Elephant arrived back at the great tree where he found Tortoise calmly waiting for him, not a drop of sweat on his brow.

"Here I am, what kept you?" said the tortoise.

"I didn't believe you could ever beat me," replied the defeated Elephant, "but it seems you are right about size."

Tortoise turned away to hide his smile, but he never felt bad about cheating the Elephant, for he felt certain he had taught him an invaluable lesson.

Tortoises Hunting Ostriches
(From South Africa)

ONE DAY, IT IS SAID, the Tortoises held a council how they might hunt Ostriches, and they said, "Let us, on both sides, stand in rows near each other, and let one go to hunt the Ostriches, so that they must flee along through the midst of us."

They did so, and as they were many, the Ostriches were obliged to run along through the midst of them. During this they did not move, but, remaining always in the same places, called each to the other, "Are you there?" and each one answered, "I am here." The Ostriches hearing this, ran so tremendously that they quite exhausted their strength, and fell down. Then the Tortoises assembled by-and-by at the place where the Ostriches had fallen, and devoured them.

Why the Worms Live Underneath the Ground
(From southern Nigeria)

WHEN EYO III WAS RULING over all men and animals, he had a very big palaver house to which he used to invite his subjects at intervals to feast. After the feast had been held and plenty of tombo had been drunk, it was the custom of the people to make speeches. One day after the feast the head driver ant got up and said he and his people were stronger than anyone, and that no one, not even the elephant, could stand before him, which was quite true. He was particularly offensive in his allusions to the worms (whom he disliked very much), and said they were poor wriggling things.

The worms were very angry and complained, so the king said that the best way to decide the question who was the stronger was for both sides to meet on the road and fight the matter out between themselves to a finish. He appointed the third day from the feast for the contest, and all the people turned out to witness the battle.

The driver ants left their nest in the early morning in thousands and millions, and, as is their custom, marched in a line about one inch broad densely packed, so that it was like a dark-brown band moving over the country. In front of the advancing column they had out their scouts, advance guard, and flankers, and the main body followed in their millions close behind.

When they came to the battlefield the moving band spread out, and as the thousands upon thousands of ants rolled up, the whole piece of ground was a moving mass of ants and bunches of struggling worms. The fight was over in a very few minutes, as the worms were bitten in pieces by the sharp pincer-like mouths of the driver ants. The few worms who survived squirmed away and buried themselves out of sight.

King Eyo decided that the driver ants were easy winners, and ever since the worms have always been afraid and have lived underground; and if they happen to come to the surface after the rain they hide themselves under the ground whenever anything approaches, as they fear all people.

How the Leopard Got His Spots
(From Sierra Leone, west Africa)

LONG AGO, Leopard and Fire were the best of friends. Every morning, without fail, Leopard made a special effort to visit his friend even though the journey took him quite a distance from his own home. It had never before bothered him that Fire did not visit him in return, until the day his wife began to mock and tease him on the subject.

"He must be a very poor friend indeed," she jeered, "if he won't come and see you even once in your own house."

Day and night, Leopard was forced to listen to his wife taunt him, until finally he began to believe that his house was somehow unworthy of his friend.

"I will prove my wife wrong," he thought to himself, and set off before dawn on the following day to beg Fire to come and visit his home.

At first, Fire presented him with every possible excuse. He never liked to travel too far, he explained to Leopard. He always felt uncomfortable leaving his family behind. But Leopard pleaded and pleaded so that eventually Fire agreed to the visit on the condition that his friend construct a path of dry leaves leading from one house to the other.

As he walked homewards, Leopard gathered as many leaves as he could find and laid them in a long line between the two houses just as Fire had instructed him. He brought his wife the good news and immediately she began to prepare the finest food to welcome their guest.

When the meal was ready and the house sparkled as if it were new, the couple sat down to await the arrival of their friend. They had been seated only a moment when suddenly they felt a strong gust of wind and heard a loud crackling noise outside their front door. Leopard jumped up in alarm and pulled open the door, anxious to discover who could be making such a dreadful commotion. He was astonished to see Fire standing before him, crackling and sparking in a haze of intense heat, his body a mass of flames that leapt menacingly in every direction.

Soon the entire house had caught fire and the smell of burning skin filled the air. Leopard grabbed hold of his squealing wife and sprang, panic-stricken, through the window, rolling in the grass to put out the flames on his back.

The two lay there exhausted, grateful to be alive. But ever since that day, their bodies were covered all over with black spots where the fingers of Fire, their reluctant house-guest, had touched them.

The Donkey Who Sinned
(From Ethiopia, northeast Africa)

ONE HOT AND SUNNY AFTERNOON, the Lion, the Leopard, the Hyena and the Donkey met together at the bottom of the field. At once, they began to discuss the drought visiting the country and the dreadful conditions that had become widespread throughout the region. No rain had fallen now for several months, the crops had shrivelled beyond recognition, and there was very little food or water to be had anywhere.

"How can this have happened to us?" they repeated over and over again, shaking their heads in disbelief. "Someone among us must have sinned very badly, or God would not be punishing us in this way."

"Perhaps we should confess our sins," the Donkey suddenly suggested, "maybe if we repent, we will be forgiven and the land will become fertile and bear healthy crops again."

They all agreed that this was a very sensible idea, and so the Lion, the most powerful of the group, immediately stood up to make his confession:

"I once committed an unforgivable crime," he told the gathering. "One day I found a young calf roaming close to a village, and even though I knew it belonged to the people, I attacked it and ate every morsel."

The other animals looked towards the Lion, whom they feared and admired for his daring and strength, and began to protest his innocence loudly:

"No, no," they reassured him. "That was no great sin! You shouldn't worry about that at all."

Next the Leopard stood up to make a clean breast of things:

"I have committed a much more dreadful sin," he announced. "One morning as I prowled through the valley, I happened upon a goat who had strayed from the rest of the herd. As soon as his back was turned, I leaped on him and devoured him."

The rest of the animals looked at the Leopard, whom they admired as a most ruthless hunter, and once again they dismissed this crime:

"No, no!" they insisted. "That is no sin! God would never hold such a thing against you."

The Hyena then spoke his piece:

"Oh, I have committed a most wicked deed," he cried. "I was so greedy one evening, I stole into the village, caught a chicken and swallowed it down in one gulp."

But again the other animals protested, judging the Hyena to be the most cunning among their friends:

"No, no! Let your conscience be at rest," they answered him. "That is no sin!"

Last of all, the Donkey came forward and began to confess:

"One day when my master was leading me along the road he met an old friend and started talking with him. While the two were deep in conversation, I crept silently to the edge of the road and began nibbling on a tuft of grass."

The Lion, the Leopard and the Hyena stared at the Donkey, whom they neither feared, nor admired. A grave silence filled the air. Slowly they formed a circle around him, shaking their heads in absolute disgust:

"That is the worst sin we have ever heard," they pronounced. "There can be no doubt now that you are the source of all our trouble."

And with that, the three of them jumped upon the donkey's back and began ripping him to pieces.

The Two Suns
(From Kenya, east Africa)

MANY HUNDREDS OF YEARS AGO, in the land now known as Kenya, the animals could speak just as well as human beings. At that time, the two species lived in harmony and agreed on most things. They even shared the same grievances, and were equally fond of complaining about the darkness, although they readily admitted that they were more than satisfied with the daylight.

"We cannot see at night," complained the men. "It is impossible to look after our cattle in the dark and we are often afraid of the great shadows that appear out of nowhere."

The animals agreed with the men and soon they arranged a meeting to decide what to do. The great elders of the people were the first to speak and they outlined various plans to defeat the darkness, some suggesting that huge fires should be lit at night throughout the land, others insisting that every man should carry his own torch. At length, however, the man considered wisest among the elders stood up and addressed the crowd:

"We must pray to God to give us two suns," he announced. "One that rises in the east and one that rises in the west. If he provides us with these, we will never have to tolerate night again."

The people immediately shouted their approval and all were in agreement with this plan, except for one small hare at the back of the crowd who ventured to challenge the speaker a little further:

"How will we get any shade?" he asked in a tiny voice.

But his question met with an impatient roar from the wisest elder who demanded to know the identity of the creature who had dared to oppose him.

"It was the Hare who spoke," said one of the warriors in the crowd, noticing that the Hare was trying to hide himself away under the bushes. Soon he was hauled out to the middle of the gathering, visibly shaking under the gaze of the people.

"How dare you disagree with me," said the elder. "What do you know of such matters anyway?"

The Hare bowed his head silently and began to whimper.

"Speak up, great prophet," said another of the elders. "Let us hear your wise words of counsel."

The people and the animals laughed loudly at the spectacle before them, all except for the warrior who had first spotted the Hare.

"Don't be afraid of them," he said gently. "Go on! Speak! Be proud of what you have to say."

The Hare stared into the eyes of the tall warrior and his courage began to return. Then, clearing his throat and raising himself up on his hind legs, he spoke the following words:

"I only wanted to say that if we had two suns there would never be any shade again. All the waters of the rivers and lakes will dry up. We shall never be able to sleep and our cattle will die of heat and thirst. There will be fires and hunger in the land and we shall all eventually perish."

The people listened and a great silence descended upon them as they considered the words of the little Hare.

At last, the wisest of the elders arose and patted the Hare warmly on the shoulder.

"Indeed you have shown greater wisdom than any of us," he said. "We are fortunate to have you among us."

Everyone agreed, and to this day the people of Kenya say that the hare is the cleverest of all animals. And they still have day and night; they still have only one sun and nobody has ever complained about it since that day.

Gihilihili: The Snake-man
(From the Tutsi people, Rwanda)

THERE WAS ONCE A MIDDLE-AGED WOMAN living in a small village who for many years had tried to conceive a child. At last, when she had almost abandoned all hope, she discovered

she was pregnant. The news filled her with great joy and she longed for the day when she could sit proudly amongst the other women holding her new-born infant in her arms.

But when nine months had passed and the time arrived for the woman to deliver her child, there was no sign of it emerging, and for several more years the infant remained within her womb, refusing to show itself. Eventually however, the woman began to suffer labour pains and was taken to her bed where she gave birth after a long and painful ordeal. She was surprised that her husband did not bring the infant to her and when she looked in his direction she saw that his eyes were filled with horror. Then she searched for the child, but no child lay on the bed. Instead she saw a long, thick-necked snake coiled up beside her, its body warm and glistening, its head lifted affectionately towards her.

Suddenly her husband grabbed hold of a shovel from a corner of the hut and began striking the snake furiously. But the woman cried out for him to stop at once:

"Do not harm the creature," she pleaded, "treat it with respect and gentleness. No matter what you may think of it, that snake is still the fruit of my womb."

The man lowered his shovel and went outdoors. Soon he returned to the hut accompanied by a group of village elders. They gathered around the bed and began to examine the snake more closely. At length, the wisest among them spoke to the husband and wife:

"We have no reason to treat this creature unkindly," he told them. "Take it to the forest and build a house for it there. Let it be free to do as it pleases. Let it grow to maturity unharmed so that it may shed its skin in the normal way."

The husband carried the snake to the heart of the forest and left it there as the elders had ordered him, making certain that it had a comfortable home to live in and a plentiful supply of food to survive on.

The years passed by quickly, and the snake grew to an impressive size, ready for the day when its old skin would be replaced by a new one. And as it wandered deeper into the forest the most wonderful transformation began to occur. The old skin started to shrink away to reveal a young man, tall, strong and handsome. The young man stood up and glanced around him. Then, lifting the snakeskin from the ground, he took a deep breath and followed the path through the forest back towards his parents' home.

Both mother and father were overjoyed to discover that the snake-creature they had abandoned so many years before had changed into such a fine and handsome youth. All the other members of the family were invited to assemble at the hut to admire their beautiful son and a great feast was held to welcome him into the community.

After their son had been with them several weeks, the father sat down with him one evening to discuss who would make the best wife for him.

"I have already chosen the daughter of Bwenge to be my wife," the young man told his father. "Even while I crawled on my belly through the forests I knew I would one day marry her. Each time she came to gather wood, I sat and watched and my love went out to her. Each time she came to get water, my love went out to her. Each time she came to cut grass for the young cattle, my love went out to her."

"You are not rich enough for such a match," his father replied. "We are poor people, and she is the daughter of a noble chief."

But the son said nothing further on the subject and called for a great fire to be made. As soon as the flames had grown quite tall, he cast the snakeskin which once covered his body into the centre of the fire, calling for his father and mother to keep a careful watch on it. They looked on in amazement as the skin crackled noisily and transformed itself into an array of valuable objects. Cattle, sheep and fowls began to leap from the flames. Drums, calabashes and churns began to appear, together with all other kinds of wealthy possessions.

Next morning the father and his son went in search of the daughter of Bwenge and presented to the chief a selection of these goods. The chief was more than satisfied by all that he saw and arranged for his daughter to be married immediately. The young man led his new wife back to his village where he made a home for them both. They were very happy together and lived long and fruitful lives, enriched by the birth of many healthy children.

The Snake-man grew old among the people who came to regard him as a man of profound wisdom and courage. Whenever there was trouble they turned to him for advice, and even after he died, his words lived on in their memory and they often recounted the story of his birth, mindful of what he had told them.

"Never allow yourself to be destroyed by misfortune," he had said.

"Never despair of yourself or of others. And above all, never condemn a person for his appearance."

The Story of the Hunters and the Big Snake

(From the Swahili-speaking peoples, east Africa)

LONG AGO THERE LIVED some hunters who one day took their bows and arrows and went with their dogs to hunt in the forest. And those hunters walked very far, looking for game, and they caught some animals, and then a very heavy rain fell upon them. So they looked for a place in which they could sit and take shelter until the rain was over, and they found a very big tree with a large hollow in it. Then those hunters and their dogs entered into that tree and sat down.

Now that hole in the tree belonged to a large snake, and that snake had gone out to look for game. The snake hunted and did not find any game, so it returned home hungry and annoyed. When it got near its hole it heard the voices of men talking in its house.

That snake was very surprised, and said to itself, "Who can it be talking in my house?" Then it said in a loud voice, "Who speaks there in my house?"

Those men inside were astonished, and asked one another, "Who can that be talking outside?"

Before they could answer, or look outside, the snake itself arrived at the entrance and blocked the way out. Then it said, "What sort of people are you to come and sit in my house? This is my house in which I sit by myself. Answer me quickly what you mean by going into it?"

Those men answered, "Please, sir, we have come from our village looking for game. We went very far and only caught some small animals, and then it rained very hard, so we came in here to escape the rain. We did not know that it was your house. Now we have nothing to say; we only ask your leave to go out. If you say 'go out' we will go our way at once."

The snake said, "You have no leave to go out."

Then those men asked, "Then what do you wish us to do?"

The snake said, "What you must do is that you must at once give that game you have caught to your dogs to eat, that they may get fat. Then you must eat your dogs, so that you become very fat, and then I will eat you."

Those men said, "We are not able to eat dogflesh, master. If this is indeed your house, perhaps you will eat us. No matter, it is the will of Allah."

Whilst they were talking thus to that big snake an elephant-nosed shrew came out of the bush and heard them talking, and came near to the door of the snake's house.

Then he asked, "What does this snake say?"

Those men said, "This snake is standing in the doorway and preventing us from going out, and he tells us we must give our game to our dogs, and then eat our dogs, that he may eat us. This is because we came to sit in here to escape from the rain."

The elephant-nosed shrew said, "Agree to what he says. When that snake has eaten you and become very fat I will eat him."

When that snake heard those words of the shrew it was very angry, and chased the shrew, and the shrew ran off into the bush, and the snake followed him very far, but did not catch him.

Then those hunters were able to come forth from that hole and escape. So they went out very quickly and ran back to their village.

When the snake came back to his house he found that those men had run away. It was indeed the elephant-nosed shrew who had saved them.

How Ra-Molo Became a Snake

(From Lesotho, southern Africa)

LONG, LONG AGO, before the time of the great chief Mosheshue, there lived, behind the mountains, a wicked chief called Ra-Molo (the father of fire), who ruled his people with the hand of

hardness. His village lay at the foot of a high hill, and down below flowed the Sinkou, deep and dark and cold.

Every year, when the harvest feasts began, would Ra-Molo cause to die the black death all those upon whom his displeasure had fallen during the past year; and when the moon was big in the heavens, he would come out from his dwelling to gaze upon his victims, and to listen to their screams of agony. Many, many times have the cries of the poor unfortunates echoed from rock to rock, while the people hid their heads in their blankets and trembled with fear and horror.

When the last feeble moans died away, the chief would return to his dwelling, and a great silence would descend upon the village. Then softly, by ones and by twos, the frightened people would creep away to some quiet spot out of sight of the village, and there offer up their prayers to the spirits of their fathers to rescue them from Ra-Molo; but for many many moons no help came.

Despair seized upon their hearts and hung in darkness over their homes. What hope was there for them when even the spirits were silent?

Now Ra-Molo had a brother who bore the name of Tau (the lion). This brother Ra-Molo hated with a great and bitter hatred, and gladly would he have put him to death, but he feared the vengeance of the spirits, for Tau was as brave and good as Ra-Molo was wicked and cruel. Then also he knew that all the people loved Tau, and would flee from the one who murdered him, as from the Evil Eye itself.

At length the evil counsels of the Ngaka (witch doctor) and the desire of Ra-Molo's heart overcame all fears, and one night, when the silence of sleep had come down upon the village, Ra-Molo called his Ngaka to bring his followers, and to enter the dwelling of Tau and put him to death.

The Ngaka needed no urging to begin his vile work. His heart glowed with delight as he thought of what a big strong man Tau was, and how long it would take him to die. Soon the whole village was aroused by the shrieks which the torturers extracted from the helpless victim. "Help, oh, help me, my brothers!" cried Tau, "lest I die, and my blood stain the hands of my father's son." They strove to rescue him, but the hut was well guarded, and their chief stood in the doorway, and forbade them to enter, using many threats to frighten them.

When the grey shadow in mercy came down to end his sufferings, Tau raised his eyes to the stars, and cried, "Oh, spirits of my fathers, receive me, and bring down upon Ra-Molo the heavy hand of vengeance, that his power may be destroyed, and no more innocent blood be spilled upon the earth to cry to the spirits. Oh, let my cry be heard, because of my great suffering!" So saying, he passed to the land of shadows, and a great darkness descended upon the village. All the people crept together and waited in tears for the dawn. At length the sun came forth, the darkness was lifted up; but what awful horror now held the people? What was that towards which all eyes were turned? Behold! at the door of the chief's dwelling lay a gigantic snake, so great that his like had never before been seen. Slowly he uncoiled himself and raised his head, when a wild cry went up from all the people. The body was the body of a snake, but the head was the head of a sheep, with a snake's tongue, which darted in and out from its wide-open mouth, while from the eyes the lightning flew. With a long loud hiss-s-s the thing began to crawl towards the river bank, then, raising its head to cast one long backward glance upon the village, it plunged into the waters of the Sinkou, there to remain a prisoner for all time. The spirits had, indeed, heard the dying cry of Tau, and had turned Ra-Molo into the awful thing the people had just beheld.

Once in each year, as the day comes round, does Ra-Molo rise to the surface of the giant pool, where he lies hid, and woe, woe to the one who sees the silver flash of his great body as he rises, for surely will that poor one be drawn by the power of those evil eyes down, down to the water's edge. Then will the serpent seize him and carry him away from the sight of men to the bottom of the pool, there to sleep cold and still till all men shall be gathered to the land of the spirits of their fathers on the day when the Great Spirit shall call from the stars.

The Ape, the Snake and the Lion

(From Zanzibar, Tanzanian coast)

LONG, LONG AGO there lived, in a village called Keejee jee, a woman whose husband died, leaving her with a little baby boy. She worked hard all day to get food for herself and child, but they lived very poorly and were most of the time half-starved.

When the boy, whose name was Mvoo Laana, began to get big, he said to his mother, one day: "Mother, we are always hungry. What work did my father do to support us?"

His mother replied: "Your father was a hunter. He set traps, and we ate what he caught in them."

"Oho!" said "Mvoo Laana; "that's not work; that's fun. I, too, will set traps, and see if we can't get enough to eat."

The next day he went into the forest and cut branches from the trees, and returned home in the evening.

The second day he spent making the branches into traps.

The third day he twisted cocoanut fiber into ropes.

The fourth day he set up as many traps as time would permit.

The fifth day he set up the remainder of the traps.

The sixth day he went to examine the traps, and they had caught so much game, beside what they needed for themselves, that he took a great quantity to the big town of Oongooja, where he sold it and bought corn and other things, and the house was full of food; and, as this good fortune continued, he and his mother lived very comfortably.

But after a while, when he went to his traps he found nothing in them day after day.

One morning, however, he found that an ape had been caught in one of the traps, and he was about to kill it, when it said: "Son of Adam, I am Neeanee, the ape; do not kill me. Take me out of this trap and let me go. Save me from the rain, that I may come and save you from the sun some day."

So Mvoo Laana took him out of the trap and let him go.

When Neeanee had climbed up in a tree, he sat on a branch and said to the youth: "For your kindness I will give you a piece of advice: Believe me, men are all bad. Never do a good turn for a man; if you do, he will do you harm at the first opportunity."

The second day, Mvoo Laana found a snake in the same trap. He started to the village to give the alarm, but the snake shouted: "Come back, son of Adam; don't call the people from the village to come and kill me. I am Neeoka, the snake. Let me out of this trap, I pray you. Save me from the rain today, that I may be able to save you from the sun tomorrow, if you should be in need of help."

So the youth let him go; and as he went he said, "I will return your kindness if I can, but do not trust any man; if you do him a kindness he will do you an injury in return at the first opportunity."

The third day, Mvoo Laana found a lion in the same trap that had caught the ape and the snake, and he was afraid to go near it. But the lion said: "Don't run away; I am Simba Kongway, the very old lion. Let me out of this trap, and I will not hurt you. Save me from the rain, that I may save you from the sun if you should need help."

So Mvoo Laana believed him and let him out of the trap, and Simba Kongway, before going his way, said: "Son of Adam, you have been kind to me, and I will repay you with kindness if I can; but never do a kindness to a man, or he will pay you back with unkindness."

The next day a man was caught in the same trap, and when the youth released him, he repeatedly assured him that he would never forget the service he had done him in restoring his liberty and saving his life.

Well, it seemed that he had caught all the game that could be taken in traps, and Mvoo Laana and his mother were hungry every day, with nothing to satisfy them, as they had been before. At last he said to his mother, one day: "Mother, make me seven cakes of the little meal we have left, and I will go hunting with my bow and arrows." So she baked him the cakes, and he took them and his bow and arrows and went into the forest.

The youth walked and walked, but could see no game, and finally he found that he had lost his way, and had eaten all his cakes but one.

And he went on and on, not knowing whether he was going away from his home or toward it, until he came to the wildest and most desolate looking wood he had ever seen. He was so wretched and tired that he felt he must lie down and die, when suddenly he heard someone calling him, and looking up he saw Neeanee, the ape, who said, "Son of Adam, where are you going?"

"I don't know," replied "Mvoo Laana, sadly; "I'm lost."

"Well, well," said the ape; "don't worry. Just sit down here and rest yourself until I come back, and I will repay with kindness the kindness you once showed me."

Then Neeanee went away off to some gardens and stole a whole lot of ripe paw-paws and bananas, and brought them to Mvoo Laana, and said: "Here's plenty of food for you. Is there anything else you want? Would you like a drink?" And before the youth could answer he ran off with a calabash and brought it back full of water. So the youth ate heartily, and drank all the water he needed, and then each said to the other, "Good-bye, till we meet again," and went their separate ways.

When Mvoo Laana had walked a great deal farther without finding which way he should go, he met Simba Kongway, who asked, "Where are you going, son of Adam?"

And the youth answered, as dolefully as before, "I don't know; I'm lost."

"Come, cheer up," said the very old lion, "and rest yourself here a little. I want to repay with kindness today the kindness you showed me on a former day."

So Mvoo Laana sat down. Simba Kongway went away, but soon returned with some game he had caught, and then he brought some fire, and the young man cooked the game and ate it. When he had finished he felt a great deal better, and they bade each other good-bye for the present, and each went his way.

After he had traveled another very long distance the youth came to a farm, and was met by a very, very old woman, who said to him: "Stranger, my husband has been taken very sick, and I am looking for someone to make him some medicine. Won't you make it?" But he answered: "My good woman, I am not a doctor, I am a hunter, and never used medicine in my life. I cannot help you."

When he came to the road leading to the principal city he saw a well, with a bucket standing near it, and he said to himself: "That's just what I want. I'll take a drink of nice well-water. Let me see if the water can be reached."

As he peeped over the edge of the well, to see if the water was high enough, what should he behold but a great big snake, which, directly it saw him, said, "Son of Adam, wait a moment." Then it came out of the well and said: "How? Don't you know me?"

"I certainly do not," said the youth, stepping back a little.

"Well, well!" said the snake; "I could never forget you. I am Neeoka, whom you released from the trap. You know I said, "Save me from the rain, and I will save you from the sun." Now, you are a stranger in the town to which you are going; therefore hand me your little bag, and I will place in it the things that will be of use to you when you arrive there."

So Mvoo Laana gave Neeoka the little bag, and he filled it with chains of gold and silver, and told him to use them freely for his own benefit. Then they parted very cordially.

When the youth reached the city, the first man he met was he whom he had released from the trap, who invited him to go home with him, which he did, and the man's wife made him supper.

As soon as he could get away unobserved, the man went to the sultan and said: "There is a stranger come to my house with a bag full of chains of silver and gold, which he says he got from a snake that lives in a well. But although he pretends to be a man, I know that he is a snake who has power to look like a man."

When the sultan heard this he sent some soldiers who brought Mvoo Laana and his little bag before him. When they opened the little bag, the man who was released from the trap persuaded the people that some evil would come out of it, and affect the children of the sultan and the children of the vizir.

Then the people became excited, and tied the hands of Mvoo Laana behind him.

But the great snake had come out of the well and arrived at the town just about this time, and he went and lay at the feet of the man who had said all those bad things about Mvoo Laana, and when the people saw this they said to that man: "How is this? There is the great snake that lives in the well, and he stays by you. Tell him to go away."

But Neeoka would not stir. So they untied the young man's hands, and tried in every way to make amends for having suspected him of being a wizard.

Then the sultan asked him, "Why should this man invite you to his home and then speak ill of you?"

And "Mvoo Laana related all that had happened to him, and how the ape, the snake, and the lion had cautioned him about the results of doing any kindness for a man.

And the sultan said: "Although men are often ungrateful, they are not always so; only the bad ones. As for this fellow, he deserves to be put in a sack and drowned in the sea. He was treated kindly, and returned evil for good."

How the Dog Came to Live with Man
(From the Bushogo people, Congo)

THERE WAS A TIME, LONG AGO, when the Dog and the Jackal lived together in the wilderness as brothers. Every day they hunted together and every evening they laid out on the grass whatever they had caught, making sure to divide the meal equally between them. But there were evenings when they both returned from a day's hunting empty-handed, and on these occasions, they would curl up side-by-side under the stars dreaming of the bush calf or the plump zebra they had come so close to killing.

They had never before gone without food for longer than two days, but then, without warning, they suffered a long spell of bad luck and for over a week they could find nothing at all to eat. On the eighth day, although they had both searched everywhere, they returned to their shelter without meat, feeling exhausted and extremely hungry. To add to their misery, a bitterly cold wind blew across the bush, scooping up the leaves they had gathered for warmth, leaving them shivering without any hope of comfort throughout the long night ahead. Curled up together, they attempted to sleep, but the wind continued to howl and they tossed and turned despairingly.

"Jackal," said the Dog after a while. "Isn't it a terrible thing to go to bed hungry after all the effort we have put in today, and isn't it an even worse thing to be both hungry and cold at the same time?"

"Yes, it is brother," replied the Jackal, "but there's very little we can do about it at the moment. Let's just curl up here and try to sleep now. Tomorrow, as soon as the sun rises, we will go out hunting again and with any luck we will be able to find some food to satisfy us."

But even though he snuggled up closer to the Jackal, the Dog could not sleep, for his teeth had begun to chatter and his stomach rumbled more loudly than ever. He lay on the cold earth, his eyes open wide, trying to recall what it was like to be warm and well-fed.

"Jackal," he piped up again, "man has a village quite close to this spot, doesn't he?"

"Yes, that is true," answered the Jackal wearily. "But what difference can that make to us right now?"

"Well," replied the Dog, "most men know how to light a fire and fire would keep us warm if we crept near enough to one."

"If you are suggesting that we take a closer look," said the Jackal, "you can forget about it. I'm not going anywhere near that village. Now go to sleep and leave me in peace."

But the Dog could not let go of the idea and as he thought about it more and more he began to imagine the delicious meal he would make of the scraps and bones left lying around by the villagers.

"Please come with me," he begged the Jackal, "my fur is not as thick as yours and I am dying here from cold and hunger."

"Go there yourself," growled the Jackal, "this was all your idea, I want nothing to do with it."

At last, the Dog could stand it no longer. Forgetting his fear, he jumped up and announced boldly:

"Right, I'm off, nothing can be worse than this. I'm going to that village to sit by the fire and perhaps I'll even come across a tasty bone. If there's any food left over, I'll bring you some. But if I don't return, please come and look for me."

So the Dog started off towards the village, slowing down when he had reached the outskirts and crawling on his belly so that nobody would notice him approach. He could see the red glow of a fire just up ahead and already he felt the warmth of its flames. Very cautiously he slid along the earth and had almost reached his goal when some fowls roosting in a tree overhead began to cackle a loud warning to their master.

At once, a man came rushing out from a nearby hut and lifting his spear high in the air, brought it down within an inch of where the dog lay.

"Please, please don't kill me," whimpered the Dog. "I haven't come here to steal your chickens or to harm you in any way. I am starving and almost frozen to death. I only wanted to lie down by the fire where I could warm myself for a short while."

The man looked at the wretched, shivering creature and could not help feeling a bit sorry for him. It was such a cold night after all, and the Dog's request was not so unreasonable under the circumstances.

"Very well," he said, withdrawing his spear. "You can warm yourself here for a few minutes if you promise to go away again as soon as you feel better."

The Dog crept forward and lay himself down by the fire, thanking the man over and over for his kindness. Soon he felt the blood begin to circulate in his limbs once more. Slowly uncurling himself, he stretched out before the flames and there, just in front of him, he noticed a fat and juicy bone, thrown there by the man at the end of his meal. He sidled up alongside it and began to devour it, feeling happier than he had done for a very long time.

He had just about finished eating when the man suddenly reappeared:

"Aren't you warm enough yet?" he asked, rather anxious to be rid of his visitor from the bush.

"No, not yet," said the Dog, who had spotted another bone he wished to gnaw on.

"Just a few more minutes then," said the man, as he disappeared inside his hut once more.

The Dog grabbed hold of the second bone and began crushing it in his strong jaws, feeling even more contented with himself. But soon the man came out of his hut and asked again:

"When are you going to get up and go? Surely you must be warm enough by now?"

But the Dog, feeling very reluctant to leave the comfort of his surroundings, pleaded with his host:

"Let me stay just a little while longer and I promise to leave you alone after that."

This time the man disappeared and failed to return for several hours, for he had fallen asleep inside his hut, quite forgetting about his guest. But as soon as he awoke, he rushed out of doors to make certain that the Dog had left him as promised. Now he became angry to see the creature snoozing by the fire in exactly the same position as before. Prodding him with his spear, he called for the Dog to get up at once. The Dog rose slowly to his feet and summoning every ounce of his courage, he looked directly into the man's eyes and spoke the following words:

"I know that you want me to go away, but I wish you would let me stay here with you. I could teach you a great many things. I could pass on to you my knowledge of the wild, help you hunt the birds of the forests, keep watch over your house at night and frighten off any intruders. I would never harm your chickens or goats like my brother, the Jackal. I would look after your women and children while you were away. All I ask in return is that you provide me with a warm bed close to your fire and the scraps from your table to satisfy my hunger."

The man now stared back into the Dog's eyes and saw that their expression was honest and trustworthy.

"I will agree to this," he replied. "You may have a home here among the villagers if you perform as you have promised."

And from that day, the Dog has lived with man, guarding his property, protecting his livestock and helping him to hunt in the fields. At night when the Dog settles down to sleep, he hears a cry from the wilderness, "Bo-ah, Bo-ah", and he knows that it is his brother, the Jackal, calling him back home. But he never answers the call, for the Dog is more than content in his new home, enjoying the comforts Jackal was once so happy to ignore.

The Truth About Cock's Comb
(From the Baganda people, central Africa)

THERE WAS A TIME, MANY YEARS AGO, when the wild cats of the forests were forced to live as servants of the fowls who frequently beat them and treated them with the utmost cruelty. The fowls, then the laziest of creatures, sat around preening their great feathers all day long, demanding that their servants supply them with food and anything else they might require. Whenever the cats caught flying ants, the fowls took four-fifths of them; whenever they had gathered millet seed, the fowls simply helped themselves to as much as they wanted. Of course, the cats did not like this arrangement, and often they considered rising up in rebellion. But one thing always held them back. They lived in

fear of the scarlet combs the fowls wore on their heads, for they had been warned that if ever they came too close to them, they would be severely burnt and scarred for life.

One day, when it had turned bitterly cold, Mother Cat discovered that her fire had gone out, and knowing that her family would not survive very long without heat, she made a brave decision to send her youngest son to the fowls to beg for fire. When the young cat arrived at the home of the Head Cock he found him stretched out on the floor of his hut, quite alone, and apparently very drunk. The young cat approached the Head Cock cautiously and announced the purpose of his visit in a tiny, terrified voice. But he received no response whatsoever as the cock continued to snore very loudly. Once more he tried, raising his voice ever so slightly, but still there was no answer.

So the young cat went back home and told his mother that he had tried to wake the cock without any success.

"You must go back there again," his mother told him. "And this time, take some dry grass with you. If you find that the cock is still asleep, stick a blade of grass into his comb and bring me back the fire."

The young cat set off once more to do as his mother had bid him. When he arrived at the Head Cock's hut, he found he had not moved an inch. Slowly he crept towards the sleeping figure and, ever so carefully, touched the comb with the grass. But surprisingly, there was no sign of any fire, not even a spark, and the blade of grass remained quite as cold as it had ever been.

Again, the young cat returned home and told his mother what had happened.

"You can't have tried hard enough," she scolded. "I suppose I will have to abandon the rest of the children and come along with you this time."

And so for the third time, the young cat set off towards the Head Cock's hut, accompanied by his mother who was determined to have her fire at any price. Luckily, the cock continued to snore as before and it was not difficult for Mother Cat to approach him and touch his comb with the grass. Gently she blew on the stalk, expecting it to burst into flame. But the result was exactly as her son had described it – there was no fire, no spark, not even the slightest glimmer of heat.

Mother Cat was now rather perplexed, and even though she was afraid of being burnt, she decided to risk placing her hands on the cock's comb to see if it was hot. Slowly and carefully she stretched out her fingers, but as soon as they rested on the scarlet comb, she found that it was stone cold.

At first astonished by the discovery, Mother Cat became very angry as she contemplated the long years of suffering her family had endured under Head Cock and the rest of the fowls. She began shaking the drunken creature violently and as soon as he had awoken she dragged him to his feet.

"We don't fear you anymore," she screamed at him. "We tested your comb while you were asleep and we know that you have deceived us all. There is no fire in it and there never has been. Now, if you value your life, you had better leave this place as quickly as you can."

The Head Cock saw that his empty boasting had been discovered and fled from his village as fast as his legs could carry him. And ever since that time, fowls have been forced to take refuge with man, squawking in fear whenever they think a cat is coming too close to them.

Chameleon Wins a Wife
(From the Kikuyu people, Kenya)

ONE DAY FROG SWAM TO THE SURFACE of a little pond and glanced around him for a place to rest: "The water is cold today," he complained, "it would do me good to bask in the sun for a little while." And so he left the water and crouched on a warm, flat stone at the edge of the pond.

After some time a beautiful young girl from the local village named Ngema came to the pond to fetch some water. The Frog remained seated on the stone without moving a muscle so that the young woman eventually began to stare at him, asking herself aloud whether or not he might be ill.

"No, I am not ill," Frog called to her irritably, "why do you imagine such a thing? Can't you see how strong I am?"

"Other frogs usually leap back into the water as soon as they see the villagers approach," replied the girl, "but you don't seem at all frightened and that is why I thought perhaps you must be sick."

The Frog turned his two big eyes towards Ngema, rose up on his hind legs and stretched himself impressively towards the sky.

"Underneath this body, I am really a fine young man," he boasted.

"I have enough cattle and goats to buy any number of beautiful girls like yourself, but a curse rests on me and I must remain here until it is lifted.

"When my father lay on his death bed, he said to me: 'My son, you will spend most of your time by the water until the day comes when you meet a girl there and ask her to marry you. If she accepts, it will mean happiness for you both, but if she refuses, she will die.' So I ask you to marry me here and now, and it is entirely up to you whether you live or die."

The girl sat down on the grass and began thinking hard. After a while she stood up again and answered the Frog worriedly:

"If that curse rests on you, then it rests on me as well. I have seen you and you have asked me to be your wife. I will not refuse you now, for I have no wish to die just yet."

So Ngema reluctantly agreed to marry the Frog and led him home to her parents' hut on the outskirts of the village.

In the courtyard at the front of her parents' house there stood a very beautiful palm tree. Among its broad, leafy branches sat a Chameleon watching the approach of the young girl and the Frog. Ngema escorted her companion indoors and left him there to discuss the wedding arrangements with her father while she sat down at the base of the tree to grind some corn for the midday meal. The Chameleon now moved cautiously towards her, descending from branch to branch slowly and carefully, his eyes darting suspiciously from side to side, until at last he stood within a few feet of her. But before he had the opportunity to address the girl, she suddenly turned towards him:

"I have been watching you all this time," she said, "and I can scarcely believe how long it took you to move such a short distance. Do you know that it has taken you over an hour to reach this spot?"

"I won't apologise for that," answered the Chameleon. "I am a stranger to you, and had I rushed upon you, you would have been frightened and called out to your people. But in this way I haven't alarmed you and now we will be able to talk quietly without anyone disturbing us."

"I have been so anxious to meet you, but wanted to choose my moment carefully. I came here early this morning to tell you I love you and my greatest wish is for you to become my wife."

The young girl set aside her bowl of corn and fell silent for several moments. At length, she raised her head and answered the Chameleon rather indifferently:

"You are too late with your request, and besides, I could never marry anyone who moves as slowly as you do. People would laugh to see us together."

"Our elders say that empty gourds make a great noise, but it amounts to very little in the end," replied the Chameleon. "Think again before you reject me."

Ngema sighed deeply as she pondered these words.

"Well," she said finally, "Frog is inside the house asking my father's permission to marry me. Whichever of you can satisfy him will earn the right to become my husband."

So Chameleon waited for Frog to emerge and then entered the house to see if he could reason with the young girl's father. Their conversation was not half so difficult as Chameleon had expected and before long he reappeared smiling to himself, having agreed with the old man that he would return to claim his bride within a few days.

As soon as he had put all his affairs in order, Chameleon returned as promised to the girl's home, anxious to get on with the wedding ceremony. But to his disgust, he found Frog still pleading for Ngema's hand, insisting that he was by far the richer of the two, and that he would make a much more suitable husband.

Chameleon stormed into the room and interrupted Frog in mid-stream:

"You call me a slow and worthless creature," he yelled furiously, "but I call you a slippery, boneless, hideous carbuncle."

And the two continued to hurl abuse at each other for some time, each of them determined to prove their worth before the young girl's family.

At last, the old man called for them both to stop and when they were ready to listen he offered them the following solution:

"I will fix a bride-price," he told the pair, "which must be delivered before the end of six days. The first of you to arrive here with everything I demand will win my daughter's hand in marriage."

Then the old man listed out the various goods he desired from each of them and without further discussion Frog and Chameleon went their separate ways, eager to assemble their respective cargoes as hastily as possible.

The Frog enlisted a great number of his friends to help him and overnight he had prepared a vast quantity of beer and food of every kind, including sweet potatoes, corn, dove-peas, shea-nuts and bananas, which he piled on to an enormous caravan ready to take to the girl's house.

Early the next morning, a long line of frogs began hopping down the road, travelling at great speed in order to ensure that they would reach their destination before the Chameleon. But as they moved along, they began to attract the sniggers of the roadside workers, for they failed to notice that at every hop, the beer spilt from the gourds, the bananas dropped from the baskets, and the food crumbled to pieces in the open bags and fell to the ground.

When the company approached Ngema's house, they received a very warm welcome from the large crowd who set off to meet them. Songs of praise were sung by the women of the village and a loud chorus of cheering could be heard for miles around. But when, later that same evening, the villagers eventually came to unfasten the loads, they were horrified to see that all the sacks were completely empty and not a drop of beer remained in the gourds. The villagers called the father of the girl and reported to him their discovery:

"Come and examine the gifts Frog has brought you," they told him, "he has arrived here with empty sacks and dry bowls."

The old man looked at the Frog sternly and raised his voice in anger:

"Why have you come here to mock us? Do you think I would exchange my precious child for such a worthless cargo? Go and seek a wife elsewhere, for I have no time for a son-in-law who would attempt to trick me like this."

The Frog did not pause to argue his case, for he knew that his impatience and arrogance had cost him his bride and that now the curse would never be reversed. He hung his head in shame and silently slunk away, hopping despondently down the road with the rest of his companions.

Three more days passed by and most of the villagers had abandoned all hope that Chameleon would ever show his face among them. But then, from the opposite direction on the fifth morning, the people spotted a caravan of carriers making very slow progress towards the village. It was mid-afternoon by the time it reached the outskirts, and as before, the villagers went forward to welcome their guests.

But this time, the women of the village were very anxious to inspect the loads before disturbing the father of the bride. They approached the caravan warily, but their fears were quickly laid to rest, for as soon as they began to unwrap the cargo, they found the sacks overflowing with food and the gourds full to the brim with beer.

Ngema smiled as she moved forward to greet the Chameleon, remembering how he had once described to her the hollow sound of an empty gourd. The celebrations now began in earnest and the satisfied father gave his daughter to the victorious Chameleon who took her for his wife the very next day.

The Chief and the Tigers
(From Lesotho, southern Africa)

THERE LIVED LONG AGO a chief whose wife was beautiful as the morning sun. Dear was she to the heart of her lord, and great was his sorrow when she grew sick. Many doctors and wise women tried to cure her, but in vain. Worse and worse she grew, till the people said she would surely die, and the heart of the chief became as water within him.

One day, as the shadows grew long on the ground, an old, old man came slowly to the village, and asked to see the chief. "Morena (Master)," he said, "I have heard of your trouble, and have come to help you. Your wife is ill of a great sickness, and she will die unless you can get a tiger's heart with which to make medicine for her to drink. See, I have here a wonderful stone which will help you, and some medicine for you to drink. Now wrap yourself in a tiger-skin. The medicine will make you wise to understand and to speak their tongue; so shall they look upon you as a brother. When you have drunk the medicine, take the stone in your hand, and set out on your journey. When you come to the home of the tigers, you must live among them as one of themselves, until you can find yourself alone with one. Him must you quickly kill, and tear from his warm body his heart unbroken, and then, throwing away your tiger skin, you must flee to your home. The tigers will chase you, but when they come too near, you must throw down the stone in front of you and jump upon it, when it will become a great rock, from whose sides fire will dart forth, and burn any who try to climb it. Thus will you be saved from the power of the tigers, and your wife be restored to health."

Gratefully the chief did as the old man desired, and set off to seek the home of the tigers. Many days he wandered across the plains and over the mountains, into the unknown valleys beyond, and there he found those he sought. They greeted him joyfully, welcoming him as a brother; only one, a young tiger of great beauty, held back, and muttered, "This is no tiger but a man. He will bring misfortune upon us. Slay him, my brothers, ere it be too late;" but they heeded him not. Not many days had passed, when all the tigers scattered themselves over the valley, and the chief found himself alone with the angry young tiger. Watching him patiently, he soon found the opportunity he sought, and, hastily killing him, he tore the still warm heart from the lifeless body, and throwing off his disguise, set off towards his home.

On, on he went, and still no sign of the tigers, but, as the sun sank to rest, they appeared in the distance, and he knew they would soon overtake him. When they were so close behind him that he heard the angry snap of their teeth, he threw down the stone the old man had given him, and sprang on to it. Instantly it became a great rock, even as the old man had said. Up came the tigers, each striving to be the first to tear the heart out of the chief, even as he had torn out their brother's heart; but the first one that reached the rock, sprang back with a howl of agony, and rolled over on his side – dead. The others all drew up in alarm, and dared not approach the stone, but spent many hours in wandering round and round the rock, and grinding their teeth at the chief, who calmly watched them from his seat on the top of the rock.

Just before dawn the tigers, now thoroughly tired, lay down, and soon were fast asleep. Carefully, silently, the chief crawled down from the rock, which immediately became again a small stone. Taking the stone in his hand, and holding close the precious heart, which was to restore his wife to health, he fled like a deer towards his village, which he now saw in the plain below. Should he reach it before the tigers caught him? The perspiration streamed from his body, his ears rang with strange noises, and his breath came in great gasps, but still he hurried on. Presently he heard the tigers coming. There was no time even to look behind. He *must* reach the village before they overtook him. On, on, stumbling blindly over every obstacle, he staggered. How far away it still looked! Would his people *never* see him? Yes, at last he is seen. He can hear the shout of his men as they rush to help him, only a few more steps now, and he is safe. Bravely he totters on, then stumbles and falls helpless, exhausted, as his men arrive, and carry him in triumph into the village, while the tigers, baffled and furious, retreat to their home beyond the mountains.

With song and dance the people keep festival, for their chief has returned in safety, and his beautiful wife, restored to perfect health, sits smiling by his side, to receive the loving congratulations of old and young; but the old man came not to join the throng, nor was he ever seen in their land again. Quietly as he came, he had gone, leaving no sign behind him.

The Lion of Manda
(From the Swahili-speaking peoples, east Africa)

ONCE UPON A TIME there was a lion who lived on the island called Manda, which is opposite Shela town, and the people of Shela heard it roaring nightly. In Shela was a rich merchant, and one day he gave out in the bazaar: "I will pay one hundred dollars to whosoever will go and sleep alone one night on the opposite shore, in Manda island." But for fear of the lion no man would do this.

Now in that same town was a youth and his wife who were very poor, for they had nothing. When this youth heard the talk of the town, he came to his wife and said, "There is a man who will give a hundred dollars to anyone who will sleep on the opposite side one night. I will go and sleep there."

His wife said to him, "Do not go, my husband, the lion will eat you."

He said, "Let me go, for if Allah loves me I will not die, and by this means we will get the wherewithal to buy some food."

Then she said to him, "Go. May Allah preserve you."

So that youth, when evening fell, took a canoe and paddled over to Manda, and there lay down on the shore.

Now, when the youth had gone, his wife there behind him was sad because she had let him go, and her heart was very heavy with fear for her husband. So she took some embers and some sticks of wood and went down on to Shela beach, and there she kindled a little fire and tended it all night, so that her young man on the opposite side might see it and not be afraid.

In the morning he returned safely to Shela and went to claim his hundred dollars. But the merchant said, "You have not earned them, for you saw the fire that your wife made, and so you were not afraid."

The youth, when he heard those words, was very angry, and went to accuse the merchant before the Sultan.

So the Sultan called that merchant and asked him why he had not paid the youth his hundred dollars.

The merchant said, "Truly, I did not pay him the dollars because he did not earn them, for he had a fire to comfort him the whole night long. Now, Sultan, see if my words are not true and judge between us."

The Sultan then asked the youth, "Did you have a fire?" The youth replied that his wife had made a fire, so the Sultan, who wished to favour the rich merchant, said, "Then you did not earn the money."

As that youth went forth from the presence of the Sultan, he jostled against a sage, who asked him his news; so he told him how he had been defrauded of his hundred dollars.

Then said the sage, "If I get your money for you, what will you give me?" The youth said, "I will give you a third." So they agreed together after that manner.

The youth then went his way, and the sage came to the Sultan and said to him, "I invite you to food at noon tomorrow in my plantation." The Sultan replied, "Thank you, I will come."

Then the sage returned to his house and made ready. He slaughtered an ox and prepared the meat in pots, but did not cook it. When the Sultan arrived next day at noon, the sage had the pots of meat placed in one place apart, and he had fires made in other places, far away from where he had put the pots. Then, having told his servants what to do, he came and sat on the verandah with the Sultan, and they conversed with one another.

After a while he arose and shouted to his servants, "Oh, Bakari and Sadi, stoke well the fires and turn over the meat."

When twelve o'clock had long passed the Sultan, feeling hungry, asked the sage, "Is not the food yet ready?"

The sage answered, "The meat is not yet done." So they continued to converse, till the Sultan became very cross owing to his hunger, and said, "Surely the food must be ready now." So the sage called out, "Oh, Bakari, and oh, Sadi, is not the food ready?"

They answered him, "Not yet, master." He then said, "Stoke up the fires well and turn the meat, that we may soon get our food;" and they answered him, "We hear and obey, master."

The Sultan then said, "Surely the meat must be cooked *now*, after all this time." So he arose to look for himself, and behold! he saw the fires all on one side of the courtyard, with servants busily feeding them, and the cooking pots all on the other side, also with servants tending them.

He turned to the sage and said, "How is the meat to become cooked, and the pots are in one place and the fires in another?" The sage replied, "They will cook like that, my master."

Then was the Sultan very wroth and said, "It is impossible to cook food like that."

"Indeed no," gravely answered the sage; "for is not the case the same between those cooking pots and their fires and the youth to whom you yesterday refused his hundred dollars and his fire, which was on the opposite shore?"

The Sultan then said, "Your words are true, oh sage! The youth did earn his hundred dollars. Send and tell the merchant to pay him at once."

So the youth got his dollars for sleeping on the island of Manda, and the sage did not accept from him the fee he had asked for. This is the story of the lion of Manda.

The Hyena and the Moonbeam

(From the Swahili-speaking peoples, east Africa)

A HYENA WENT FORTH to drink water one day, and he came to a well and stooped down to quench his thirst. Now where he stooped down there was a moonbeam shining on the water.

The Hyena saw that moonshine there in the water and he thought it was a bone. He tried to reach it, but he could not, so he said to himself, "Now if I drink all this water I will get that bone which is at the bottom."

So he drank and drank, and the water was not finished. So he drank and drank again, till he was so full of water that he died.

The Jackal and the Wolf

(From South Africa)

ONCE ON A TIME, JACKAL, who lived on the borders of the colony, saw a wagon returning from the seaside laden with fish; he tried to get into the wagon from behind, but he could not; he then ran on before and lay in the road as if dead. The wagon came up to him, and the leader cried to the driver, "Here is a fine kaross for your wife!"

"Throw it into the wagon," said the driver, and Jackal was thrown in.

The wagon travelled on, through a moonlight night, and all the while Jackal was throwing out the fish into the road; he then jumped out himself and secured a great prize.

But stupid old Wolf (hyena), coming by, ate more than his share, for which Jackal owed him a grudge, and he said to him, "You can get plenty of fish, too, if you lie in the way of a wagon as I did, and keep quite still whatever happens."

"So!" mumbled Wolf.

Accordingly, when the next wagon came from the sea, Wolf stretched himself out in the road. "What ugly thing is this?" cried the leader, and kicked Wolf. He then took a stick and thrashed him within an inch of his life. Wolf, according to the directions of Jackal, lay quiet as long as he could; he then got up and hobbled off to tell his misfortune to Jackal, who pretended to comfort him.

"What a pity," said Wolf, "I have not got such a handsome skin as you have!"

Cloud Eating
(From South Africa)

JACKAL AND HYENA WERE TOGETHER, it is said, when a white cloud rose. Jackal descended upon it, and ate of the cloud as if it were fat.

When he wanted to come down, he said to Hyena, "My sister, as I am going to divide with thee, catch me well." So she caught him, and broke his fall. Then she also went up and ate there, high up on the top of the cloud.

When she was satisfied, she said, "My greyish brother, now catch me well." The greyish rogue said to his friend, "My sister, I shall catch thee well. Come therefore down."

He held up his hands, and she came down from the cloud, and when she was near, Jackal cried out (painfully jumping to one side), "My sister, do not take it ill. Oh me! Oh me! A thorn has pricked me and sticks in me." Thus she fell down from above, and was sadly hurt.

Since that day, it is said that Hyena's hind feet have been shorter and smaller than the front ones.

Cock and Jackal
(From South Africa)

COCK, IT IS SAID, was once overtaken by Jackal, and caught. Cock said to Jackal, "Please, pray first (before you kill me), as the white man does."

Jackal asked, "In what manner does he pray? Tell me."

"He folds his hands in praying," said Cock. Jackal folded his hands and prayed. Then Cock spoke again; "You ought not to look about you as you do. You had better shut your eyes." He did so; and Cock flew away, upbraiding at the same time Jackal with these words, "You rogue! do you also pray?"

There sat Jackal, speechless, because he had been outdone.

The Lion, the Hyena and the Hare
(From the Swahili-speaking peoples, east Africa)

ONCE IT HAPPENED that a lion, a hyena and a hare set out on a journey together. The way was long, and they suffered much from hunger. Till one day, when they were as yet far distant from the end of the journey, they were so sorely pressed by hunger that they gave up all hope of getting any further.

Then they took counsel together and said, "Now we shall all die, and not one of us will escape. It were better that we eat one of our number, so that the other two may get the strength to proceed."

So they all agreed that this must be done, but they could not agree as to who should be eaten and who should be saved. At last it was decided that the youngest amongst them should be eaten by the other two.

Then said the lion to the hare, "Now tell us your age, that we may know."

The hare replied, "Am I not the smallest and weakest here? It would not be fitting for me to speak before the great ones. You, my masters, tell your ages first, and then I will speak."

So the lion turned to the hyena and said, "You must then speak first."

The hyena thought awhile and then said, "My age is five hundred years old."

The lion then said to the hare, "You have heard the hyena, now you must speak."

But the hare said, "How can I speak before you, my lord, have spoken?"

The lion thought and then said, "I am two thousand years old."

When the hare heard these words he wept. The other two asked him why he wept, and he said, "Oh, my friends, I weep to think of my eldest son, my first born, for it was on a day just two thousand years ago that he died."

So the lion killed the hyena, and when he and the hare had eaten him they were able to get strength to go on, and they finished their journey in safety.

Why the Bat Flies by Night
(From southern Nigeria)

A BUSH RAT CALLED OYOT was a great friend of Emiong, the bat; they always fed together, but the bat was jealous of the bush rat. When the bat cooked the food it was always very good, and the bush rat said, "How is it that when you make the soup it is so tasty?"

The bat replied, "I always boil myself in the water, and my flesh is so sweet, that the soup is good."

He then told the bush rat that he would show him how it was done; so he got a pot of warm water, which he told the bush rat was boiling water, and jumped into it, and very shortly afterwards came out again. When the soup was brought it was as strong and good as usual, as the bat had prepared it beforehand.

The bush rat then went home and told his wife that he was going to make good soup like the bat's. He therefore told her to boil some water, which she did. Then, when his wife was not looking, he jumped into the pot, and was very soon dead.

When his wife looked into the pot and saw the dead body of her husband boiling she was very angry, and reported the matter to the king, who gave orders that the bat should be made a prisoner. Everyone turned out to catch the bat, but as he expected trouble he flew away into the bush and hid himself. All day long the people tried to catch him, so he had to change his habits, and only came out to feed when it was dark, and that is why you never see a bat in the daytime.

The Fish and the Leopard's Wife; or, Why the Fish Lives in the Water

(From southern Nigeria)

MANY YEARS AGO, when King Eyo was ruler of Calabar, the Fish used to live on the land; he was a great friend of the Leopard, and frequently used to go to his house in the bush, where the Leopard entertained him.

Now the Leopard had a very fine wife, with whom the Fish fell in love. And after a time, whenever the Leopard was absent in the bush, the Fish used to go to his house and make love to the Leopard's wife, until at last an old woman who lived near informed the Leopard what happened whenever he went away.

At first the leopard would not believe that the Fish, who had been his friend for so long, would play such a low trick, but one night he came back unexpectedly, and found the Fish and his wife together; at this the Leopard was very angry, and was going to kill the Fish, but he thought as the Fish had been his friend for so long, he would not deal with him himself, but would report his behaviour to King Eyo.

This he did, and the king held a big palaver, at which the Leopard stated his case quite shortly, but when the Fish was put upon his defence he had nothing to say, so the king addressing his subjects said, "This is a very bad case, as the Fish has been the Leopard's friend, and has been trusted by him, but the Fish has taken advantage of his friend's absence, and has betrayed him." The king, therefore, made an order that for the future the Fish should live in the water, and that if he ever came on the land he should die; he also said that all men and animals should kill and eat the Fish whenever they could catch him, as a punishment for his behaviour with his friend's wife.

Why the Flies Bother the Cows
(From southern Nigeria)

WHEN ADIAHA UMO WAS QUEEN OF CALABAR, being very rich and hospitable, she used to give big feasts to all the domestic animals, but never invited the wild beasts, as she was afraid of them.

At one feast she gave there were three large tables, and she told the cow to sit at the head of the table, as she was the biggest animal present, and share out the food. The cow was quite ready to do this, and the first course was passed, which the cow shared out amongst the people, but forgot the fly, because he was so small.

When the fly saw this, he called out to the cow to give him his share, but the cow said: "Be quiet, my friend, you must have patience."

When the second course arrived, the fly again called out to the cow, but the cow merely pointed to her eye, and told the fly to look there, and he would get food later.

At last all the dishes were finished, and the fly, having been given no food by the cow, went supperless to bed.

The next day the fly complained to the queen, who decided that, as the cow had presided at the feast, and had not given the fly his share, but had pointed to her eye, for the future the fly could always get his food from the cow's eyes wherever she went; and even at the present time, wherever the cows are, the flies can always be seen feeding off their eyes in accordance with the queen's orders.

Why the Cat Kills Rats
(From southern Nigeria)

ANSA WAS KING OF CALABAR for fifty years. He had a very faithful cat as a housekeeper, and a rat was his house-boy. The king was an obstinate, headstrong man, but was very fond of the cat, who had been in his store for many years.

The rat, who was very poor, fell in love with one of the king's servant girls, but was unable to give her any presents, as he had no money.

At last he thought of the king's store, so in the night-time, being quite small, he had little difficulty, having made a hole in the roof, in getting into the store. He then stole corn and native pears, and presented them to his sweetheart.

At the end of the month, when the cat had to render her account of the things in the store to the king, it was found that a lot of corn and native pears were missing. The king was very angry at this, and asked the cat for an explanation. But the cat could not account for the loss, until one of her friends told her that the rat had been stealing the corn and giving it to the girl.

When the cat told the king, he called the girl before him and had her flogged. The rat he handed over to the cat to deal with, and dismissed them both from his service. The cat was so angry at this that she killed and ate the rat, and ever since that time whenever a cat sees a rat she kills and eats it.

Segu the Honey Guide
(From the Swahili-speaking peoples, east Africa)

SEGU IS THE HONEY GUIDE. His work is that he lives in the forest and flies about looking for bees' nests, and when he finds one he goes to look for men. When he finds them he says,

"Che! che! che! che!" until those sons of men look up and say, "Ah, there is Segu. Let us go with him that he may show us honey."

So these people follow Segu, who flies in front from tree to tree saying, "Che! che! che! che!"

When he comes to that tree where the honey is he flies round, saying, "Che! che! che! che!" very fast, and then he goes and sits by himself.

Then these men come to the tree and look up and see where the bees' nest is; so they climb up with their axe and cut a hole and get out the honey.

They take that honey and are very pleased, but a little of it they leave for Segu as his share.

On these people going away, Segu comes out and finds the honey which they have left him; so he sits and eats and fills himself, and arises and flies away. This is, indeed, Segu's manner of living.

Another day Segu sees a lion asleep, and he looks for people, and when he finds them he twitters and says, "Che! che! che! che!"

Then these people follow him thinking, "Today Segu is going to show us much honey."

They follow him up there to where the lion is lying, and when they suddenly see him they are unable to stand, if there is running away to be done instead.

The lion frightens these people, so they run swiftly away, saying, "Today Segu has done evil; every day he shows us honey, and today he comes to show us a lion."

That is all.

Why a Hawk Kills Chickens

(From southern Nigeria)

IN THE OLDEN DAYS there was a very fine young hen who lived with her parents in the bush. One day a hawk was hovering round, about eleven o'clock in the morning, as was his custom,

making large circles in the air and scarcely moving his wings. His keen eyes were wide open, taking in everything (for nothing moving ever escapes the eyes of a hawk, no matter how small it may be or how high up in the air the hawk may be circling).

This hawk saw the pretty hen picking up some corn near her father's house. He therefore closed his wings slightly, and in a second of time was close to the ground; then spreading his wings out to check his flight, he alighted close to the hen and perched himself on the fence, as a hawk does not like to walk on the ground if he can help it.

He then greeted the young hen with his most enticing whistle, and offered to marry her. She agreed, so the hawk spoke to the parents, and paid the agreed amount of dowry, which consisted mostly of corn, and the next day took the young hen off to his home.

Shortly after this a young cock who lived near the hen's former home found out where she was living, and having been in love with her for some months – in fact, ever since his spurs had grown – determined to try and make her return to her own country. He therefore went at dawn, and, having flapped his wings once or twice, crowed in his best voice to the young hen. When she heard the sweet voice of the cock she could not resist his invitation, so she went out to him, and they walked off together to her parent's house, the young cock strutting in front crowing at intervals.

The hawk, who was hovering high up in the sky, quite out of sight of any ordinary eye, saw what had happened, and was very angry. He made up his mind at once that he would obtain justice from the king, and flew off to Calabar, where he told the whole story, and asked for immediate redress. So the king sent for the parents of the hen, and told them they must repay to the hawk the amount of dowry they had received from him on the marriage of their daughter, according to the native custom; but the hen's parents said that they were so poor that they could not possibly afford to pay. So the king told the hawk that he could kill and eat any of the cock's children whenever and wherever he found them as payment of his dowry, and, if the cock made any complaint, the king would not listen to him.

From that time until now, whenever a hawk sees a chicken he swoops down and carries it off in part-payment of his dowry.

The King and the Nsiat Bird
(From southern Nigeria)

WHEN NDARAKE WAS KING OF IDU, being young and rich, he was very fond of fine girls, and had plenty of slaves. The Nsiat bird was then living at Idu, and had a very pretty daughter, whom Ndarake wished to marry.

When he spoke to the father about the matter, he replied that of course he had no objection personally, as it would be a great honour for his daughter to marry the king, but, unfortunately, when any of his family had children, they always gave birth to twins, which, as the king knew, was not allowed in the country; the native custom being to kill both the children and throw them into the bush, the mother being driven away and allowed to starve. The king, however, being greatly struck with Adit, the bird's daughter, insisted on marrying her, so the Nsiat bird had to agree. A large amount of dowry was paid by the king, and a big play and feast was held. One strong slave was told to carry Adit Nsiat during the whole play, and she sat on his shoulders with her legs around his neck; this was done to show what a rich and powerful man the king was.

After the marriage, in due course Adit gave birth to twins, as her mother had done before her. The king immediately became very fond of the two babies, but according to the native custom, which was too strong for anyone to resist, he had to give them up to be killed. When the Nsiat bird heard this, he went to the king and reminded him that he had warned the king before he married what would happen if he married Adit, and rather than that the twins should be killed, he and the whole of his family would leave the earth and dwell in the air, taking the twins with them. As the king was so fond of Adit and the two children, and did not want them to be killed, he gladly consented, and the Nsiat bird took the whole of his family, as well as Adit and her two children, away, and left the earth to live and make their home in the trees; but as they had formerly lived in the town with all the people, they did not like to go into the forest, so they made their nests in the trees which grew in the town, and that is why you always see the Nsiat birds living and making their nests only in places where human beings are. The black birds are the cocks, and the golden-coloured ones are the hens. It was the beautiful colour of Adit which first attracted the attention of Ndarake and caused him to marry her.

The Kites and the Crows
(From Zanzibar, Tanzanian coast)

ONE DAY KOONGOOROO, sultan of the crows, sent a letter to Mwayway, sultan of the kites, containing these few words: "I want you folks to be my soldiers." To this brief message Mwayway at once wrote this short reply: "I should say not." Thereupon, thinking to scare Mwayway, the sultan of the crows sent him word, "If you refuse to obey me I'll make war upon you." To which the sultan of the kites replied, "That suits me; let us fight, and if you beat us we will obey you, but if we are victors you shall be our servants."

So they gathered their forces and engaged in a great battle, and in a little while it became evident that the crows were being badly beaten.

As it appeared certain that, if something were not done pretty quickly, they would all be killed, one old crow, named Jeeoosee, suddenly proposed that they should fly away.

Directly the suggestion was made it was acted upon, and the crows left their homes and flew far away, where they set up another town. So, when the kites entered the place, they found no one there, and they took up their residence in Crowtown.

One day, when the crows had gathered in council, Koongooroo stood up and said: "My people, do as I command you, and all will be well. Pluck out some of my feathers and throw me into the town of the kites; then come back and stay here until you hear from me."

Without argument or questioning the crows obeyed their sultan's command.

Koongooroo had lain in the street but a short time, when some passing kites saw him and inquired threateningly, "What are you doing here in our town?"

With many a moan he replied, "My companions have beaten me and turned me out of their town because I advised them to obey Mwayway, sultan of the kites."

When they heard this they picked him up and took him before the sultan, to whom they said, "We found this fellow lying in the street, and he attributes his involuntary presence in our town to so singular a circumstance that we thought you should hear his story."

Koongooroo was then bidden to repeat his statement, which he did, adding the remark that, much as he had suffered, he still held to his opinion that Mwayway was his rightful sultan.

This, of course, made a very favorable impression, and the sultan said, "You have more sense than all the rest of your tribe put together; I guess you can stay here and live with us."

So Koongooroo, expressing much gratitude, settled down, apparently, to spend the remainder of his life with the kites.

One day his neighbors took him to church with them, and when they returned home they asked him, "Who have the best kind of religion, the kites or the crows?"

To which crafty old Koongooroo replied, with great enthusiasm, "Oh, the kites, by long odds!"

This answer tickled the kites like anything, and Koongooroo was looked upon as a bird of remarkable discernment.

When almost another week had passed, the sultan of the crows slipped away in the night, went to his own town, and called his people together.

"Tomorrow," said he, "is the great annual religious festival of the kites, and they will all go to church in the morning. Go, now, and get some wood and some fire, and wait near their town until I call you; then come quickly and set fire to the church."

Then he hurried back to Mwayway's town.

The crows were very busy indeed all that night, and by dawn they had an abundance of wood and fire at hand, and were lying in wait near the town of their victorious enemies.

So in the morning every kite went to church. There was not one person left at home except old Koongooroo.

When his neighbours called for him they found him lying down. "Why!" they exclaimed with surprise, "are you not going to church today?"

"Oh," said he, "I wish I could; but my stomach aches so badly I can't move!" And he groaned dreadfully.

"Ah, poor fellow!" said they; "you will be better in bed;" and they left him to himself.

As soon as everybody was out of sight he flew swiftly to his soldiers and cried, "Come on; they're all in the church."

Then they all crept quickly but quietly to the church, and while some piled wood about the door, others applied fire.

The wood caught readily, and the fire was burning fiercely before the kites were aware of their danger; but when the church began to fill with smoke, and tongues of flame shot through the cracks, they tried to escape through the windows. The greater part of them, however, were suffocated, or, having their wings singed, could not fly away, and so were burned to death, among them their sultan, Mwayway; and Koongooroo and his crows got their old town back again.

From that day to this the kites fly away from the crows.

Tink-Tinkje
(From South Africa)

THE BIRDS WANTED A KING. Men have a king, so have animals, and why shouldn't they? All had assembled.

"The Ostrich, because he is the largest," one called out.

"No, he can't fly."

"Eagle, on account of his strength."

"Not he, he is too ugly."

"Vulture, because he can fly the highest."

"No, Vulture is too dirty, his odor is terrible."

"Peacock, he is so beautiful."

"His feet are too ugly, and also his voice."

"Owl, because he can see well."

"Not Owl, he is ashamed of the light."

And so they got no further. Then one shouted aloud, "He who can fly the highest will be king." "Yes, yes," they all screamed, and at a given signal they all ascended straight up into the sky.

Vulture flew for three whole days without stopping, straight toward the sun. Then he cried aloud, "I am the highest, I am king."

"T-sie, t-sie, t-sie," he heard above him. There Tink-tinkje was flying. He had held fast to one of the great wing feathers of Vulture, and had never been felt, he was so light. "T-sie, t-sie, t-sie, I am the highest, I am king," piped Tink-tinkje.

Vulture flew for another day still ascending. "I am highest, I am king."

"T-sie, t-sie, t-sie, I am the highest, I am king," Tink-tinkje mocked. There he was again, having crept out from under the wing of Vulture.

Vulture flew on the fifth day straight up in the air. "I am the highest, I am king," he called.

"T-sie, t-sie, t-sie," piped the little fellow above him. "I am the highest, I am king."

Vulture was tired and now flew direct to earth. The other birds were mad through and through. Tink-tinkje must die because he had taken advantage of Vulture's feathers and there hidden himself. All flew after him and he had to take refuge in a mouse hole. But how were they to get him out? Someone must stand guard to seize him the moment he put out his head.

"Owl must keep guard; he has the largest eyes; he can see well," they exclaimed.

Owl went and took up his position before the hole. The sun was warm and soon Owl became sleepy and presently he was fast asleep.

Tink-tinkje peeped, saw that Owl was asleep, and z-zip away he went. Shortly afterwards the other birds came to see if Tink-tinkje were still in the hole. "T-sie, t-sie," they heard in a tree; and there the little vagabond was sitting.

White-crow, perfectly disgusted, turned around and exclaimed, "Now I won't say a single word more." And from that day to this White-crow has never spoken. Even though you strike him, he makes no sound, he utters no cry.

The Lost Message
(From South Africa)

THE ANT HAS HAD from time immemorial many enemies, and because he is small and destructive, there have been a great many slaughters among them. Not only were most of the birds their enemies, but Anteater lived almost wholly from them, and Centipede beset them every time and at all places when he had the chance.

So now there were a few among them who thought it would be well to hold council together and see if they could not come to some arrangement whereby they could retreat to some place of safety when attacked by robber birds and animals.

But at the gathering their opinions were most discordant, and they could come to no decision.

There was Red-ant, Rice-ant, Black-ant, Wagtail-ant, Gray-ant, Shining-ant, and many other varieties. The discussion was a true babel of diversity, which continued for a long time and came to nothing.

A part desired that they should all go into a small hole in the ground, and live there; another part wanted to have a large and strong dwelling built on the ground, where nobody could enter but an ant; still another wanted to dwell in trees, so as to get rid of Anteater, forgetting entirely that there they would be the prey of birds; another part seemed inclined to have wings and fly.

And, as has already been said, this deliberation amounted to nothing, and each party resolved to go to work in its own way, and on its own responsibility.

Greater unity than that which existed in each separate faction could be seen nowhere in the world; each had his appointed task, each did his work regularly and well. And all worked together in the same way. From among them they chose a king – that is to say some of the groups did – and they divided the labour so that all went as smoothly as it possibly could.

But each group did it in its own way, and not one of them thought of protecting themselves against the onslaught of birds or Anteater.

The Red-ants built their house on the ground and lived under it, but Anteater levelled to the ground in a minute what had cost them many days of precious labour. The Rice-ants lived under the ground, and with them it went no better. For whenever they came out, Anteater visited them and took them out sack and pack. The Wagtail-ants fled to the trees, but there on many occasions sat Centipede waiting for them, or the birds gobbled them up. The Gray-ants had intended to save themselves from extermination by taking to flight, but this also availed them nothing, because the Lizard, the Hunting-spider, and the birds went a great deal faster than they.

When the Insect-king heard that they could come to no agreement he sent them the secret of unity, and the message of Work-together. But unfortunately he chose for his messenger the Beetle, and he has never yet arrived at the Ants, so that they are still today the embodiment of discord and consequently the prey of enemies.

The Monkey's Fiddle
(From South Africa)

HUNGER AND WANT forced Monkey one day to forsake his land and to seek elsewhere among strangers for much-needed work. Bulbs, earth beans, scorpions, insects, and such things were completely exhausted in his own land. But fortunately he received, for the time being, shelter with a great uncle of his, Orang Outang, who lived in another part of the country.

When he had worked for quite a while he wanted to return home, and as recompense his great uncle gave him a fiddle and a bow and arrow and told him that with the bow and arrow he could hit and kill anything he desired, and with the fiddle he could force anything to dance.

The first he met upon his return to his own land was Brer Wolf. This old fellow told him all the news and also that he had since early morning been attempting to stalk a deer, but all in vain.

Then Monkey laid before him all the wonders of the bow and arrow that he carried on his back and assured him if he could but see the deer he would bring it down for him. When Wolf showed him the deer, Monkey was ready and down fell the deer.

They made a good meal together, but instead of Wolf being thankful, jealousy overmastered him and he begged for the bow and arrow. When Monkey refused to give it to him, he thereupon began to threaten him with his greater strength, and so when Jackal passed by, Wolf told him that Monkey had stolen his bow and arrow. After Jackal had heard both of them, he declared himself unqualified to settle the case alone, and he proposed that they bring the matter to the court of Lion, Tiger, and the other animals. In the meantime he declared he would take possession of what had been the cause of their quarrel, so that it would be safe, as he said. But he immediately brought to earth all that was eatable, so there was a long time of slaughter before Monkey and Wolf agreed to have the affair in court.

Monkey's evidence was weak, and to make it worse, Jackal's testimony was against him. Jackal thought that in this way it would be easier to obtain the bow and arrow from Wolf for himself.

And so fell the sentence against Monkey. Theft was looked upon as a great wrong; he must hang.

The fiddle was still at his side, and he received as a last favor from the court the right to play a tune on it.

He was a master player of his time, and in addition to this came the wonderful power of his charmed fiddle. Thus, when he struck the first note of 'Cockcrow' upon it, the court began at once to show an unusual and spontaneous liveliness, and before he came to the first waltzing turn of the old tune the whole court was dancing like a whirlwind.

Over and over, quicker and quicker, sounded the tune of 'Cockcrow' on the charmed fiddle, until some of the dancers, exhausted, fell down, although still keeping their feet in motion. But Monkey, musician as he was, heard and saw nothing of what had happened around him. With his head placed lovingly against the instrument, and his eyes half closed, he played on, keeping time ever with his foot.

Wolf was the first to cry out in pleading tones breathlessly, "Please stop, Cousin Monkey! For love's sake, please stop!"

But Monkey did not even hear him. Over and over sounded the resistless waltz of 'Cockcrow'.

After a while Lion showed signs of fatigue, and when he had gone the round once more with his young lion wife, he growled as he passed Monkey, "My whole kingdom is yours, ape, if you just stop playing."

"I do not want it," answered Monkey, "but withdraw the sentence and give me my bow and arrow, and you, Wolf, acknowledge that you stole it from me."

"I acknowledge, I acknowledge!" cried Wolf, while Lion cried, at the same instant, that he withdrew the sentence.

Monkey gave them just a few more turns of the 'Cockcrow', gathered up his bow and arrow, and seated himself high up in the nearest camel thorn tree.

The court and other animals were so afraid that he might begin again that they hastily disbanded to new parts of the world.

The Lioness and the Ostrich
(From South Africa)

IT IS SAID, once a lioness roared, and the ostrich also roared. The lioness went toward the place where the ostrich was. They met. The lioness said to the ostrich, "Please to roar." The ostrich roared. Then the lioness roared. The voices were equal. The lioness said to the ostrich, "You are my match."

Then the lioness said to the ostrich, "Let us hunt game together." They saw eland and made toward it. The lioness caught only one; the ostrich killed a great many by striking them with the claw which was on his leg; but the lioness killed only one. When they had met after the hunting they went to the game, and the lioness saw that the ostrich had killed a great deal.

Now, the lioness also had young cubs. They went to the shade to rest themselves. The lioness said to the ostrich, "Get up and rip open; let us eat." Said the ostrich, "Go and rip open; I shall eat the blood." The lioness stood up and ripped open, and ate with the cubs. And when she had eaten, the ostrich got up and ate the blood. They went to sleep.

The cubs played about. While they were playing, they went to the ostrich, who was asleep. When he went to sleep he also opened his mouth. The young lions saw that the ostrich had no teeth. They went to their mother and said, "This fellow, who says he is your equal, has no teeth; he is insulting you." Then the lioness went to wake the ostrich, and said, "Get up, let us fight"; and they fought. And the ostrich said, "Go to that side of the ant-hill, and I will go to this side of it." The ostrich struck the ant-hill, and sent it toward the lioness. But the second time he struck the lioness in a vulnerable spot, near the liver, and killed her.

Crocodile's Treason
(From South Africa)

CROCODILE WAS, in the days when animals still could talk, the acknowledged foreman of all water creatures and if one should judge from appearances one would say that he still is. But in those days it was his especial duty to have a general care of all water animals, and when one year it was exceedingly dry, and the water of the river where they had lived dried up and became scarce, he was forced to make a plan to trek over to another river a short distance from there.

He first sent Otter out to spy. He stayed away two days and brought back a report that there was still good water in the other river, real sea-cow holes, that not even a drought of several years could dry up.

After he had ascertained this, Crocodile called to his side Tortoise and Alligator.

"Look here," said he, "I need you two to-night to carry a report to Lion. So then get ready; the veldt is dry, and you will probably have to travel for a few days without any water. We must make peace with Lion and his subjects, otherwise we utterly perish this year. And he must help us to trek over to the other river, especially past the Boer's farm that lies in between, and to travel unmolested by any of the animals of the veldt, so long as the trek lasts. A fish on land is sometimes a very helpless thing, as you all know." The two had it mighty hard in the burning sun, and on the dry veldt, but eventually they reached Lion and handed him the treaty.

"What is going on now?" thought Lion to himself, when he had read it. "I must consult Jackal first," said he. But to the commissioners he gave back an answer that he would be the following evening with his advisers at the appointed place, at the big vaarland willow tree, at the farther end of the hole of water, where Crocodile had his headquarters.

When Tortoise and Alligator came back, Crocodile was exceedingly pleased with himself at the turn the case had taken.

He allowed Otter and a few others to be present and ordered them on that evening to have ready plenty of fish and other eatables for their guests under the vaarland willow.

That evening as it grew dark Lion appeared with Wolf, Jackal, Baboon, and a few other important animals, at the appointed place, and they were received in the most open-hearted manner by Crocodile and the other water creatures.

Crocodile was so glad at the meeting of the animals that he now and then let fall a great tear of joy that disappeared into the sand. After the other animals had done well by the fish, Crocodile laid bare to them the condition of affairs and opened up his plan. He wanted only peace among all animals; for they not only destroyed one another, but the Boer, too, would in time destroy them all.

The Boer had already stationed at the source of the river no less than three steam pumps to irrigate his land, and the water was becoming scarcer every day. More than this, he took advantage of their unfortunate position by making them sit in the shallow water and then, one after the other, bringing about their death. As Lion was, on this account, inclined to make peace, it was to his glory to take this opportunity and give his hand to these peace-making water creatures, and carry out their part of the contract, namely, escort them from the dried-up water, past the Boer's farm and to the long sea-cow pools.

"And what benefit shall we receive from it?" asked Jackal.

"Well," answered Crocodile, "the peace made is of great benefit to both sides. We will not exterminate each other. If you desire to come and drink water, you can do so with an easy mind, and not be the least bit nervous that I, or any one of us will seize you by the nose; and so also with all the other animals. And from your side we are to be freed from Elephant, who has the habit, whenever he gets the opportunity, of tossing us with his trunk up into some open and narrow fork of a tree and there allowing us to become biltong."

Lion and Jackal stepped aside to consult with one another, and then Lion wanted to know what form of security he would have that Crocodile would keep to his part of the contract.

"I stake my word of honour," was the prompt answer from Crocodile, and he let drop a few more long tears of honesty into the sand.

Baboon then said it was all square and honest as far as he could see into the case. He thought it was nonsense to attempt to dig pitfalls for one another; because he personally was well aware that his race would benefit somewhat from this contract of peace and friendship. And more than this, they must consider that use must be made of the fast disappearing water, for even in the best of times it was an unpleasant thing to be always carrying your life about in your hands. He would, however, like to suggest to the King that it would be well to have everything put down in writing, so that there would be nothing to regret in case it was needed.

Jackal did not want to listen to the agreement. He could not see that it would benefit the animals of the veldt. But Wolf, who had fully satisfied himself with the fish, was in an exceptionally peace-loving mood, and he advised Lion again to close the agreement.

After Lion had listened to all his advisers, and also the pleading tones of Crocodile's followers, he held forth in a speech in which he said that he was inclined to enter into the agreement, seeing that it was clear that Crocodile and his subjects were in a very tight place.

There and then a document was drawn up, and it was resolved, before midnight, to begin the trek. Crocodile's messengers swam in all directions to summon together the water animals for the trek.

Frogs croaked and crickets chirped in the long water grass. It was not long before all the animals had assembled at the vaarland willow. In the meantime Lion had sent out a few despatch riders to his subjects to raise a commando for an escort, and long ere midnight these also were at the vaarland willow in the moonlight.

The trek then was regulated by Lion and Jackal. Jackal was to take the lead to act as spy, and when he was able to draw Lion to one side, he said to him:

"See here, I do not trust this affair one bit, and I want to tell you straight out, I am going to make tracks! I will spy for you until you reach the sea-cow pool, but I am not going to be the one to await your arrival there."

Elephant had to act as advance guard because he could walk so softly and could hear and smell so well. Then came Lion with one division of the animals, then Crocodile's trek with a flank protection of both sides, and Wolf received orders to bring up the rear.

Meanwhile, while all this was being arranged, Crocodile was smoothly preparing his treason. He called Yellow Snake to one side and said to him: "It is to our advantage to have these animals, who go among us every day, and who will continue to do so, fall into the hands of the Boer. Listen, now! You remain behind unnoticed, and when you hear me shout you will know that we have arrived safely at the sea-cow pool. Then you must harass the Boer's dogs as much as you can, and the rest will look out for themselves."

Thereupon the trek moved on. It was necessary to go very slowly as many of the water animals were not accustomed to the journey on land; but they trekked past the Boer's farm in safety, and toward break of day they were all safely at the sea-cow pool. There most of the water animals disappeared suddenly into the deep water, and Crocodile also began to make preparations to follow their example. With tearful eyes he said to Lion that he was, oh, so thankful for the help, that, from pure relief and joy, he must first give vent to his feelings by a few screams. Thereupon he suited his words to actions so that even the mountains echoed, and then thanked Lion on behalf of his subjects, and purposely continued with a long speech, dwelling on all the benefits both sides would derive from the agreement of peace.

Lion was just about to say good day and take his departure, when the first shot fell, and with it Elephant and a few other animals.

"I told you all so!" shouted Jackal from the other side of the sea-cow pool. "Why did you allow yourselves to be misled by a few Crocodile tears?"

Crocodile had disappeared long ago into the water. All one saw was just a lot of bubbles; and on the banks there was an actual war against the animals. It simply crackled the way the Boers shot them.

But most of them, fortunately, came out of it alive.

Shortly after, they say, Crocodile received his well-earned reward, when he met a driver with a load of dynamite. And even now when the Elephant gets the chance he pitches them up into the highest forks of the trees.

The Judgment of Baboon
(From South Africa)

ONE DAY, IT IS SAID, the following story happened. Mouse had torn the clothes of Itkler (the tailor), who then went to Baboon, and accused Mouse with these words:

"In this manner I come to thee: Mouse has torn my clothes, but will not know anything of it, and accuses Cat; Cat protests likewise her innocence, and says, 'Dog must have done it'; but Dog denies it also, and declares Wood has done it; and Wood throws the blame on Fire, and says, 'Fire did it'; Fire says, 'I have not, Water did it'; Water says, 'Elephant tore the clothes'; and Elephant says, 'Ant tore them.' Thus a dispute has arisen among them. Therefore, I, Itkler, come to thee with this proposition: Assemble the people and try them in order that I may get satisfaction."

Thus he spake, and Baboon assembled them for trial. Then they made the same excuses which had been mentioned by Itkler, each one putting the blame upon the other.

So Baboon did not see any other way of punishing them, save through making them punish each other; he therefore said,

"Mouse, give Itkler satisfaction."

Mouse, however, pleaded not guilty. But Baboon said, "Cat, bite Mouse." She did so.

He then put the same question to Cat, and when she exculpated herself, Baboon called to Dog, "Here, bite Cat."

In this manner Baboon questioned them all, one after the other, but they each denied the charge. Then he addressed the following words to them, and said,

"Wood, beat Dog.
Fire, burn Wood.
Water, quench Fire.
Elephant, drink Water.
Ant, bite Elephant in his most tender parts."

They did so, and since that day they cannot any longer agree with each other.

Ant enters into Elephant's most tender parts and bites him.

Elephant swallows Water.
Water quenches Fire.
Fire consumes Wood.
Wood beats Dog.
Dog bites Cat.
And Cat bites Mouse.

Through this judgment Itkler got satisfaction and addressed Baboon in the following manner:

"Yes! Now I am content, since I have received satisfaction, and with all my heart I thank thee, Baboon, because thou hast exercised justice on my behalf and given me redress."

Then Baboon said, "From today I will not any longer be called Jan, but Baboon shall be my name."

Since that time Baboon walks on all fours, having probably lost the privilege of walking erect through this foolish judgment.

The Zebra Stallion
(From South Africa)

THE BABOONS, IT IS SAID, used to disturb the Zebra Mares in drinking. But one of the Mares became the mother of a foal. The others then helped her to suckle (the young stallion), that he might soon grow up.

When he was grown up and they were in want of water, he brought them to the water. The Baboons, seeing this, came, as they formerly were used to do, into their way, and kept them from the water.

While the Mares stood thus, the Stallion stepped forward, and spoke to one of the Baboons, "Thou gum-eater's child!"

The Baboon said to the Stallion, "Please open thy mouth, that I may see what thou livest on." The Stallion opened his mouth, and it was milky.

Then the Stallion said to the Baboon, "Please open thy mouth also, that I may see." The Baboon did so, and there was some gum in it. But the Baboon quickly licked some milk off the Stallion's tongue. The Stallion on this became angry, took the Baboon by his shoulders, and pressed him upon a hot, flat rock. Since that day the Baboon has a bald place on his back.

The Baboon said, lamenting, "I, my mother's child, I, the gum-eater, am outdone by this milk-eater!"

When Lion Could Fly
(From South Africa)

LION, IT IS SAID, used once to fly, and at that time nothing could live before him. As he was unwilling that the bones of what he caught should be broken into pieces, he made a pair of White Crows watch the bones, leaving them behind at the kraal

whilst he went a-hunting. But one day Great Frog came there, broke the bones in pieces, and said, "Why can men and animals live no longer?" And he added these words, "When he comes, tell him that I live at yonder pool; if he wishes to see me, he must come there."

Lion, lying in wait (for game), wanted to fly up, but found he could not fly. Then he got angry, thinking that at the kraal something was wrong, and returned home. When he arrived he asked, "What have you done that I cannot fly?" Then they answered and said, "Someone came here, broke the bones into pieces, and said, "If he want me, he may look for me at yonder pool!" Lion went, and arrived while Frog was sitting at the water's edge, and he tried to creep stealthily upon him. When he was about to get hold of him, Frog said, "Ho!" and, diving, went to the other side of the pool, and sat there. Lion pursued him; but as he could not catch him he returned home.

From that day, it is said, Lion walked on his feet, and also began to creep upon (his game); and the White Crows became entirely dumb since the day that they said, "Nothing can be said of that matter."

Why Has Jackal a Long Black Stripe on His Back?

(From South Africa)

THE SUN, IT IS SAID, was one day on earth, and the men who were travelling saw him sitting by the wayside, but passed him without notice.

Jackal, however, who came after them, and saw him also sitting, went to him and said, "Such a fine little child is left behind by the men." He then took Sun up, and put it into his awa-skin (on his back). When it burnt him, he said, "Get down," and shook himself; but Sun stuck fast to his back, and burnt Jackal's back black from that day.

Horse Cursed By Sun
(From South Africa)

IT IS SAID THAT ONCE Sun was on earth, and caught Horse to ride it. But it was unable to bear his weight, and therefore Ox took the place of Horse, and carried Sun on its back. Since that time Horse is cursed in these words, because it could not carry Sun's weight:

"From today thou shalt have a (certain) time of dying.
This is thy curse, that thou hast a (certain) time of dying.
And day and night shalt thou eat,
But the desire of thy heart shall not be at rest,
Though thou grazest till morning and again until sunset.
Behold, this is the judgment which I pass upon thee,"

said Sun. Since that day Horse's (certain) time of dying commenced.

Lion's Defeat
(From South Africa)

THE WILD ANIMALS, it is said, were once assembled at Lion's. When Lion was asleep, Jackal persuaded Little Fox to twist a rope of ostrich sinews, in order to play Lion a trick. They took ostrich sinews, twisted them, and fastened the rope to Lion's tail, and the other end of the rope they tied to a shrub.

When Lion awoke, and saw that he was tied up, he became angry, and called the animals together. When they had assembled, Lion said (using this form of conjuration):

"What child of his mother and father's love,
Whose mother and father's love has tied me?"

Then answered the animal to whom the question was first put:

"I, child of my mother and father's love,
I, mother and father's love, I have not done it."

All answered the same; but when he asked Little Fox, Little Fox said:

"I, child of my mother and father's love,
I, mother and father's love, have tied thee!"

Then Lion tore the rope made of sinews, and ran after Little Fox. But Jackal said:

"My boy, thou son of lean Mrs Fox, thou wilt never be caught."

Truly Lion was thus beaten in running by Little Fox.

The Monkey, the Shark and the Washerman's Donkey

(From Zanzibar, Tanzanian coast)

ONCE UPON A TIME Keema, the monkey, and Papa, the shark, became great friends. The monkey lived in an immense mkooyoo tree which grew by the margin of the sea – half of its branches being over the water and half over the land.

Every morning, when the monkey was breakfasting on the kooyoo nuts, the shark would put in an appearance under the tree and call out, "Throw me some food, my friend;" with which request the monkey complied most willingly.

This continued for many months, until one day Papa said, "Keema, you have done me many kindnesses: I would like you to go with me to my home, that I may repay you."

"How can I go?" said the monkey; "we land beasts cannot go about in the water."

"Don't trouble yourself about that," replied the shark; "I will carry you. Not a drop of water shall get to you."

"Oh, all right, then," said Mr Keema; "let's go."

When they had gone about half-way the shark stopped, and said: "You are my friend. I will tell you the truth."

"Why, what is there to tell?" asked the monkey, with surprise.

"Well, you see, the fact is that our sultan is very sick, and we have been told that the only medicine that will do him any good is a monkey's heart."

"Well," exclaimed Keema, "you were very foolish not to tell me that before we started!"

"How so?" asked Papa.

But the monkey was busy thinking up some means of saving himself, and made no reply.

"Well?" said the shark, anxiously; "why don't you speak?"

"Oh, I've nothing to say now. It's too late. But if you had told me this before we started, I might have brought my heart with me."

"What? Haven't you your heart here?"

"Huh!" ejaculated Keema; "don't you know about us? When we go out we leave our hearts in the trees, and go about with only our bodies. But I see you don't believe me. You think I'm scared. Come on; let's go to your home, where you can kill me and search for my heart in vain."

The shark did believe him, though, and exclaimed, "Oh, no; let's go back and get your heart."

"Indeed, no," protested Keema; "let us go on to your home."

But the shark insisted that they should go back, get the heart, and start afresh.

At last, with great apparent reluctance, the monkey consented, grumbling sulkily at the unnecessary trouble he was being put to.

When they got back to the tree, he climbed up in a great hurry, calling out, "Wait there, Papa, my friend, while I get my heart, and we'll start off properly next time."

When he had got well up among the branches, he sat down and kept quite still.

After waiting what he considered a reasonable length of time, the shark called, "Come along, Keema!" But Keema just kept still and said nothing.

In a little while he called again: "Oh, Keema! Let's be going."

At this the monkey poked his head out from among the upper

branches and asked, in great surprise, “Going? Where?”

“To my home, of course.”

“Are you mad?” queried Keema.

“Mad? Why, what do you mean?” cried Papa.

“What’s the matter with you?” said the monkey. “Do you take me for a washerman’s donkey?”

“What peculiarity is there about a washerman’s donkey?”

“It is a creature that has neither heart nor ears.”

The shark, his curiosity overcoming his haste, thereupon begged to be told the story of the washerman’s donkey, which the monkey related as follows:

“A washerman owned a donkey, of which he was very fond. One day, however, it ran away, and took up its abode in the forest, where it led a lazy life, and consequently grew very fat.

“At length Soongoora, the hare, by chance passed that way, and saw Poonda, the donkey.

“Now, the hare is the most cunning of all beasts – if you look at his mouth you will see that he is always talking to himself about everything.

“So when Soongoora saw Poonda he said to himself, ‘My, this donkey is fat!’ Then he went and told Simba, the lion.

“As Simba was just recovering from a severe illness, he was still so weak that he could not go hunting. He was consequently pretty hungry.

“Said Mr Soongoora, ‘I’ll bring enough meat tomorrow for both of us to have a great feast, but you’ll have to do the killing.’

“‘All right, good friend,’ exclaimed Simba, joyfully; ‘you’re very kind.’

“So the hare scampered off to the forest, found the donkey, and said to her, in his most courtly manner, ‘Miss Poonda, I am sent to ask your hand in marriage.’

“‘By whom?’ simpered the donkey.

“‘By Simba, the lion.’

“The donkey was greatly elated at this, and exclaimed: ‘Let’s go at once. This is a first-class offer.’

“They soon arrived at the lion’s home, were cordially invited in, and sat down. Soongoora gave Simba a signal with his eyebrow, to the effect that this was the promised feast, and that he would wait outside. Then he said to Poonda: ‘I must leave you for a while to attend to some private business. You stay here and converse with your husband that is to be.'

"As soon as Soongoora got outside, the lion sprang at Poonda, and they had a great fight. Simba was kicked very hard, and he struck with his claws as well as his weak health would permit him. At last the donkey threw the lion down, and ran away to her home in the forest.

"Shortly after, the hare came back, and called, 'Haya! Simba! have you got it?'

"'I have not got it,' growled the lion; 'she kicked me and ran away; but I warrant you I made her feel pretty sore, though I'm not strong.'

"'Oh, well,' remarked Soongoora; 'don't put yourself out of the way about it.'

"Then Soongoora waited many days, until the lion and the donkey were both well and strong, when he said: 'What do you think now, Simba? Shall I bring you your meat?'

"'Ay,' growled the lion, fiercely; 'bring it to me. I'll tear it in two pieces!'

"So the hare went off to the forest, where the donkey welcomed him and asked the news.

"'You are invited to call again and see your lover,' said Soongoora.

"'Oh, dear!' cried Poonda; 'that day you took me to him he scratched me awfully. I'm afraid to go near him now.'

"'Ah, pshaw!' said Soongoora; 'that's nothing. That's only Simba's way of caressing.'

"'Oh, well,' said the donkey, 'let's go.'

"So off they started again; but as soon as the lion caught sight of Poonda he sprang upon her and tore her in two pieces.

"When the hare came up, Simba said to him: 'Take this meat and roast it. As for myself, all I want is the heart and ears.'

"'Thanks,' said Soongoora. Then he went away and roasted the meat in a place where the lion could not see him, and he took the heart and ears and hid them. Then he ate all the meat he needed, and put the rest away.

"Presently the lion came to him and said, 'Bring me the heart and ears.'

"'Where are they?' said the hare.

"'What does this mean?' growled Simba.

"'Why, didn't you know this was a washerman's donkey?'

"'Well, what's that to do with there being no heart or ears?'

"'For goodness' sake, Simba, aren't you old enough to know that if this beast had possessed a heart and ears it wouldn't have come back the second time?'

"Of course the lion had to admit that what Soongoora, the hare, said was true.

"And now," said Keema to the shark, "you want to make a washerman's donkey of me. Get out of there, and go home by yourself. You are not going to get me again, and our friendship is ended. Good-bye, Papa."

A Hospitable Gorilla
(From the Congo and central Africa)

ONCE THERE WAS A TRIBE that dwelt on the banks of the Black River just above Basoko town, and at that time of the far past the thick forest round about them was haunted by many monstrous animals; big apes, chimpanzees, gorillas and such creatures, which are not often seen nowadays.

Not far from the village, in a darksome spot where the branches met overhead and formed a thick screen, and the lower wood hedged it closely round about so that a tortoise could scarcely penetrate it, there lived the Father of the Gorillas. He had housed himself in the fork of one of the tallest trees, and many men had seen the nest as they passed by, but none as yet had seen the owner.

But one day a fisherman in search of rattans to make his nets, wandered far into the woods, and in trying to recover the direction home struck the Black River high up. As he stood wondering whether this was the black stream that flowed past his village, he saw, a little to the right of him, an immense gorilla, who on account of the long dark fur on his chest appeared to be bigger than he really was. A cold sweat caused by his great fear began to come out of the man, and his knees trembled so that he could hardly stand, but when he perceived that the gorilla did not move, but continued eating his bananas, he became comforted a little, and his senses came back. He turned his head around, in order to see the clearest way for a run; but as he was about to start, he saw that the gorilla's eyes were fixed on him. Then the gorilla broke out into speech and said:

"Come to me, and let me look at thee."

The fisherman's fear came back to him, but he did as he was told, and when he thought he was near enough, he stood still.

Then the gorilla said:

"If thou art kin to me, thou art safe from harm; if not, thou canst not pass. How many fingers hast thou?" he asked.

"Four," the fisherman answered, and he held a hand up with its back towards the gorilla, and his thumb was folded in on the palm so that it could not be seen by the beast.

"Ay – true indeed. Why, thou must be a kinsman of ours, though thy fur is somewhat scanty. Sit down and take thy share of this food, and eat."

The fisherman sat down, and broke off bananas from the stalk and ate heartily.

"Now mind," said the gorilla, "thou hast eaten food with me. Shouldst thou ever meet in thy wanderings any of my brothers, thou must be kind to them in memory of this day. Our tribe has no quarrel with any of thine, and thy tribe must have none against any of mine. I live alone far down this river, and thy tribe lives further still. Mind our password, "*Tu-wheli, Tu-wheli*." By that we know who is friendly and who is against us."

The fisherman departed, and speeding on his way reached his village safely; but he kept secret what he had seen and met that day.

Some little time after, the tribe resolved to have a grand hunt around their village, to scare the beasts of the forest away; for in some things they resemble us. If we leave a district undisturbed for a moon or so, the animals think that we have either departed the country or are afraid of them. The apes and the elephants are the worst in that respect, and always lead the way, pressing on our heels, and often sending their scouts ahead to report, or as a hint to us that we are lingering too long.

The people loaded themselves with their great nets, and first chose the district where the Gorilla Father lived. They set their nets around a wide space, and then the beaters were directed to make a large sweep and drive all the game towards the nets, and here and there where the netting was weak, the hunters stood behind a thick bush, their heavy spears ready for the fling.

Well, it just happened that at that very time the Father of the Gorillas was holding forth to his kinsmen, and the first they knew of the hunt, and that a multitude of men were in the woods, was when they heard the horrid yells of the beaters, the sound of horns, the jingle of iron, and the all-round swish of bushes.

The fisherman, like the rest of his friends, was well armed, and he was as keen as the others for the hunt, but soon after he heard the cries of the beaters, he saw a large gorilla rushing out of the bushes, and knew him instantly for his friend, and he cried out "*Tu-wheli! Tu-wheli*!" At the sound of it the gorilla led his kinsmen towards him, and passed the word to those behind, saying, "Ah, this is our friend. Do not hurt him."

The gorillas passed in a long line of mighty fellows, close by the fisherman, and as they heard the voice of their father, they only whispered to him, "*Tu-wheli, Tu-wheli*," but the last of all was a big, sour-faced gorilla, who, when he saw that the pass was only guarded by one man, made a rush at him. His roar of rage was heard by the father, and turning back he knew that his human brother was in danger, and he cried out to those nearest to part them, "The man is our brother;" but as the fierce gorilla was deaf to words, the father loped back to them, and slew him, and then hastened away as the hunters were pressing up.

These, when they came up and observed that the fisherman's spear was still in his hand, and not painted with blood, were furious, and they agreed together that he should not have a share of the meat, "For," said they, "he must have been in a league against us." Neither did he obtain any share of the spoil.

A few days after this the fisherman was proceeding through a part of the forest, and a gorilla met him in the path, and said:

"Stay, I seem to know thee. Art thou not our brother?"

"*Tu-wheli, Tu-wheli*!" he cried.

"Ah, it is true, follow me;" and they went together to the gorilla's nesting-tree, where the fisherman was feasted on ripe bananas, berries, and nuts, and juicy roots, and he was shown which roots and berries were sweet, and which were bitter, and so great was the variety of food he saw, that he came to know that though lost in the forest a wise man need not starve.

When the fisherman returned to his village he called the elders together, and he laid the whole story of his adventures before his people, and when the elders heard that the berries and roots, nuts, and mushrooms in the forest, of which they had hitherto been afraid, were sweet and wholesome, they exclaimed with one voice, that the gorillas had proved themselves true friends, and had given them much useful knowledge; and it was agreed among them that in future the gorillas should be reckoned among those, against whom it would not be lawful to raise their spears.

Ever since the tribes on the Black River avoid harming the gorilla, and all his kind big and little; neither will any of the gorilla trespass on their plantations, or molest any of the people.

Stories of Wit & Wisdom

STORIES WHICH EXPLORE HUMAN EXPERIENCE – man's strengths and weaknesses, his relationship with his fellow beings and his correct place within society, form an intrinsic part of the African mythological tradition.

Many of the stories included here may be described as 'proverbial'. They offer instruction, often culminating in some form of moral punch line, which demonstrates well the African storyteller's use of tales as a vehicle to teach man correct social values, responsibility, humility, and a sense of justice. 'The Young Man and the Skull', for example, is characteristic of the group. It embodies a simple proverb, linked to the protagonist's unhappy fate, warning us that boastfulness is a sign of moral decadence which cannot go unpunished. Similarly, 'The Rich Man and the Poor Man' demonstrates the fact that greed will never be rewarded.

Other stories, among them 'How Walakuga Answered the King' and 'The Two Rogues', have a less serious intention and focus rather more light-heartedly on man's cunning, commending it as an essential tool for his survival.

Tales of punishment and retribution figure prominently in many African tales, demonstrating that wrongdoers will always suffer the consequences of their actions (and how), but also that the wronged are entitled to avenge themselves. It is also made clear that crimes will always be discovered – such as in 'Out of the Mouths of Babes', in which the baby reveals the truth.

The Rich Man and the Poor Man
(From the Akamba people, Kenya)

IN A CERTAIN VILLAGE OF THE AKAMBA there lived two men, one rich and one poor. Yet in spite of their different circumstances, they lived together as neighbours. The rich man always supported his poor friend in times of trouble and in return, the poor man worked hard on the rich man's farm, ploughing the fields and carrying out as many odd jobs as he could manage.

But there came a time when a severe famine spread throughout the land, causing widespread hardship and misery. Even the rich man could not escape the suffering, and as he watched his wealth decline, he grew hard-hearted towards his fellow men. Soon he had forgotten all about the poor man and when, one day, his old friend arrived on his doorstep to beg the scraps from his table, the rich man dismissed him as a common beggar and warned him never to trespass on his land again.

The poor man watched his children die of starvation one by one until only himself and his wife remained. But even though his spirit was almost broken, he was determined to keep his wife alive, and so he swallowed his pride and set off one evening towards the village where he began searching through other people's waste for even an old bone to chew on. Before long, he was approached by a well-dressed woman who took pity on him and presented him with a handful of maize. The poor man carried the maize home to his wife and she set a great pot of water over the fire to boil. She had intended to make a hot, nourishing soup for them both, but this proved an impossible task, since they had no meat to add to the broth and no salt with which to season it.

The poor man sat at his table trying to figure out how he might improve the flavour of his meal when suddenly an idea came to him he thought might be worth trying.

"I wonder if my rich friend is having a nice dinner tonight," he said to himself, and he promptly arose from the table and set off in the direction of the rich man's farmhouse. He crept close enough to take a good look through the kitchen window and there, right in front of him, he saw a steaming-hot chicken lying on a plate of thick gravy. The delicious smell of the cooked meat wafted on the breeze towards him, causing the poor man's stomach to grumble loudly. Without wasting another second, he rushed back to his hut, grabbed his bowl of watery soup, and sat down against the outside wall of the rich man's house. Then, as he spooned the thin liquid down his throat, he breathed in the aroma of the meat and began to imagine that he was chewing on the most tender pieces of chicken flesh. When he had finished his meal, he felt very satisfied and hurried off home to tell his wife how clever he had been.

A few days later, the poor man saw the rich man and could not prevent himself boasting of his cleverness once again.

"I came to your house a few days ago," he told the rich man, "and while I drank my watery soup I breathed in the delicious smell rising up from your table. I might as well have sat alongside you sharing the same chicken. My own meal tasted equally good."

"So that is why my food tasted so dull," roared the rich man, "you stole all its flavour from me. Well, you must pay for what you have taken. I order you to come with me to the judge. We will let him decide your punishment."

The poor man was hauled that same day before the judge who ordered him to pay one goat to the rich man for having stolen the aroma from his food. But the poor man could not even afford to pay the rich man a single grain of wheat, let alone a goat, and he drifted slowly homewards, his head bowed in despair, wondering how he could possibly break the distressing news to his wife.

While he walked towards his hut, he met a wise old man hobbling along the road. And as the two were headed in the same direction, they soon struck up a conversation. The poor man revealed to his companion the whole sad story of what had happened and the wise man agreed with him that he had been most unfairly treated.

"I have a goat I will give you," said the old man, "I will go and fetch it for you. Take it home and look after it until the day you are called upon to make your payment. When that day arrives, I promise I will reappear to help you."

And saying this, the wise man went off to fetch the goat, leaving the poor man a little bewildered, yet relieved to know that all was not entirely lost.

Less than a week later, the judge sent a message to the poor man telling him that he should appear before him to deliver the promised payment. By midday a large group of people had gathered in front of the judge's house to witness the proceedings. At the centre of the crowd stood the wise man, listening intently to all that was said. He behaved as if he knew nothing of the whole affair and began asking the people to explain to him what was happening.

"The poor man is supposed to pay the rich man a goat for having stolen the smell from his food," they told him.

"But why make so much fuss over such a trivial incident?" the wise man asked.

"The poor man must pay the rich man his goat," the people repeated, "that is the judge's decision and we must stand by it."

"And would you accept another judgement on this case?" the old man enquired politely.

"We would," replied the people, "if you can prove yourself a good enough judge."

So the old man moved forward to the front of the crowd and addressed the people with the following words:

"A man who steals should be forced to repay only as much as he has taken. If the poor man had eaten the food, he should be made to pay back that food. But if he has only breathed the smell, he should only pay back the smell, nothing more, nothing less."

"Yes, that is very true," answered the people, "but how can a man give back just the smell of the food?"

"I will show you a way," answered the wise man. Then he turned to the rich man and said to him:

"The goat you have asked for has been brought to you. But you may not have it unless the poor man has taken your food. Beat this goat with your staff instead and when the animal bleats, take the sound of its bleating as payment for the smell of your food. Surely you will agree with me that this is a fair exchange!"

The rich man could not argue against this judgement and all around him the people began to clap their hands, delighted to have experienced such wisdom at first hand.

And so the poor man was saved from an unfair sentence and was allowed to go home. But the rich man was made to appear a selfish and greedy individual before the entire village. He slunk away silently and hoped that the whole affair would blow over, but whenever he appeared again in public, the people pointed at him and whispered among themselves:

"He who rides the horse of greed at a gallop will be forced to dismount at the door of shame."

How Walukaga Answered the King

(From the Baganda people, central Africa)

WALUKAGA, THE BLACKSMITH, was by far the most gifted craftsman in the village, capable of turning his hand to all kinds of metalwork. Every morning a crowd usually gathered at his home, gasping in amazement at the speed with which he produced spears and axes, shovels and hoes, armlets and collars, and a whole variety of objects for the benefit of the villagers. The blacksmith's fame had spread far and wide so that even the king took a particular interest in his work and lined his courtyards with wonderful iron figures Walukaga had created specially for him.

One day a messenger from the palace arrived at the blacksmith's home to announce that the king wished him to perform a very special task. Walukaga was delighted by the news, for nothing pleased him more than to serve the king with his craft. He hurried off into a back room where he put on his finest crimson robe and a beautifully decorated head-dress. Then he followed the messenger to the palace, trying to imagine as he went along what kind of exciting work lay in store for him.

He was immediately shown to the king's private chamber and as soon as the king clapped his hands a group of servants appeared carrying several trays of iron pieces in various shapes.

"I have a very special job for you, Walukaga," the king announced enthusiastically. "I was staring at those fine figures you made for me just the other day when it occurred to me how nice it would be to have a life-size metal man for a companion. But I don't just mean a statue. What I want is an iron man who can walk and talk, who has blood in his veins, wisdom in his head and feelings in his heart."

Walukaga almost collapsed with the shock. He stared long and hard into the king's eyes looking for a sign that the whole thing was some kind of joke, but the king's stern expression filled him with despair. From that moment onwards, the blacksmith had no peace of mind, for he well knew that failure to obey his sovereign's wishes would certainly mean death for himself and his family.

"I will do my very best to please you," he answered mournfully and arranged for the iron to be delivered to his forge later that same day.

Next morning, Walukuga arose earlier than usual and made a tour of the neighbouring houses hoping that someone among his friends would be able to help him out of the terrible situation he now found himself in. But every last person he turned to for advice could only offer the most impractical suggestions. One friend recommended that he build a metal shell and put a real man inside it, refusing to believe that the king would ever notice the difference. Another suggested that he flee the country and remain in hiding until the whole affair had been forgotten, entirely overlooking the fact that Walukaga had a wife and children to think of. A third even advised him to persuade the palace cook to poison the king's food. Walukaga listened to each neighbour in turn and fell into a deep depression. He returned home in the afternoon and shut himself away in his room, knowing that his days were numbered and trying desperately hard to come to terms with that fact.

A few days later, as Walukaga walked through the bush deep in thought, he managed to stray from his usual path and found himself wandering through a deserted stretch in search of a familiar landmark. Suddenly he thought he heard voices up ahead and moving closer to investigate, discovered a filthy-looking man sitting cross-legged on the ground chatting away to himself. The blacksmith recognized the man as someone once well-known in the village who had suffered so much misfortune as a youth he had gone completely mad and taken refuge in the wilderness.

Although frightened at first, Walukaga soon realized that the madman was in fact perfectly harmless and decided to accept the cup of water offered him as a sign of friendship. Soon the pair began chatting, and as the conversation turned to more important things, the blacksmith felt he would have nothing to lose if he unburdened himself and told the madman all about the king's impossible command. His companion sat and listened quietly to the very end without interruption and when Walukaga, only half-seriously, asked him whether he had any advice to spare, he was surprised to see the madman's eyes narrow almost to a squint and his face take on a grave and purposeful expression.

"I will tell you precisely what you should do," the madman spoke clearly and decidedly. "I want you to go to the king and tell him if he really wants you to make this remarkable iron man, you must have only the very finest materials. Say to him that you will need a very special charcoal and a plentiful supply of water from a most unusual source. Let him send word to the people of the village that they must shave their heads and burn their hair until they have produced a thousand loads of charcoal, and let him order them to weep into their water-bowls until they have given him a hundred pots of tears."

The blacksmith pondered this advice and rapidly concluded it was by far the best he had received to date. But when he turned to thank the madman, he saw that he had begun rocking back and forth, laughing hysterically and shaking his head uncontrollably. Walukaga felt he had no more time to lose, and in spite of the late hour, he hurried off towards the palace, anxious to say his piece before his courage failed him.

Bowing low before the king, he timidly listed off all the things he would need to complete the work requested of him. But the king listened patiently and agreed to everything demanded, promising that the materials would be collected as smoothly and swiftly as possible.

So the very next day, messengers were sent out to every part of the kingdom ordering the people to shave their heads and weep into their bowls. Nobody dared disobey the king's command and even the women and children came forward without complaint. The people did their very best to comply with the king's wishes, but after seven days, when all of them had shaved their heads and wept until their eyes were red and raw, there was still not enough charcoal to make up even a single load, or enough tears to fill half a water-pot.

The elders of the kingdom had little choice but to appear before their leader and confess to him their lack of success. But as they stood before the king, quaking at the thought of the punishment he would deal them, they were relieved to discover that his response was more than reasonable. The king accepted that the people's efforts had been sincere and he sighed deeply and sent for the blacksmith to appear before him.

"Walukaga," he said, "you may stop your work on the iron man I asked you to build me. You have requested something impossible and my people cannot deliver the materials you need. Go home now and continue on with the work you are best at."

Walukaga approached the king and smiled a little nervously.

"I hope you will not be angry with me, Your Majesty," he said, "but because you asked the impossible of me, I knew I had to do the same in return. I could never have made you a living man of iron, no more than your people could have delivered the charcoal and the water I demanded."

But the king was not in the least bit angry, for he was delighted to have such a clever and honest man among his subjects.

The Young Man and the Skull
(From the Mbundu people, southwest Africa)

ONE DAY A YOUNG HUNTER had journeyed far into the bush in search of antelope when he accidentally stumbled upon a skull lying in the earth. Drawing nearer, he stooped to the ground to examine the object and began muttering to himself:

"How did you manage to get here my friend? What can have brought you to this unhappy end?"

To the young man's absolute astonishment, the skull opened its jaws and began speaking:

"Talking brought me here, my friend. Talking brought me to this place."

The hunter raced back towards his village to tell the people all about his discovery.

"Friends," he cried excitedly, "I have just come across a human skull in the bush and it has spoken to me. It must be a wonderful sign."

"Nonsense," they replied, "how can you possibly hold a conversation with the head of a dead man?"

"But it really did speak to me," the young man insisted, "you only refuse to believe me because you are jealous."

But still the people continued to jeer him.

"Why not go and tell the chief all about your discovery," one mocked, "I'm sure he'll be overjoyed by the news!"

"I will do precisely that," retorted the young man angrily, and off he marched towards the chief's house to tell him all about the skull.

But the chief, who had been taking his afternoon nap, was extremely unhappy that he had been disturbed.

"Why have you come here with your tall stories?" he shouted. "You had better be telling the truth or I will see to it that your own head comes off. Now, take me to this wretched place and let me hear the skull's message for myself."

A small crowd set off from the village, arriving shortly afterwards at the place where the young man had made his discovery. And sure enough, they soon spotted the skull sitting in the earth.

"It looks perfectly ordinary," complained the people after a time, "when are we going to hear it speak?"

The young man crouched to the ground and repeated the words he had first spoken to the skull. But no answer came and the skull's jaws remained firmly shut. Again, the hunter spoke to it, raising his voice more loudly, but only silence followed.

Now the crowd began to grow restless and when a third and fourth attempt produced exactly the same result, they leapt on the young man and chopped off his head as the chief had ordered.

The head fell to the ground and rolled alongside the skull. For a long time afterwards all remained quiet as the villagers disappeared over the hill bearing the body homewards for burial. Then the skull opened its jaws and spoke up:

"How did you manage to get here my friend? What can have brought you to this unhappy end?"

"Talking brought me here," replied the head. "Talking brought me to this place."

The Story of the Glutton
(From the Bantu-speaking peoples, east Africa)

SEBGUGUGU WAS A POOR MAN who lived with his wife and children in one of the shabbiest huts in the village. He had very few possessions worth speaking of and certainly nothing of any great value to his name, apart from a white cow and calf he had inherited from his bride many years before on their wedding day.

One morning, as Sebgugugu sat outside his hut lazing in the warm sunshine, he observed a brightly coloured bird hopping towards him. The bird drew closer and, perching itself on the gate-post, began to chirp a little song. Sebgugugu listened attentively, and after a time he became convinced that the bird was speaking to him through the melody.

"Kill the White One," he heard it say. "Kill the white one and you will get a hundred in return."

Sebgugugu stood up excitedly and called to his wife across the fields to come and hear the strange song. Obediently, she stopped her work and hurried back towards the hut. But after she had listened to the bird singing for a few minutes she turned and said to her husband:

"I cannot hear anything unusual. It is only a sweet little song. Perhaps you have had too much hot sun for one day."

"That bird is definitely speaking to us," her husband argued, "and I'm certain he is trying to deliver a message from the great Imana. [Imana is the name given to the High God of the Bantu people, who commands everything, even Death.] He is telling us that we will get a hundred fat cows if only we kill the white one we own."

"Surely you would never consider doing such a thing!" his wife cried out in alarm. "We depend on that cow for milk to feed our children and if anything happens to it they will die of starvation."

But Sebgugugu chose to ignore these words and marched off, axe in hand, towards the field to kill the white cow.

That evening, the family feasted on freshly roasted beef and for several weeks afterwards they had enough food to keep them satisfied. Soon, however, the meat began to run out and their stomachs felt very empty. There was still no sign of the hundred cows intended to replace the one they had slaughtered, but Sebgugugu would not accept any of the blame for this and carried on as before, basking lazily in the sun while his wife struggled to feed their children and keep the household together.

A few weeks later, the strange bird made a second visit to Sebgugugu's hut and this time he heard it advise him to kill the calf of the white cow. Though his wife pleaded with him, Sebgugugu went ahead as before and slaughtered the young animal, cutting up the carcass for food. But there was far less meat on this occasion, and it lasted only a few days. The children, thirsty without milk, and hungrier than ever, began to grow pale and thin. And when he saw that the hundred cows had still failed to appear, Sebgugugu became slightly fearful for the first time.

"The children are starving," he said to his wife anxiously, "there is nothing else here for them to eat."

"Didn't I warn you this would happen when you slaughtered the first of our precious cattle," his wife replied angrily. "You have left us with little choice now but to abandon our home and roam the countryside in search of food."

Next morning, the family gathered together what few belongings remained in their hut and started off in search of food. By midday, they had travelled a long distance and sat down by the roadside to recover their strength. Weary and footsore, Sebgugugu buried his head in his hands, ready to give up the fight:

"What can I do to save my children?" he cried out despondently. "I have been a very foolish creature."

But the Great Creator, Imana, who had been watching over the family from above, now appeared before the sobbing man and spoke to him encouragingly:

"What is your trouble, Sebgugugu?" he enquired. "You should know by now that you have only to ask and I will do my best to help you."

Sebgugugu raised his eyes and confessed to the High God every detail of his selfish behaviour.

"I can see that you are sorry," Imana responded, "and I will give you the chance to prove to me that you are a man of worth. Walk towards that cattle-kraal beyond the hill and there you will find an old crow guarding the herd. Say to him that I have given you permission to drink the milk. Do not forget to thank him for his hospitality and remember to treat him always with the utmost respect."

Sebgugugu promised to do all this and headed off towards the kraal. He could not find any trace of the old crow when he arrived, but his eyes soon lit up at the sight of four large churns standing nearby, full to the brim with creamy, white milk. Sebgugugu bent over the milk and helped himself to as much as he wanted, leaving just about enough for his wife and children.

Suddenly, in the distance, he caught sight of the old crow driving the cattle homewards, flying back and forth and squawking over their heads to keep them together. Remembering what Imana had said, Sebgugugu ran forward to greet the herdsman, apologizing for the fact that his wife had drunk so much of the milk.

"But I will see to it that she repays you in some way," he reassured the crow. And as the two of them sat down to chat for the evening, he ordered his wife to fetch a pail and begin milking the cows. When she had done this, he ordered her to build a fire to drive the mosquitoes away. Then, he instructed her to bring the crow a bowl full of milk for his supper. Although exhausted, his wife performed all of these tasks without complaint, grateful for the fact that her children had found a place of refuge where they could be restored to health under the crow's protection.

For a long time, things went on well in this way, but then, without warning, Sebgugugu began to grow restless and discontented.

"That old crow is beginning to annoy me," he said to his wife one day. "There really couldn't be a better time to do away with him, you know. Our own children are now old enough to herd the cattle for me, so we really have no use for him anymore."

His wife was appalled to hear him say such a thing, but although she protested loudly, Sebgugugu took his bow and arrows and went outdoors to lie in wait for the crow as he returned home with the cattle that evening. When the crow came near enough, he took aim and shot an arrow in his direction. But the arrow missed its target and the startled crow took to the skies. As he did so, the cattle began to disappear into thin air one by one until there was not so much as a stray calf remaining to satisfy the needs of the family. Sebgugugu looked to his wife for comfort, but she could not give him any. Reduced to destitution once more, she led her children by the hand along the road away from the kraal, her head bowed in disappointment and misery.

They had not gone very far, however, before the benevolent Imana appeared before them once more.

"You have behaved very badly," he chastised Sebgugugu, "but I am prepared to give you another chance. If you walk a little deeper into the bush you will come across a long, twisted vine lying in the earth. Sprinkle a little water on the vine, and soon you will be able to gather from it not only the most succulent melons, but also delicious gourds and fruits of every variety and colour. But you must never attempt to prune the vine or do anything to it other than gather the produce it yields. Do exactly as I say and you will never be short of food."

Again Sebgugugu thanked the High God and promised to behave as he had been commanded. He quickly found the vine, watered it, and ordered his wife to harvest the fruit and vegetables it yielded. That evening, Sebgugugu sat down to a large helping of the wholesome food, and while his wife and children stood by, waiting to take their share of whatever he left behind, he patted his stomach contentedly and smiled at his good fortune.

But after a few weeks the same pattern repeated itself, and for no good reason, Sebgugugu became fidgety and began looking around him for some sort of diversion. Stooping to examine the vine one morning, he decided that it would be a far more productive plant if only its branches were thinned out to produce healthier shoots. He took his knife and without consulting anyone, began hacking at the stalks. But almost immediately, the vine withered away into the earth like a sun-scorched seedling.

This time when Imana appeared before Sebgugugu, he was fuming with anger. Sebgugugu fell on his knees and begged for forgiveness, but the High God spoke sternly, his voice as loud as the fiercest thunder:

"I have watched you disobey me repeatedly without any show of remorse," he yelled, "and it is only for the sake of your honest wife and children that I am prepared to give you a third and final chance. Leave this place now and a little further down the road you will come across a large rock embedded in the soil. The rock will provide you with every kind of food – corn, milk, beans and other grains. Never attempt to force the food from the rock. Be patient and you will always be given as much as you need."

Sebgugugu stood up, his heart pounding in his breast, and scuttled off in search of the rock, taking with him a basket and a jar. He soon reached the spot Imana had described and saw before him an enormous grey boulder. Moving closer to inspect it, he observed that its surface was covered in a number of small cracks. He held up his jar and at once, through the cracks, a thin stream of milk began to flow, followed by a long, steady line of corn. He carried this food back home to his family and they all sat down together to enjoy a very pleasant meal.

It seemed as if Sebgugugu had thoroughly mended his ways and for several months after the High God had admonished him, he remained an attentive and considerate husband and father. But one morning he awoke in a very bad mood, for his wife had taken ill, and now the responsibility of feeding and caring for the family fell on his shoulders alone. Sebgugugu set off towards the rock, but as he stood waiting for the milk to flow and the grain to appear, he became very impatient and kicked the rock furiously. By sunset, when he had finally gathered all he needed, his anger had multiplied tenfold, and he shouted in exasperation to his sick wife:

"I have wasted the entire day waiting for that rock to deliver the food. I can stand it no longer. I am going to find a way to widen those cracks no matter what it takes."

And with his usual disregard for the welfare of his wife and family, Sebgugugu stormed outside where he cut some stout poles and hardened them in the fire.

Next morning, he returned to the rock, and using the great poles as levers, attempted to enlarge the cracks. The task was far easier than he had imagined and soon he had created a wide gap, large enough for him to pop his head through to take a closer look at the food. He pushed his nose towards the opening, but as he did so he was sucked further and further inwards until, with a crash like thunder, the gap closed up and the cracks disappeared, leaving not even the slightest trace on the smooth surface of the rock.

Sebgugugu's wife did not mourn his disappearance for very long and within a few months she had married a modest and respectable man from a neighbouring village. And if ever her children asked about their father, she told them the story of the glutton, who had pushed Imana's patience to the limit and had met with his just reward.

The Feast
(From the Cameroon, west Africa)

ONCE THERE LIVED A KIND AND GENEROUS CHIEF who wished to repay his people for the long hours they had worked for him on his farm. An idea came to him that he should hold a great feast and so he sent messengers to all of the surrounding villages inviting the men, women and children to attend his home the following evening, asking only that each man bring a calabash of wine along to the celebrations.

Next day, there was great excitement among the people. They chatted noisily about the event as they worked in the fields and when they had finished their labour they returned home to bathe and dress themselves in their finest robes. By sunset, more than a hundred men and their families lined the roadside. They laughed happily as they moved along, beating their drums and dancing in time to the rhythm. When they arrived at the chief's compound, the head of every household emptied his calabash into a large earthenware pot that stood in the centre of the courtyard. Soon the pot was more than half full and they all looked forward to their fair share of the refreshing liquid.

Among the chief's subjects there was a poor man who very much wanted to attend the feast, but he had no wine to take to the festivities and was too proud to appear empty-handed before his friends.

"Why don't you buy some wine from our neighbour?" his wife asked him, "he looks as though he has plenty to spare."

"But why should we spend money on a feast that is free?" the poor man answered her. "No, there must be another way."

And after he had thought about it hard for a few minutes he turned to his wife and said:

"There will be a great many people attending this feast, each of them carrying a calabash of wine. I'm sure that if I added to the pot just one calabash of water, nobody would notice the difference."

His wife was most impressed by this plan, and while her husband went and filled his calabash with water, she stepped indoors and put on her best tunic and what little jewellery she possessed, delighted at the prospect of a good meal and an evening's free entertainment.

When the couple arrived at the chief's house they saw all the other guests empty the wine they had brought into the large earthen pot. The poor man moved forward nervously and followed their example. Then he went to where the men were gathered and sat down with them to await the serving of the wine.

As soon as the chief was satisfied that all the guests had arrived, he gave the order for his servants to begin filling everyone's bowl. The vessels were filled and the men looked to their host for the signal to begin the drinking. The poor man grew impatient, for he was quite desperate to have the taste of the wine on his lips, and could scarcely remember when he had last enjoyed such a pleasant experience for free.

At length, the chief stood up and delivered a toast to his people. Then he called for his guests to raise their bowls to their lips. Each of them tasted their wine, swallowed it, and waited to feel a warm glow inside.

They swallowed some more of the wine, allowing it to trickle slowly over their tongues, and waited for the flavour to release itself. But the wine tasted as plain as any water. And now, all around the room, the guests began to shuffle their feet and cough with embarrassment.

"This is really very good wine," one of the men spoke up eventually.

"Indeed it is the best I've ever tasted," agreed another.

"Quite the finest harvest I've ever come across," added his neighbour.

But the chief of the people knew precisely what had happened, and he smiled at the comical spectacle as each man tried to hide the fact that he had filled his calabash that morning from the village spring.

The enormous earthen pot contained nothing but water, and it was water that the people were given to drink at the chief's great feast. For the chief had very wisely decided in his own mind:

"When only water is brought to the feast, water is all that should be served."

The Three Tests

(From the Swahili-speaking peoples, east Africa)

THERE ONCE LIVED A KING who had seven strong sons. When the day arrived for the eldest of them to leave the family home, he explained to his father that he longed to travel to a distant land and requested a sailing boat, together with some food and money. The king provided him with these things and the young man set sail across the ocean, promising to return to his family as soon as he had completed his great adventure.

He had been on the seas for some weeks when he spotted an island up ahead, and as he wished to rest awhile on dry land, he moored his boat and swam ashore. He found it a very pleasant spot, and strolled happily among the fruit-trees, helping himself to large handfuls of the juicy berries hanging from almost every branch. The berries satisfied not only his hunger, but also his thirst, and when the young man spat out the seeds, he noticed that they transformed themselves instantly into new plants laden with deliciously ripe fruit. Delighted with this discovery, he collected several baskets of the berries and took them on board his boat. He drew up his anchor and set sail once more, hoping that the next stage of his voyage would prove just as rewarding.

After several more days at sea, he approached another strange land, this time populated by a race of tall and powerful men, and discovered that it was ruled by a great sultan. Wishing to make a favourable impression, the young man offered the sultan some of the wonderful berries he had gathered, explaining how the seeds could bear fruit as soon as they touched fertile soil. The sultan was immediately suspicious and refused to believe a word until he had seen the evidence with his own eyes.

"If what you say is true," the sultan declared, "I will reward you handsomely. But if I find that you are lying, I will throw you in prison for having wasted my time."

So the young man brought a basket of fruit from his boat, ate some of it and spat the seeds upon the ground. But to his great disappointment, the seeds lay there without altering their shape in any way. The sultan gave the signal, and at once a group of guards seized the young man, bound him, and carried him away to prison, promising that he would never again see the light of day.

When six months had passed and the king had still not received word of his eldest son, he began to grow extremely worried.

His brothers were also very concerned for his safety and so it was agreed that the next eldest should go in search of him. It was not long before he, too, arrived on the island bearing the wonderful fruit-trees and when he had eaten some of the fruit and found that the seeds sprang to life as soon as they touched the soil, he gathered several baskets of the berries and took them on board his boat.

Shortly afterwards, the second son approached the sultan's kingdom and, as his brother had done before him, he began to boast of the miraculous fruit he had discovered, offering to demonstrate its remarkable magic to the sultan. He ate some of the berries and threw the seeds upon the ground. But the seeds failed to spring up, and the sultan, enraged that he had been made to look a fool a second time, immediately ordered him to be imprisoned in a chamber next to his eldest brother.

One by one, the king's sons set sail from the palace. Each landed on the island and gathered the enchanted berries. Each boasted of their wonderful magic when they arrived in the sultan's kingdom, and each was immediately thrown into prison when the seeds failed to sprout.

At last, only the youngest son remained. The boy's name was Sadaka, and although he was scarcely a youth, he could not be persuaded to abandon the thought of going in search of his brothers. The king eventually agreed to give him a boat and when he had loaded it with millet, rice and cattle, he embraced his mother and his father and took to the waves.

After a long, storm-tossed journey, Sadaka arrived on a cold, desolate island and climbed ashore hoping to find some trace of his brothers. But the first sight to greet him was a flock of weather-beaten birds, perilously close to starvation. Without any hesitation, the young boy hauled a sack of millet ashore and scattered it all around for the dying creatures to feed on. Soon the birds had recovered their strength, and in return for Sadaka's kindness, they begged him to accept from them an incense stick:

"Burn this stick if at any time you need us," they told him, "and we will smell it and come to help you."

Sadaka accepted the gift and walked on towards the trees. He had not gone very far before he encountered a swarm of flies, weak with hunger and unable to take to the air. The boy immediately slaughtered the cattle he had on board and threw them on to the island. Soon the flies were buzzing around him gratefully. Their leader thanked Sadaka and gave him a second incense stick:

"If at any time you need us," the flies told him, "burn this stick and we will come to your aid."

Sadaka explored a little further. Eventually he came upon a family of jinns who were also without food. He stopped to light a great fire and began cooking a large pot of rice for them to eat. The jinns marvelled at this generosity and when they had eaten their fill, they handed him an incense stick, identical to the other two, instructing him to burn it if ever he ran into trouble.

Sadaka sailed away and before he had even lost sight of the island, the sun began to shine, the sea grew calmer, and soon he had arrived at the place where his brothers had gathered the enchanted berries. He could not quite believe his eyes when the seeds he spat out blossomed into new trees, and so he decided to gather some of the fruit and take it to the jinns to show them.

"O yes," said the sultan of the jinns, "we have heard all about these berries and they are very real. But if you intend to show them to anyone else, it is important to know that the miracle will only happen when the seeds fall on special soil."

The young boy considered this information for a time, then he thanked the jinns and returned to the island of the fruit trees. Here he gathered up enough of the precious soil to fill three wooden barrels. He rolled the barrels on to his boat, hoisted his sails and set out to sea once more.

After he had travelled only a short stretch of the ocean he came upon the sultan's kingdom and presented himself before the great ruler.

"I have journeyed here in search of my brothers," he informed the sultan, "and if any of your people can help me find them, I will reward them with a very special tree that will always bear more fruit than they can eat, and whose branches will always remain strong and productive even in times of famine."

But the sultan laughed uproariously for some minutes at the young man's speech.

"Listen to this fool," he called to his attendants. "There are six men in my prison who came here boasting exactly the same thing. See to it that this one joins them."

But Sadaka began to protest noisily:

"Give me a chance to prove myself," he pleaded. "Tomorrow I will show you this wonder, but please be patient with me until then."

"So be it," replied the sultan indifferently, "but remember, if you fail, I will show no mercy and you will be cast into prison with the others."

That night, when he was certain that everyone lay sleeping , Sadaka crept from his chamber and headed towards the shore. He dragged the first of the three barrels from his boat and began sprinkling the soil thinly and evenly upon the ground. The work took several long hours and he had only just emptied the last of the barrels when the first rays of sunshine peered over the horizon. Silently and carefully, he crawled back to his bed and waited there anxiously for the people to stir.

As soon as the sultan and the wise men of the kingdom had awoken, Sadaka was summoned to appear before him. He carried a small basket of fruit with him and set it down on the ground. Slowly he lifted a handful of the ripe berries and began chewing on them. The sultan yawned aloud and twisted in his seat. The wise men glanced around them and took very little notice. But when Sadaka spat the seeds upon the earth and they began to rise up before their eyes, the sultan and all the people on the island cried out in sheer delight. Again Sadaka performed his great miracle and soon he was joined by others who ate the fruit and spat out the seeds until the whole kingdom blossomed with the magic trees.

From that moment onwards, the sultan took Sadaka under his wing and saw to it that everything he needed was provided for him. Almost immediately, he arranged for his brothers to be released from prison and ordered a great feast to be held to celebrate their freedom. And as time moved on, the sultan grew very fond of the young man and wished that he had been blessed with an equally wise and generous son of his own.

The sultan possessed a daughter, however, whose extraordinary beauty and talent were famous throughout the land. It was not long before Sadaka came to hear of her many virtues and when, one day, he spotted her strolling through the palace gardens, his heart was filled with a deep desire to be with her. He went before the sultan and asked if he might make her his wife, but to his surprise, the sultan grew very angry and declared that he had yet to encounter a man even half good enough to marry his daughter.

"What would I have to do to prove my worth to you?" Sadaka asked him, "I will do anything you ask, for now that I have seen her, my heart will never be at peace."

The sultan led Sadaka to a very large storeroom and pointed to the hundreds of sacks containing all kinds of mixed grain.

"If you can separate these different kinds of grain and place each kind in its own sack by tomorrow morning, then you may marry the princess," he announced.

Sadaka eyes widened in disbelief at the sight of the huge task facing him, but he so badly wanted the sultan's daughter, he agreed at least to try his hand. So he sat down on the floor and began sorting through the first sack. But after a very short time, he realized how hopeless the situation was and buried his head in his hands. Then he suddenly remembered the incense stick the birds on the lonely island had given him. He took the stick from beneath his robe, and as soon as the pungent odour filled the air, a flock of birds appeared out of nowhere asking what they might do to help him. After the birds had heard what the sultan had ordered, they flew around the room and began picking up the grain in their beaks, separating each kind into its own sack.

Next morning, when the sultan arrived at his storehouse, he saw that all the grain was separated as he had ordered. But he walked away, shaking his head and gathered his wise men around him. At length, he came and spoke to Sadaka:

"We cannot quite believe what we have seen," he told the young man, "and so you must prove yourself once more if you wish to marry my daughter. If you can cut through the trunk of that Baobab tree over there, with one stroke of your sword, you can take her."

Sadaka saw that the tree was of an enormous size and knew that he could not possibly perform what was required of him without help. So he asked to be allowed to go back to his room to get his weapon and here he burned the second incense stick. At once the family of jinns appeared before him and when he told them what the sultan wanted him to do, they flew away and returned with an army of white ants that marched towards the tree. The ants gnawed at the trunk leaving only the bark so that when Sadaka approached and drew his sword, he easily cut the tree in half and it fell to the ground effortlessly.

But the sultan was still not satisfied:

"Tomorrow will be your final test," he told Sadaka. "In the afternoon all the maidens of the kingdom will pass in front of you one by one, each of them wearing identical veils over their faces. You must pick the princess from among them and if you choose correctly, you shall have her for your wife."

Then Sadaka retired once more to his chamber and burnt his last incense stick. Immediately, the leader of the flies appeared and Sadaka explained what had been demanded of him.

"When the maidens of the city pass before you," said the fly, "I will stand in front of you and you must keep watch on me. When the princess draws near, I will drum my wings and alight on her shoulder as she passes by."

So the next afternoon all the maidens of the kingdom passed in a procession before the sultan and his attendants and, as promised, the leader of the flies took to the air and landed on the shoulder of the princess as she walked past. Sadaka stood up and walked forward to where the princess stood, planting a kiss on her cheek for everyone around to see.

Sadaka had now passed his three tests and the sultan could not deny he was more than a fitting son-in-law. Proudly he took the princess by the arm and led her away. They were married the very next day and the sultan built for them a fine palace where they lived a long and happy life together.

The Two Rogues

(From the Hausa-speaking peoples, west Africa)

AMONG THE HAUSA PEOPLE, there were two men, each as devious as the other, who spent most of their time plotting and planning how best to earn a living by dishonest means. One rogue lived in Kano, while the other lived in Katsina, and although they had never actually met, news of their trickery travelled back and forth between the villages, so that even with some distance between them, they considered themselves powerful rivals.

One morning, when the rogue from Kano had run rather short of money, he sat down by a palm tree to consider his next crooked scheme. Suddenly an idea came to him and, taking his hunting knife, he began peeling a long length of bark from the tree. After he had trimmed it carefully, he took it to one of the women at the dye-pit and asked her to dip it in blue ink for him. The wood looked impressive when it had been stained, but in order to improve it even more, the rogue from Kano painted it with a glaze, giving it the appearance of the finest blue broadcloth. Then he wrapped it up in paper, placed it in his leather bag and set out for market, confident that the cloth would fetch a very favourable price.

But while the rogue from Kano had been doing all of this, the rogue from Katsina had also kept himself busy, for he, too, had recently run short of funds and had only a couple of hundred cowries left to his name. So he took a goatskin, laid it flat on the ground and heaped several loads of pebbles on to it. Then he sprinkled the cowries on top, drew the four corners together and set off with his bundle to market.

Half way along the road, the two rogues happened to meet and soon fell into conversation as they walked along.

"Where are you off to, my friend?" asked the rogue from Kano.

"I'm on my way to market," said the rogue from Katsina. "I've got all my money here in cowries, twenty thousand of them, and I intend to purchase something very special for my wife."

"Well, fancy that! I was just heading in the same direction myself," said the rogue from Kano, "and I have with me the very best blue broadcloth to sell to the highest bidder."

"Wouldn't it be nice to avoid such a long journey in this heat," said the rogue from Katsina. "You look almost as weary as I feel and we still have exactly the same distance to go."

And so the two men rapidly abandoned all thought of going to market. They struck a bargain on the spot and exchanged their wares before parting in great friendship, each one believing he had got the better of the other.

When they had moved off a short distance, each man stopped in his path to examine the bargain he had carried away. But, of course, the rogue from Kano discovered that he had been handed a bag of stones, while the rogue from Katsina found that he had purchased little more than a parcel of bark.

As soon as they discovered they had been duped, they each turned back and retraced their steps until eventually they came face to face once more. At first angry and belligerent, they soon realized they had much in common and grew calmer at the thought of putting this to lucrative use:

"We are each as crafty as the other," they said, "and it would be wisest from now on to join forces and seek our fortune together."

Shaking hands on this arrangement, they took to the road without further hostility and walked on until they had arrived at a neighbouring town. Here they found an old woman who sold them water-bottles, staffs and begging-bowls, and when they had equipped themselves with these items, they set off once more, pretending to be blind beggars as they hobbled along in the afternoon sunshine.

They followed a dusty trail deep into the bush and before long stumbled upon a party of traders pitching camp among the trees. The traders had only just begun to unload their caravan and as the two rogues hid in the undergrowth feasting their eyes on the rich cargo, they began discussing a plan which would enable them to get their hands on as much of the goods as possible.

Later that evening, when darkness had descended upon the camp, the two rogues came out of hiding and moved slowly towards the fire where the traders had just gathered together for their evening meal, beating their staffs on the ground before them and squeezing their eyes tightly shut. The pitiful sight they presented earned them immediate sympathy and without delay they were handed platefuls of hot food and encouraged to spend the night at the camp.

Soon the traders retired to their beds accompanied by the blind men who complained aloud of the great weariness that had suddenly overtaken them. They pretended to be the very first to fall asleep, but as soon as they were certain everyone else had followed their example, they opened their eyes again and crept from their beds. Very quietly, they began to rummage through the traders' property, carrying off quantities of food, drink, precious jewellery and money to a dry well a short distance away into which they very carefully dropped them.

Next morning when the party awoke and found they had been robbed of everything, they were quite devastated and began an immediate search for the thieves. The two rogues did not escape suspicion, but having anticipated that their innocence might be questioned, they had already made certain that some of their own possessions had been carried off.

"Where are our water-bottles?" they cried out in mock-despair, "and our staffs! They are missing also. How will we manage to walk without them?"

But the traders grew angry to hear them voice such petty concerns.

"Here we are," they cried, "robbed of everything we own, and all you miserable beggars can think about are your water-bottles and your walking sticks. Get out of here before we throw you out."

But as they groped their way through the bush, the two rogues smiled at one another, knowing that as soon as the coast was clear, they would hurry off to the well and help themselves to the stolen goods.

"Why don't you go down into the well," said the rogue from Kano to his companion. "I have strong labourer's hands and I can use a rope to haul up the goods more skilfully than you."

"No, you go down," said the rogue from Katsina, "I have much better eyesight and can keep a more careful watch up here in case any of the traders return."

"No, you go," said the rogue from Kano.

"No, you," replied the rogue from Katsina.

And they continued to argue back and forth in this manner for several minutes until, finally, the rogue from Katsina reluctantly agreed to go down into the well. Soon his companion had lowered a strong rope to which he tied the goods, allowing them to be hauled to the top swiftly and smoothly. The rogue from Kano worked as quickly as possible above the surface, trying hard to conceal the fact that while he stacked the stolen goods, he was also gathering together a mound of boulders at the mouth of the well. But his companion below had a pretty shrewd idea of what the rogue from Kano intended for him and was resolved to keep his head about him at all times.

When, at long last, the work of retrieving the stolen property had almost come to an end, the rogue from Kano shouted into the well:

"My friend, when you have secured the last item to the rope and are ready to come up yourself, give me a shout. That way, I can haul you up very carefully so that you don't tear yourself on the jagged stones along the sides."

But the rogue from Katsina did not trust this gesture of friendship and shouted back:

"The next load will be a pretty heavy one, but it is the only thing left down here."

Then he crawled into the last of the bales of wheat and hid himself inside.

The rogue from Kano now hauled up the remaining bale and carried it over to where he had stacked the other goods, not suspecting for one moment that his companion lay concealed within it. He then walked to the mouth of the well and began hurling the boulders into the opening one by one until he was satisfied that he had completely covered the base and crushed anything resting at the bottom.

But while he was busy doing this, the rogue from Katsina crawled out of hiding and started to divide up the stolen property, placing some in the bushes, some underneath the rocks and some beneath his robes. The hoard had been reduced to little or nothing by the time he heard his companion walking back from the well. He had no wish to be discovered alive, and so he decided to retreat to the bush until nightfall, at which time he intended to return and gather up everything for himself alone.

The rogue from Kano scratched his head in dismay and sat down on the ground trying to solve the riddle of the missing goods he had so carefully stacked by the side of the well.

"Someone must have come in the last few minutes and taken the stuff away," he exclaimed to himself, but then it occurred to him that the thief could not be very far away and that, in all probability, he would be in desperate need of a pack-horse to help him carry his load.

The thought had no sooner entered his head when he leaped into the shelter of the trees and began braying like a donkey. Sure enough, after a few minutes, he saw a figure hurrying towards him calling out:

"Steady there donkey! Hold on until I can get to you. Don't run away now, boy!"

The figure reached through the branches and seized him by the collar. Within seconds, the rogue from Kano found himself pinned to the ground staring into the eyes of the rogue from Katsina. The two men remained speechless for a time, but then they stood up, smiled knowingly at one another and began dusting down their clothes.

Silently, they gathered up their booty and continued on their travels once more. The road they now followed happened to take them past the rogue of Kano's house and here the two men sat down and finally divided up the stolen property fairly and squarely.

Some days later, however, the rogue of Katsina announced his wish to visit his own family.

"I cannot possibly carry my share of the goods with me," he told his companion, "but I will leave them here and in three months" time I will come back and collect what is mine."

And so he set off, believing he had seen the last of his friend's trickery and that he had nothing more to fear.

Two months passed by and the rogue of Kano kept his word and never once laid a finger on his friend's share of the stolen property. But when the third month had almost come to an end, he ordered his family to dig a grave in the field close to their hut. Then, on the night before the rogue of Katsina was due to return, he gathered up all of the goods, including his friend's portion, crammed them into a sack, and threw them into the grave, instructing his family to bury him alive alongside them.

"Cover the grave over with fresh earth," he told his family, "and when Katsina returns, say that I have passed away and that you have buried the contents of the house with me."

And so, next morning, as soon as the family saw the rogue from Katsina appear in the distance, they ran towards him weeping and wailing:

"You have arrived too late!" they cried. "Our brother is dead. We buried him four days ago."

"Really?" said the rogue from Katsina, rather taken aback by the news. "So he has gone the way of all flesh and taken his most valuable possessions with him, I suppose."

"O yes!" replied the family, "everything was cast into the grave, for we were uncertain which items belonged to him."

"Take me to the grave so that I may see this for myself," said the rogue from Katsina, his suspicion increasing every moment. "I must pay my last respects even if I have missed out on the burial."

When he was taken to the grave the rogue from Katsina broke into loud lamentations, but after a few minutes, when he had recovered himself, he spoke to the family:

"You really ought to cut some thorn-bushes and cover the mound well," he told them, "otherwise the hyenas may come and dig up the body and scatter the bones."

"We'll do it tomorrow," promised the family, and saying this, they led the rogue of Katsina into their hut and provided him with supper and a comfortable bed for the night.

At the first sign of darkness, when the household had grown very quiet, the rogue from Katsina stole from his bed and walked to his friend's grave. He crouched to the ground and began to growl ferociously, dropping on his hands and knees and scrabbling at the earth as if he were a hyena trying to get at the corpse underneath.

Inside the grave the rogue from Kano awoke from his sleep, and as soon as he heard the loud scratching and growling sounds he screamed out in terror:

"Help, help! Someone save me! The hyenas have come for me. They are trying to eat me. Let me out of here!"

The rogue from Katsina continued to dig, until he caught sight of his friend's ghostly face, lifted towards the opening in sheer horror.

"All right," he said, "out you come, Kano. I think you have finally learned your lesson."

The rogue from Kano seized his friend's hand and was lifted to the surface. He was more relieved to see the rogue from Katsina than he had ever believed possible and as it began to dawn on him, once and for all, that he had finally met his match, he suddenly burst into a fit of laughter:

"Katsina, you are a scoundrel," he said as he tittered away to himself.

"Yes, and you are another!" Katsina replied smiling from ear to ear.

The Girls Who Wanted New Teeth

(From the Banyarwanda people, Rwanda)

A NUMBER OF YOUNG GIRLS agreed together to go and get teeth created for them. But one of their companions was unable to join the party. This girl's mother was dead, and she had a stepmother who kept her hard at work and otherwise made

her life a burden, so that she had become a poor, stunted drudge, ill-clothed and usually dirty. As for going to ask for new teeth, this was quite out of the question.

So when her friends came back and showed her their beautiful teeth she said nothing, but felt the more, and went on with her work. When the cows came home in the evening she lit the fire in the kraal, so that the smoke might drive away the mosquitoes, and then helped with the milking, and when that was done served the evening meal. After supper she slipped away, took a bath, oiled herself, and started out without anyone seeing her.

Before she had gone very far in the dark she met a hyena, who said to her, "You, maiden, where are you going?" She answered, "I'm going where all the other girls went. Father's wife would not let me go with them, so I'm going by myself." The hyena said, "Go on, then, child of lmana!" and let her go in peace. She walked on, and after a while met a lion, who asked her the same question. She answered him as she had done the hyena, and he too said, "Go on, child of lmana!" She walked on through the night, and just as dawn was breaking she met Imana himself, looking like a great, old chief with a kind face. He said to her, "Little maid, where are you going?" She answered, "I have been living with my stepmother, and she always gives me so much to do that I could not get away when the other girls came to ask you for new teeth, and so I came by myself." And Imana said, "You shall have them," and gave her not only new teeth, but a new skin, and made her beautiful all over. And he gave her new clothes and brass armlets and anklets and bead ornaments, so that she looked quite a different girl, and then, like a careful father, he saw her on her way home, till they had come so near that she could point out her village. Then he said, "When you get home whatever you do you must not laugh or smile at anyone, your father or your stepmother or anyone else." And so he left her.

When her stepmother saw her coming she did not at first recognize her, but as soon as she realized who the girl was she cried out, "She's been stealing things at the chief's place! Where did she get those beads and those bangles? She must have been driving off her father's cows to sell them. Look at that cloth! Where did you get it?" The girl did not answer. Her father asked her, "Where did you pick up these things?" – and still she did not answer. After a while they let her alone. The stepmother's spiteful speeches did not impress the neighbours, who soon got to know of the girl's good fortune, and before three days had passed a respectable man called on her father to ask her in marriage for his son. The wedding took place in the usual way, and she followed her young husband to his home. There everything went well, but they all – his mother and sisters and he himself – thought it strange that they never saw her laugh.

After the usual time a little boy was born, to the great joy of his parents and grandparents. Again all went well, till the child was four or five years old, when, according to custom, he began to go out and herd the calves near the hut. One day his grandmother, who had never been able to satisfy her curiosity, said to him, "Next time your mother gives you milk say you will not take it unless she smiles at you. Tell her, if she does not smile you will cry, and if she does not do so then you will die!" He did as she told him, but his mother would not smile; he began to cry, and she paid no attention; he went on screaming, and presently died. They came and wrapped his body in a mat, and carried it out into the bush – for the Banyaruanda do not bury their dead – and left it there. The poor mother mourned, but felt she could not help herself. She must not disobey Imana's commandment. After a time, another boy was born. When he was old enough to talk and run about his grandmother made the same suggestion to him as she had done to his brother, and with the same result. The boy died, and was carried out to the bush. Again, a baby was born – this time a bonny little girl.

When she was about three years old her mother one evening took her on her back and went out to the bush where the two little bodies had been laid long ago. There, in her great trouble, she cried to Imana, "*Yee, baba wee!* Oh my father! Oh Imana, lord of Ruanda, I have never once disobeyed you; will you not save this little one?" She looked up, and, behold! There was Imana standing before her, looking as kind as when she had first seen him, and he said, "Come here and see your children. I have brought them back to life. You may smile at them now." And so she did, and they ran to her, crying, "Mother! Mother!" Then Imana touched her poor, worn face and eyes dimmed with crying and her bowed shoulders, and she was young again, tall and straight and more beautiful than ever; he gave her a new body and new teeth. He gave her a beautiful cloth and beads to wear, and he sent his servants to fetch some cows, so many for each of the boys. Then he went with them to their home.

The husband saw them coming, and could not believe his eyes – he was too much astonished to speak. He brought out the one stool which every hut contains, and offered it to the guest, but Imana would not sit down yet. He said, "Send out for four more stools." So the man sent and borrowed them from the neighbours, and they all sat down, he and his wife and the two boys, and Imana in the place of honour. Then Imana said, "Now look at your wife and your children. You have got to make them happy and live comfortably with them. You will soon enough see her smiling at you and at them. It was I who forbade her to laugh, and then some wicked people went and set the children on to try to make her do so, and they died. Now I have brought them back to life. Here they are with their mother. Now see that you live happily together. And as for your mother, I am going to burn her in her house, because she did a wicked thing. I leave you to enjoy all her belongings, because you have done no wrong." Then he vanished from their sight, and while they were still gazing in astonishment a great black cloud gathered over the grandmother's hut; there was a dazzling flash, followed by a terrible clap of thunder, and the hut, with everyone and everything in it, was burned to ashes. Before they had quite recovered from the shock Imana once more appeared to them, in blinding light, and said to the husband, "Remember my words, and all shall be well with you!" A moment later he was gone.

The Kinyamkela's Bananas
(From the Zaramo people, Tanzania)

NEAR MKONGOLE, IN THE ZARAMO COUNTRY, there was once a hollow tree haunted by a *kinyamkela*. Two boys from Mkongole, Mahimbwa and Kibwana, strolling through the woods, happened to come upon this tree, and saw that the ground had been swept clean all round it and that there was a bunch of bananas hanging from a branch. They took the bananas down, ate them, and went home quite happy.

But that night, when they were both asleep in the 'boys' house' of their village, they were awakened by a queer noise, and saw the one-legged, one-armed *kinyamkela* standing in the doorway. He called out to them: "You have eaten my bananas! You must die!" And with that they were suddenly hit by stones flying out of the darkness. There was a regular rain of stones, lumps of earth, and even human bones. The boys jumped up, ran out, and took refuge in another hut, but the stones followed them there. This went on for four nights, and then a doctor named Kikwilo decided to take the matter in hand. He said to the boys, "You have eaten the *kinyamkela's* bananas; that is why he comes after you." He took a gourd, twice seven small loaves of bread, a fowl, some rice, and some bananas, and went to the *kinyamkela's* tree, where he laid the things down, saying, "The boys are sorry for what they did. Can you not leave them alone now?" That night the *kinyamkela* appeared again to Mahimbwa and Kibwana, and said, "It's all right now; the matter is settled; but don't let it happen again."

So there was peace in the village, and all would have been well if the business had stopped there. But there was a certain man named Mataula, a woodcarver, addicted to hemp-smoking, who was, unluckily, absent at the time. When he came back and heard the story he declared that someone must have been playing a trick on the boys, and announced that he would sit up that night and see what happened. So he loaded his gun and waited. The *kinyamkela* must have heard his words, for as soon as it was dark he began to be pelted with bones and all sorts of dirt, and at last an invisible hand began to beat him with a legbone. He could not fire, as he could see no one, and was quite helpless to defend himself against the missiles. The neighbours had no cause to bless him, for they began to be persecuted similarly, and at last the whole population had to emigrate, as life in the village had become unendurable.

The Two Brothers
(From the Bantu-speaking people of South Africa)

TWO BROTHERS, Masilo and Masilonyane, went hunting together and happened upon a ruined village. The younger, Masilonyane, went straight on through the ruins with his dogs, while his brother turned aside and skirted round them.

In the middle of the ruins Masilonyane found a number of large earthen pots turned upside down. He tried to turn up one of the largest, but it resisted all his efforts. After he had tried in vain several times he called to his brother for help, but Masilo refused, saying, "Pass on. Why do you trouble about pots?" Masilonyane persevered, however, and at length succeeded in heaving up the pot, and in doing so uncovered a little old woman who was grinding red ochre between two stones. Masilonyane, startled at this apparition, was about to turn the pot over her again, but she remonstrated: "My grandchild, do you turn me up and then turn me upside down again?" She then requested him to carry her on his back. Before he had time to refuse she jumped up and clung to him, so that he could not get rid of her. He called Masilo, but Masilo only jeered and refused to help him.

Masilo had to walk on with his burden, till, at last, seeing a herd of springbok, he thought he had found a way of escape, and said, "Grandmother, get down, that I may go and kill one of these long-legged animals, so that I may carry you easily in its skin." She consented, and sat down on the ground, while Masilonyane called his dogs and made off at full speed after the game. But as soon as he was out of her sight he turned aside and hid in the hole of an ant-bear. The old woman, however, was not to be defeated. After waiting for a time and finding that he did not come back she got up and tracked him by his footprints, till she came to his hiding-place. He had to come out and take her up again, and so he plodded on for another weary mile or two, till the sight of some hartebeests gave him another excuse for putting her down. Once more he hid, and once more she tracked him; but this time he set his dogs on her, and they killed her. He told the dogs to eat her, all but her great toe, which they did. He then took an axe and chopped at the toe, when out came many cattle, and, last of all, a beautiful cow, spotted like a guinea-fowl.

Now Masilo, who had shirked all the unpleasant part of the day's adventures, came running up and demanded a share of the cattle. Masilonyane, not unnaturally, refused, and they went on together.

After a while Masilonyane said he was very thirsty, and his brother said he knew of a water-hole not far off. They went there, and found that it was covered with a large, flat stone. They levered up the stone with their spears, and Masilonyane held it while Masilo stooped to drink. When he, in his turn, stooped to reach the water Masilo dropped the stone on him and crushed him to death. Then he collected the cattle and started to drive them home.

Suddenly he saw a small bird perching on the horn of the speckled cow; it sang:

"Clzwidi! Clzwidi! Masilo has killed Masilonyane,
because of his speckled cow!"

(People say it was Masilonyane's heart which was changed into a bird.) Masilo threw a stone at the bird, and seemed to have killed it, but it came to life again, and before he had one very far he saw it sitting on the cow's horn, and killed it once more, as he thought.

When he reached his home all the people crowded together and greeted him. "*Dumela!* Chief's son! *Dumela!* Chief's son! Where is Masilonyane?" He answered, "I don't know; we parted at the water-hole, and I have not seen him since." They went to look at the cattle, and exclaimed in admiration, "What a beautiful cow! Just look at her markings!"

While they were standing there the little bird flew up with a great whirring of wings and perched on the horn of the speckled cow and sang:

"Clzwidi! Clzwidi! Masilo has killed
Masilonyane, all for his speckled cow!"

Masilo threw a stone at the bird, but missed it, and the men said, "Just leave that bird alone and let us hear." The bird sang the same words over and over again, and the people heard them clearly. They said, "So that is what you have done! You have killed your younger brother." And Masilo had nothing to say. So they drove him out of the village, and he became an outcast.

The Tale of Nyengebule
(From the Xhosa people of Southern Africa)

NYENGEBULE HAD TWO WIVES, who, one day, went out together to collect firewood in the forest. The younger found a bees' nest in a hollow tree, and called her companion to help

her take out the honeycomb. When they had done so they sat down and ate it, the younger thoughtlessly finishing her share, while the elder kept putting some aside, which she wrapped up in leaves to take home for her husband.

Arriving at the kraal, each went to her own hut. The elder, on entering, found her husband seated there, and gave him the honeycomb. Nyengebule thanked her for the attention, and ate the honey, thinking all the time that Nqandamate, the younger wife, who was his favourite, would also have brought him some, especially as he was just then staying in her hut. When he had finished eating he hastened thither and sat down, expecting that she would presently produce the titbit. But he waited in vain, and at last, becoming impatient, he asked, "Where is the honey?" She said, "I have not brought any." Thereupon he lost his temper and struck her with his stick, again and again. The little bunch of feathers which she was wearing on her head (as a sign that she was training for initiation as a doctor) fell to the ground; he struck once more in his rage; she fell, and he found that she was dead. He made haste to bury her, and then he gathered up his sticks and set out for her parents' kraal, to report the death (which he would represent as an accident) and demand his *lobolo*-cattle back (a man who loses his wife before she has had any children is entitled to get back the cattle he paid on his marriage-unless her parents can give him another daughter instead of her). But the little plume which had fallen from her head when he struck her turned into a bird and flew after him.

When he had gone some distance he noticed a bird sitting on a bush by the wayside, and heard it singing these words:

"I am the little plume of the diligent wood-gatherer,
The wife of Nyengebule.
I am the one who was killed by the house-owner, wantonly!
He asking me for morsels of honeycomb."

It kept up with him, flying alongside the path, till at last he threw a stick at it. It paid no attention, but kept on as before, so he hit it with his knobkerrie, killed it, threw it away, and walked on.

But after a while it came back again and repeated its song. Blind with rage, he again threw a stick at it, killed it, stopped to bury it, and went on his way.

As he was still going on it came up again and sang:

"I am the little plume of the diligent wood-gatherer..."

At that he became quite desperate, and said, "What shall I do with this bird, which keeps on tormenting me about a matter I don't want to hear about? I will kill it now, once for all, and put it into my bag to take with me." Once more he threw his stick at the little bird and killed it, picked it up, and put it into his *inxowa*. He tied the bag up tightly with a thong of hide, and thought he had now completely disposed of his enemy.

So he went on till he came to the kraal of his wife's relations, where he found a dance going on. He became so excited that he forgot the business about which he had come, and hurried in to join in the fun. He had just greeted his sisters-in-law when one of them asked him for snuff. He told her – being in a hurry to begin dancing and entirely forgetful of what the bag contained – to untie the *inxowa*, which he had laid aside. She did so, and out flew the bird – *dri-i-i!* It flew up to the gate-post, and, perching there, began to sing:

"Ndi 'salama sika' Tezateza
'Mfazi Unyengebule;
Ndingobulewe 'Mninindhlu ngamabom,
Ebendibuza amanqatanqata obusi."

He heard it, and, seeing that everyone else had also heard it, started to run away. Some of the men jumped up and seized hold of him, saying, "What are you running away for?" He answered – his guilty conscience giving him away against his will – "Me! I was only coming to the dance. I don't know what that bird is talking about."

It began again, and its song rang out clearly over the heads of the men who were holding him:

"Ndi 'salama sika' Tezateza...

They listened, the meaning of the song began to dawn on them, and they grew suspicious. They asked him, "What is this bird saying?" He said, "I don't know."

They killed him.

The Story of Takane
(From Lesotho, southern Africa)

ONCE LONG AGO there lived in Basutoland a chief who had many herds of cattle and flocks of sheep, and also a beautiful daughter called Takane, the joy of his heart, and her mother's pride. Takane was loved by Masilo, her cousin, who secretly sought to marry her, but she liked him not, neither would she pay heed to his entreaties.

At length Masilo wearied her so, that her anger broke forth, and with scorn she said: "Masilo, I like you not. Talk not to me of marriage, for I would rather die than be your wife." "Ho! is that true?" asked Masilo, the evil spirit shining out of his eyes. "Wait a little while, proud daughter of our chief; I will yet repay you for those words." Takane laughed a scornful laugh, and, taking up her pitcher, stepped blithely down to the well. How stupid Masilo was, and why did he keep on troubling her? Did he think, the great baboon, that she would ever marry him? Ho! How stupid men were, after all!

But in Masilo's heart there raged a devil prompting him to deeds of revenge. It whispered in his ear, and, as he listened, he smiled, well pleased, for already he saw the desire of his heart within his reach. Patience and a little cunning, and she should be his.

The next day Masilo obtained his uncle's consent to his giving a feast at a small village across the river for youths and maidens, as was the custom of his tribe. He then paid a visit to the old witch-doctor, who promised to send a terrible hailstorm upon the village in the middle of the feast. Next he went to all the people of the village, and, because he was a chief's son, and had power in the land, and they were afraid to offend him, he made them promise that none of them would allow Takane to enter their huts; but he said no word of the hailstorm, only he told the people the evil eye would smite them if they disobeyed him.

Early the next day all the villages were astir with excitement; the youths set out in companies by themselves, the maidens following later, singing and dancing as they went. How lovely Takane looked, her face and beautifully rounded limbs shining with fat and red clay; the bangles on her arms and ankles burnished until human endeavour could do no more. Soon all were assembled, and dancing, singing, feasting, and gladness held sway. Suddenly the sky grew dark, the rain-god frowned upon the village, and hail poured in fury down upon the feast. Away ran old and young, seeking shelter in the friendly huts. Takane alone remained outside. As she ran from hut to hut, the people crowded to the doorway, and, when she implored them to take her in, they replied that indeed they would gladly do so, but how could they find room for even one more? Did she not see how some of them were almost outside the door already? At length she came to a hut in which there was only one old woman, sitting shivering over a small fire. "Mother," exclaimed Takane, "I pray you, let me come in, for I am nearly dead already." The old woman placed herself in the doorway, exclaiming, "Go away; don't you see my house is full?" But the girl gently pushed her aside and entered.

After the storm had passed, the merrymakers returned to their homes, Masilo alone remaining behind, in the hope of discovering Takane's dead body, or hearing something of her fate. As he wandered here and there, he saw her coming towards him, unconscious of his presence, and evidently on her way to cross the river. Quickly he hid behind a huge boulder until she had passed, when he cautiously followed her, overtaking her just as she reached the bank of the river. Now by this time the river was getting almost too full to cross in safety, and the Water Spirit was angrily murmuring, for he wanted a sacrifice of a human being to satisfy him. Masilo went up to Takane, who stood hesitating whether to cross or not, and, seizing her by the hand, drew her into the river, until the water came up to her neck.

"Will you marry me now, Takane, or shall I let the Water Spirit have you? I know you cannot swim; so if you won't marry me, I shall take you into the deep hole by that tree and push you in. Say, now, will you marry me?"

"No, Masilo, I will never marry you, never. Let the Water Spirit take me first;" and she struggled to free her hand, but he was strong, and he held her fast. Again he drew her farther into the river, until the water reached her lips.

"Now, Takane, is not life with me better than death with the Water Spirit for husband? Say, will you marry me now?"

"I choose rather death in the black pool, with the cold stones for my bed and the water for my covering, than life with you as my husband. Haste, haste, for I am weary and would sleep."

Her continued refusal to marry him so infuriated Masilo, that, seizing her by the hair of her head, he swam out towards the pool, into which he pushed her with a fierce laugh, saying, "There! Go drown! It is too late now to change your mind." He then turned, and in a few moments reached the bank, and, without one backward glance, walked off to his hut.

Now a wonderful thing happened to Takane. When Masilo pushed her into the pool, the hungry water took her swiftly down towards the tree which grew out of the middle of the river. She did not sink, because her 'blanket' (literally the skin mantle worn by Basuto before the introduction of blankets) was not yet wet through, and, as she passed under the tree, the blanket caught in a low branch and held her firmly. There she remained for some time, vainly trying to pull herself up into the tree. At length she succeeded in doing so, and for the moment at any rate was safe, but, as she looked at the water all round her, and realized that even when the river was low she could not reach the bank unaided, she felt that it would be better to drown at once than to die a slow death from starvation, which seemed the only fate before her if she remained in the tree. Still, something might happen, someone might pass and see her. Yes, she would wait at least a little while; so, arranging herself as comfortably as she could, she prepared to pass the night in the tree.

The next morning Masilo came down to the river with the cows. Takane hid herself as much as possible, but his sharp eyes soon discovered her.

"Oh, ho! What strange bird is that?" he exclaimed. "How came it in the tree? I must try to catch it." Then, seeing that Takane remained motionless, he sat down on the bank and began to eat his 'bogobe' with great enjoyment. "See what nice bread I have. Are you not hungry, Takane? Shall I send you some? But no, you do not need it. You are so fat, you will live for a long time. Well, I must go away now, but I will come again tomorrow. It is nice to see the dear little Takane so happy."

The next day Masilo came again, and ate his breakfast on the river bank, taunting Takane all the while. This he did on several following days, until Takane became so weak that she neither heard nor saw him, and would have fallen into the water were it not that her blanket held her firmly to the tree. Meanwhile, there was mourning in her father's house and village, for all thought she had been drowned in trying to cross the river after the storm.

One day, Takane's little brother followed Masilo when he took the cattle out to graze. When they came near the river, Masilo told the child not to come any farther, saying if he was a good boy, and did what he was told, he would get a present of some little birds which were in a tree in the river. Masilo then left the child and paid his daily visit to Takane, but the little boy, full of curiosity, followed unseen, and to his great astonishment saw, not a birds nest, with the promised young, but his sister Takane, almost unrecognisable from starvation. He listened for a little while to the conversation, then, fearing Masilo's anger if he were discovered, he crept back to the herd. When Masilo returned, he told the child the birds were not quite big enough to leave their nest.

The little boy then went home and told his parents what he had seen. They made him promise to keep his secret; then, calling their medicine man, they hurriedly took counsel together. Late that night, when the village was wrapped in darkness, the parents of Takane and the medicine man set out for the spot where the girl was hidden. The medicine man called upon the spirit of the water to aid them, and soon Takane lay in her mother's arms, too weak even to speak. Slowly and tenderly they bore her back to her home, where for days she lay between life and death. Masilo and the other villagers were told that a sick stranger was in the hut, therefore they must not enter, and, as this is the custom of the people, they thought nothing more of it. Masilo, it is true, had been down to the river and had found Takane gone, but he only thought that at last she had fallen into the water and been drowned. Several times he went down to see if the Water Spirit had given up its victim, but no sign of Takane's real fate came to warn him.

When two moons had come and gone, the old chief saw that the time to punish Masilo had come, so, calling all his people to assemble on a certain day, he made preparations for a great feast. When the day came, the people all assembled in the open space in front of the *khotla* (court-house), leaving a wide path from the chief's hut to the centre of the open space. This path was carpeted with new mats, and skin karosses were laid on the ground for the chief and his family to sit upon. Masilo, by right of his near relationship to the chief, took a prominent place in the inner circle, while, unknown to him, several warriors quietly took their stand immediately behind him. Presently the old chief issued from his hut, followed by his chief councillor and medicine man; behind them came Takane's mother, leading by the hand Takane herself, no longer a living skeleton, but plump, smiling, and lovely as ever. A stir like the beginning of a storm shook the people, while Masilo, with a wild cry, turned to escape, but was quickly caught by the armed warriors, who had remained motionless behind him. Briefly the old chief related the story; then, raising his hand and pointing at the terrified Masilo, he cried, "What, my children, shall be the fate of this toad?" With one voice, the people answered, "The cruel death for him! The cruel death for him!"

A smile of approval passed over the chief's face, and, making a sign to the warriors who held Masilo, he turned his back on the trembling wretch, who was dragged off to a distance and tortured to death, while the village feasted and danced.

When darkness once again enfolded the land, the dead body of Masilo was taken to a secret spot and buried, and life at the village returned to its daily duties; but the spirit of Masilo could not rest, and still strove to possess Takane, as his body had longed for her.

One day the daughters of the village, accompanied by Takane, went forth to gather reeds for the making of mats. They wandered far in their search, and were growing weary, when one of them cried: "See! There are reeds, beautiful reeds, as many as we shall need;" and they looking, saw, even as their companion had said, a small bed of beautiful reeds. Soon all were busily engaged in cutting down armfuls of the desired plant; but Takane, being a chief's daughter, was not allowed to work as hard as the other girls, and soon seated herself down to rest in the middle of the reed bed.

When the sun was low in the sky the girls prepared to return home, but Takane could not rise from the ground, nor could her companions lift her. Again and again they tried to move her, but to no purpose; she seemed to have become rooted to the ground. Finally, she persuaded them all to return and obtain help from the village.

"Will you not be afraid, sister, if we leave you alone?" they asked.

"Of what shall I be afraid?" Takane replied. "It is yet light, and the home is near. Haste, for I am hungry, and the night is coming."

The girls then left her and ran home. No sooner had they disappeared, than Takane heard a noise amongst the reeds behind her, and, looking round, she saw Masilo standing there.

"Oh, ho! Takane! You are mine at last! Guessed you not that this was my grave, and that it was I who held you firmly to the ground, so that not even all your companions could raise you? Come now, for we must hasten, lest we be caught by your father's people. By the spirits of my fathers, I have sworn that you shall be my wife."

"But you yourself are a spirit. How, then, can you marry me, and what need have you of a wife? Are you going to kill me even as you were killed?"

"True, I *was* a spirit, but I am now a man, and you are my wife. Come, for I tarry no longer." So saying, he seized her hand and began to run with her away from their old home, while she, filled with superstitious dread, offered only slight resistance. On they ran, ever onward, all through the night and far into the new day. At length, utterly weary, Takane lay down, and refused to go any farther. All around them were strange mountains and valleys, but no sign of human habitation. Here, then, Masilo resolved to remain, and here he built his hut, with the aid of Takane, who, now that she was powerless to escape, became a happy and devoted wife, obeying Masilo as even a wife should. Soon other wanderers came to dwell near them, and ere many years passed Masilo was chief of a happy, prosperous little village, and Takane the mother of sons and daughters whose beauty made her heart glad.

How Khosi Chose a Wife
(From Lesotho, southern Africa)

IN THE DAYS OF OUR FATHERS' FATHERS there lived a rich chief who had only one wife, whom he loved so much that he would not take even one of the beautiful daughters of the great chief to wife, not even when, after many years, no child was born to them.

"I will wait," said the old chief, "the spirits will relent before I die, for we will offer many sacrifices to them."

Accordingly the best of the flocks and herds were sacrificed, and the woman found favour in the eyes of the gods, and a daughter, beautiful as the morning, was born. So precious was this child in the eyes of her parents that they hid her from the sight of men, wrapping her in the skin of the crocodile, the sacred beast of the people. Because of this the people called her 'Polomahache' (the crocodile scale), and very few believed in her beauty, for they thought she must be deformed or terribly ugly to be hidden away under a covering always; but the maiden grew in beauty and grace, until her parents felt they must strive to find a youth worthy of her, if one was to be had upon the earth.

Now the great chief had a son who was dearer to him than all his wives or his other children, or even his flocks and herds; a son tall and straight as the spear, fleet of foot as the wild deer, and brave as the mighty lion of the mountains. This youth the people called Khosi, the fleet one.

At the time when Polomahache had become old enough to marry, Khosi had begun to think of taking a wife, and had sent round to the neighbouring villages requesting the people to send the prettiest girls for his inspection, naming a certain day upon which he would receive them. Upon the day named, very early in the morning, Polomahache, enveloped in her crocodile skin and accompanied by two female attendants, set out for Khosi's village. Many other damsels passed them with jest and laughter, bidding Polomahache remain at home, as her looks were enough to frighten even the bravest lover. Now the custom was that each damsel should wash in the pool below the village of the expectant bridegroom-elect; accordingly the pool below Khosi's village was soon thronged with merry, laughing girls, who were quite unconscious of the fact that Khosi was hidden in the branches of a tree close by, from whence he could, unseen, inspect his would-be wives. While the other girls bathed, Polomahache remained quietly in the background, but when they had departed she stepped timidly down to the water's edge, where she stood hesitatingly, as if afraid to throw off her hideous covering. Khosi, upon seeing her, hid himself more securely in the tree, exclaiming, "Ah! what wild beast have we here? Surely she does not hope that I shall choose her?"

"My child," said one of the attendants, "why do you stand in fear? Know you not that it is the custom of our tribe for the damsels to wash ere they approach their master's house. Remove your covering, then, and be not afraid, for we are alone."

Reluctantly Polomahache did so, and stepped into the clear, cold water, revealing herself in all her beauty to the enraptured gaze of the spectator in the tree.

"Ha," exclaimed Khosi, "what beauty, what eyes, what a face! She, and she alone, shall be my bride." And he continued to gaze upon her until, her bathing completed, she once more enveloped herself in the crocodile skin and departed to the village, when Khosi descended from his hiding-place and returned by another path to his home.

When all the maidens were assembled, Khosi, accompanied by his father and mother, came out from the hut and walked slowly along, carefully studying each maid as he passed. Many bright glances were shot at him; many maiden hearts fluttered in hopeful expectation; but one by one he passed them all until he came to little Polomahache, who had hidden herself away at the end of the row of maidens.

"Ho! Hèla! what is this?" exclaimed Khosi. "Surely this is no maiden, but some wild beast."

"Indeed, Chief Khosi," replied a gentle voice from behind the skin, "I am but a poor maid who fears she cannot hope to find favour in the eyes of the Great One."

"Now truly, mother, this is the wife for me. Send all the other maidens away, for I will have none of them." So saying, Khosi turned and re-entered the hut. His mother trembled with rage, for she thought Polomahache had bewitched her son, so she followed him into the hut; but when she heard what he had to tell her, she promised to try to arrange the marriage on condition that Khosi would manage to let her see Polomahache without the skin. Accordingly they arranged that Khosi was to see his bride alone, and if he could persuade her to throw off the crocodile skin he was to clap three times as if in pleasure, and his mother would come in.

When the sun was low in the heavens Khosi conducted Polomahache to his father's hut, where at length he persuaded her to throw off the skin. As it fell to the ground he clapped three times, exclaiming, "Oh! beautiful as the dawn is my beloved; her eyes are tender as the eyes of a deer; her voice is like many waters." As he spoke his mother entered, and being quite satisfied with the maiden's beauty, the marriage was soon arranged, and Khosi and his beautiful bride dwelt long in happiness and prosperity in the land of their fathers.

Lelimo and the Magic Cap
(From Lesotho, southern Africa)

ONCE LONG AGO, when giants dwelt upon the earth, there lived in a little village, far up in the mountains, a woman who had the power of making magic caps. When her daughter Siloane grew old enough to please the eyes of men, her mother made her a magic cap. "Keep this cap safely, my child, for it will protect you from the power of Lelimo (the giant). If you lose it, he will surely seize you and carry you away to his dwelling in the mountains, where he and his children will eat you."

Siloane promised to be very careful, and for a long time always carried the magic cap with her whenever she went beyond the village.

Now it was the custom each year for the maidens of the village to go to a certain spot, where the 'tuani' or long rushes grew, there to gather great bundles with which to make new mats for the floors of the houses. When the time came, Siloane and many more maidens set out for the place. The distance was great, and as they must reach their destination at the rising of the sun, they set off from the village at midnight.

Just as the sun rose from sleep, the maidens arrived at the graves on which the rushes grew. Soon all were busy cutting rushes and making mats. Siloane laid down her cap on one of the graves by which she was working. All day the maidens worked, and at sunset they started on their homeward journey. Soon the moon arose and lighted the land, and the light-hearted maidens went gaily singing on their way.

When they had gone some way, Siloane suddenly remembered she had left the magic cap on the grave where she had been sitting. Afraid to face her mother without it, she asked her companions to wait for her while she hurried back to fetch it.

Long the maidens waited, amusing themselves by telling stories and singing songs in the moonlight, but Siloane returned not. At length two girls set out to look for her, but when they reached the spot, no trace of her was to be found. Great was their dismay. How could they tell the news to her parents? Still there was nothing else to be done, and, with heavy hearts, they all returned to the village.

When Ma-Batu, the mother of Siloane, heard their story, she immediately set to work to make another magic cap, which she gave to her younger daughter Sieng, telling her to have it always by her, in case Siloane should need her help.

Meanwhile, Siloane had been taken captive by the giant as she was making her way back to recover her magic cap. When she felt Lelimo's heavy hand on her shoulder, she struggled frantically to get away, but her strength was as water against such a man, and he soon had her securely tied up in his big bag, made out of the skin of an ox.

Now when Lelimo saw Siloane, he was returning from a feast, and was very drunk, so that he mistook his way, and wandered long and far, until, in the morning, he came to a large hut, where he threw down the sack containing Siloane, and demanded a drink of the woman who stood in the door. She gave him some very strong 'juala' (beer), which made him more drunk than before. While he was drinking, Siloane called softly from the sack, for she had recognised her mother's voice talking to the giant, and knew that he had brought her in some wonderful way to her father's house. Again she called, and this time her sister heard her, and hastened to undo the sack. She then hid Siloane, and, by the aid of the magic cap, she filled the sack with bees and wasps and closed it firmly. When the giant came out from the hut, he picked up the sack and started for his own home. On his arrival there he again threw down the sack, and ordered his wife to kill and cook the captive girl he imagined he had brought home. His wife began to feel the sack in order to find out how big the girl was, but the bees became angry and stung her through the sack, which frightened her, and she refused to open it. Thereupon Lelimo called his son, but he also refused. In a great rage, the giant turned them both out of the house, and closed all the openings. He then made a great fire, and prepared to roast the girl.

When he opened the sack, the bees and wasps, who were by this time thoroughly furious, swarmed upon him, and stung him till he howled with agony, and, mad with pain, he broke down the door of the hut and rushed down to the river, into which he flung himself head first. In this position he was afterwards found by his wife, his feet resting on a rock above the water, his head buried in the mud of the river.

Such was the end of this wicked giant, who had been the terror of that part of the country for many, many years.

The Famine

(From Lesotho, southern Africa)

IN THE YEARS WHEN the locusts visited the lands of the chief Makaota, and devoured all the food, the people grew thin and ill from starvation, and many of them died. When their food was all gone, they wandered in the lands and up the mountains, searching for roots upon which to feed. Now as they searched, Mamokete, the wife of the Chief Makoata, chanced to wander near some bushes, when suddenly she heard the most exquisite singing. She stopped to listen, but could see nothing. So she walked up to the bushes and looked in, and there she saw the most beautiful bird she had ever seen. "Oh! Ho! Little bird," she cried, "help me, for I and my husband and children are starving. Our cattle are all dead, and we know not where to find food."

"Take me," sang the bird, "and I will be your food. Keep me safely, guard me well, and you shall never starve as long as I remain with you."

Thankfully the poor woman took the bird and hurried home with it. She placed it in an earthen pitcher and went to call her husband. When they returned, they opened the pitcher to look at the bird, when lo! milk poured from the mouth of the pitcher, and the hungry people drank. How their hearts rejoiced over the gift which had been given them!

One day Makaota and his wife were going out to the lands to work, but before leaving they called their children, and bade them be good, and guard the pitcher well. The children promised to obey, but soon began to quarrel. Each wished to drink out of the pitcher first, and in their greediness they upset and broke the pitcher, and the bird flew out of the open door. Terrified at what they had done, the children ran after it; but when they got outside, there was no sign of the beautiful bird. It had completely vanished.

What grief now filled their hearts and the hearts of Makaota and Mamokete his wife! Hunger seized once more upon them, and despair filled their hearts. Day by day they sought the wonderful bird, but found her not. At length, when the two children lay sick for want of food, and the parents' hearts were heavy with grief, there came again the wonderful singing, borne upon the evening wind. Nearer and nearer it came, and then, lo! at the open door stood the lovely bird.

"I have come back," she said, "because the punishment has been enough. Take me, and your house shall prosper."

Gladly they took the beautiful bird in their hands, and vowed never again to let anger and greed drive her away from them; and so their house did thrive, even as the bird had said, and peace and plenty dwelt not only in the house of Makaota, but in the whole village for ever after.

The Cat's Tail

(From the Swahili-speaking peoples, east Africa)

AT A PLACE CALLED LAMU lived a woman and her husband. One day, whilst they were at meal, a cat came in and looked at them. Now these two people loved to disagree with each other. So that woman said to the man, "I say that the tail of a cat is stuck in." The man said to his wife, "No, it is not stuck in; it sprouts out."

So they wrangled together about this matter for many days. At last they disputed so noisily that their neighbours threatened to drive them out of the village. Then, as neither the husband nor the wife would give in, they decided to seek the wise man who lived at Shela, for sure he would know and could settle this great question.

So they each took a dollar and tied it in the corner of their robes and set out for Shela, quarrelling so hard all the way that everybody turned round to stare at them.

At last they arrived at the town of Shela and found the wise man at his house. When he saw the big round dollars bulging out of their clothes he smiled upon them and invited them in.

Then the woman asked him, "Look up for us in your learned books whether a cat's tail is stuck in or whether it sprouts out."

The man said, "No. Look up whether it does not sprout out or whether it is stuck in."

The wise man saw that they were fools, so he replied: "Give me my fee: one dollar for the answer to the question as to whether the cat's tail is stuck in or whether it sprouts out, and one dollar for the answer as to whether it sprouts out or is stuck in."

So they each gave him a dollar, and the wise man made great pretence at looking through his books. Finally he said, "You are both wrong; the cat's tail is neither stuck in nor does it sprout out, and it neither sprouts out nor is it stuck in, but it is just stuck on."

They then returned home in silence, and the wise man stuck to their dollars.

The Young Thief

(From the Swahili-speaking peoples, east Africa)

ONCE UPON A TIME there was a man and he wished to marry. So he went to the Seers and asked them to foretell his future. The Seers looked at their books and said to him, "If you marry

you will certainly have a child, a very beautiful boy, but with one blemish; he will be a thief, the biggest thief that ever was."

So that man said, "Never mind, even if he be a thief; I should like to have a son." So he married, and in due time a child was born, a beautiful boy.

The child was carefully brought up till he was old enough to have a teacher. Then the father engaged a professor to come and teach him every day. He built a house a little distance from the town and put him in it, and that professor came every morning and taught him during the day, and in the evening returned home. Now the father ordered the professor never to let his son see any other soul but himself, and he thought by that means that his son would escape the fate that had been decreed by the Seers; for if he never saw any other person he could have no one to teach him to steal.

One day the professor came, and he told the lad about a horse of the Sultan's, which used to go out to exercise by itself and return by itself, and was of great strength and speed.

Then that youth asked where was the Sultan's palace, and his professor took him up on to the flat roof and pointed out to him the palace and its neighbourhood.

That night, after the professor left, the youth slipped out and came to the Sultan's stables, stole the horse, and returned home with it.

Next day the professor was a little late in coming, so the lad asked him, "Sheikh, why have you delayed today?" The professor said, "I stayed to hear the news. Behold, someone has stolen the Sultan's horse which I told you about yesterday."

Then that lad asked, "What does the Sultan propose to do?"

The old man replied, "He thought of sending out his soldiers, but then he heard of a seer who is able to detect a thief by looking at his books, so he is going to ask him first."

So the youth asked, "Where does that seer live?"

The professor then pointed out the seer's house and its neighbourhood.

That night the youth slipped out and came to the seer's house and found that the seer was out. He saw his wife and said to her: "My mistress, the seer has sent me to fetch his box of books."

So the wife brought out the box containing all his books of magic and gave them to him, and he took them and returned with them to his house.

Next day his professor was late, and when he came he said to him, "Father, why have you delayed?"

The old man said, "I stopped to hear the news. Do you remember the seer of whom I told you yesterday, who was to find out the thief for the Sultan? Well, he has now been robbed of his books of magic."

The youth asked, "What does the Sultan intend to do?"

The old man replied, "He was about to send out his soldiers, and then he heard that there was a magician who is able to detect a thief by casting charms, so he is going to consult him."

Then the youth asked, "Where does the magician live?"

So the old man took him on the roof and pointed out the magician's house and its neighbourhood.

That night, after the professor had gone, the youth went out and came to the house of the magician. He found him out, but saw his wife and said to her, "Mother, I fear to ask you, for was not the seer robbed in like manner yesterday? but the magician has sent me to fetch his bag of charms."

That woman said, "Have no fear; the thief's not you, my child;" and she gave him the bag of charms, and he took them and went to his house.

Next day, when the professor came, he asked for the news, and he said, "Did I not tell you yesterday that the Sultan was going to get a magician to tell him the thief by casting his charms? Well, last night the magician had his bag of charms stolen."

Then the youth asked, "What is the Sultan going to do?"

The old man answered, "He was going to send out his soldiers to catch the thief, but he heard that a certain woman said she knew who the thief was, and so he is going to pay her to tell him."

The youth asked where the woman lived, and the old man pointed out her house to him.

That evening the youth went out, and came to the house of that woman and found her outside, and he said to her, "Mother, I am thirsty; give me a drink of water."

So she went to the well to draw some water, and the youth came behind her and pushed her in. Then he went into the house and took her clothes and jewellery and brought them back to his house.

Next day, when the professor came, he asked the news, and he said, "My son, I told you yesterday that there was a woman who said that she could tell the Sultan the name of the thief. Well, last night the thief came and pushed her into the well and stole her things."

Then that youth asked, "What does the Sultan propose to do?"

The old man replied, "He is sending his soldiers out to look for the thief."

That night, after the professor had gone, the youth dressed up as a soldier, and went out and met the soldiers of the Sultan looking for the thief.

He said to them, "That is not the way to look for a thief. The way to look for a thief is to sit down very quietly in a place, and then perhaps you will see or hear him."

So he brought them all to one place and made them sit down, and one by one they all fell asleep. When they were all asleep he took their weapons and all their clothes he could carry and came with them to his house.

Next day, when the professor came, he asked him the news, and he said, "Last night the Sultan sent his soldiers out to look for the thief and behold, the thief stole their arms and their clothes, so that they returned naked."

Then the youth asked, "And now, what does the Sultan propose to do?"

The old man said, "Tonight the Sultan goes himself to look for the thief."

The youth said, "That is good, for the wisdom of Sultans is great."

That night the youth dressed up as a woman and scented himself and went out. He saw in the distance a lamp, and knew that it was the Sultan looking for the thief, so he passed near. When the Sultan smelt those goodly scents, he turned round to see whence they came, and he saw a very beautiful woman.

He asked, "Who are you?"

The lad replied, "I was just returning home when I saw your light, so I stepped aside to let you pass."

The Sultan said, "You must come and talk with me a little."

That lad said, "No, I must go home."

They were just outside the prison, so at last the youth consented to go in and talk for a little while with the Sultan.

When they got inside the courtyard, the youth took a pair of leg-irons and asked the Sultan, "What are these?"

The Sultan replied, "Those are the leg-irons with which we fasten our prisoners."

Then that youth said, "Oh, fasten them on me, that I may see how they work."

The Sultan said, "No, you are a woman, but I will put them on to show you," and he put them on.

The youth looked up and saw a gang-chain and asked, "What is that?"

The Sultan said, "That is what we put round their necks, and the end is fastened to the wall."

So the youth said, "Oh, put it on my neck, that I may see what it is like."

The Sultan replied, "No, you are a woman, but I will put it on my neck to show you;" so he put it on.

Then the youth took the key of the leg-irons and of the gang-chain, and looked up and saw a whip and said, "What is that?"

"That," said the Sultan, "is a whip with which we whip our prisoners if they are bad."

So the youth picked up the whip and began beating the Sultan. After the first few strokes the Sultan said, "Stop, that is enough fun-making."

But the youth went on and beat him soundly, and then went out, leaving the Sultan in chains and chained to the wall, and he also locked the door of the prison and took the key and went home. Next day the Sultan was found to be in the prison, and they could not get in to let him out or free him.

So a crier was sent round the town to cry, "Anyone who can deliver the Sultan from prison will be given a free pardon for any offence he has committed."

So, when the cries came to that youth's house, he said, "Oho, I want that as a certificate in writing before I will say what I know."

When these words were brought to the Wazir, he had a document drawn up, giving a free pardon to anyone who would deliver the Sultan. Then he brought it round to the prison for the Sultan's signature, and as they could not get it in they pushed it through the window on the end of a long pole. Then the Sultan signed it, and it was given to that youth, who handed over the key of the prison and of the chains and fetters. After the Sultan had been released he called that youth to his palace, and the youth took the horse, and the sage's books of magic, and the magician's bag of charms, and the woman's clothes and jewellery, and the soldiers' arms and clothes, and came to the palace.

When the Sultan heard his story he said that he was indeed a very clever youth, so he made him his Wazir.

This is the story of the man who would have a child, even though he should be a thief.

The Woodcutter and His Donkey
(From the Swahili-speaking peoples, east Africa)

ONCE UPON A TIME there was a poor woodcutter, and his work was to go out every day into the forest and cut wood. In the evening, he used to load up his donkey with the wood he had cut and return to the town, where he sold it. The money he got each day was only sufficient for the food of himself and his wife for that day.

They lived like that many months and many days, and they were very, very poor; till one day the woodcutter went out to the forest as usual to cut wood. As he was at work he looked up and saw a number of birds sitting on the top of a tree, with their beaks wide open. And there was a cloud of insects about the tree, and they fell into the birds' mouths.

Then the woodcutter said to himself, "Behold these birds, they sit on the top of a tree with their mouths open, and God feeds them by bringing insects to fall into their mouths. They do not have to work or even to move from their perch; they just open their mouths and are fed. Why should I have to work hard all day and then only get just enough to eat? Why should not God feed me like that?"

So he loaded up his donkey with the wood he had already cut and returned to the town. When he reached his house he went in and got into bed.

His wife went out and sold the wood, and then bought some food and returned home. When she found her husband in bed she said, "My husband, are you ill?"

He replied, "No, my wife, I am waiting for God to feed me as I saw Him feed the birds today."

So she cooked the food and then called to him, "The food is ready, my husband."

He replied, "No. Today I saw that God fed the birds without them having to move. They just opened their mouths and the food dropped in, so now I am not going to move out of bed, but am just going to wait here in bed to be fed also."

So his wife brought his food in to him there in bed and he ate and slept. Next morning his wife said to him, "Arise, my husband, for it is time that you went to work."

He replied, "No, I am not going to work; I am just going to stop here in bed and wait to be fed."

His wife said, "But, my husband, we have no food and no money in the house. What are we to do if you do not go and work?"

He answered, "Never mind. God is able to feed the birds when they are hungry, and so He is able to feed me."

So he stopped there in bed. Now a neighbour of his had a vision that night that in a certain cave was a great treasure stored. He wanted to go and search for it, and when he heard that the woodcutter was not going to work that day he thought that he would borrow his donkey to bring back the wealth, if his vision came true.

So he came to borrow the donkey; but as he was a very mean man he did not want to tell of his vision or for what purpose he wanted the donkey. He knocked at the door, and the wife came and opened it, and he asked to see the woodcutter.

The wife went to call her husband, but he said, "Tell him to come in here; I will not get up."

So the neighbour came in and asked the woodcutter to lend him his donkey, and said, "If I have a prosperous journey I will give you a few coppers."

The woodcutter agreed, and he took the donkey and went to the place about which he had dreamed. There he found the cave, and when he entered he saw piles of money, gold, silver and copper.

So he gathered up first all the gold and then all the silver and filled the donkey's saddle-bags, till at last they would hold no more.

He was loth to leave the copper, so he left the donkey outside the cave and went back and began to stuff his clothes with the copper coins. Whilst he was doing this the mouth of the cave fell in, and he was unable to get out.

The donkey waited and waited till at last, when evening was near, seeing no one coming, it set off and returned home, and came to the door of the house. The wife heard a noise at the door and said, "My husband, there is someone at the door; get up and open it to see who it is."

He replied, "No, my wife, I am going to stop just here in bed till God brings me my food."

So the wife opened the door, and the donkey walked in to where the woodcutter was lying in bed. When he looked at it he saw that the saddle-bags were stuffed full of gold and silver.

The man and his wife waited for the return of the neighbour, but when he did not come back they made plans together what they should do.

The husband said to his wife, "Behold, my wife, the neighbours all know that we are very poor and have no money in the house. Even if we were to take a little money and buy food tomorrow they will say that we have stolen it, so how are we to spend all this wealth? Even if we go away they will know that we have not the money to expend on a journey, so what shall we do?"

So they planned together, and then they crept out, when everybody was asleep, and put a little money on the doorstep of each house near them. On one they put ten reals, on another five, and so on.

In the morning when everyone opened their doors, behold, some silver coins on the doorstep. So the neighbours said to one another, "I got five reals; what did you get?" and so on. Another said, "Surely some Jin must have put all this money here in the night."

Then were the neighbours not surprised when they saw that the woodcutter and his wife had a little money wherewith to buy food. So the woodcutter said to his neighbours, "I found twenty reals on my doorstep this morning, and I and my wife are going to expend this money on travelling to a far country, where perhaps we will meet with better fortune than here."

So they bought the necessaries for a long journey with a little of that money, and then the greater part they packed up on the donkey and journeyed off.

They travelled on and on, till at last they came to a country where they were not known, and there they bought a house and settled down, and the people said, "Behold, these must be some rich folk who have come from a far country."

So they lived there in great splendour, and spent their money and gave praise to God.

This is the story of the woodcutter who had trust in God, and it finishes here.

Kitangatanga of the Sea
(From the Swahili-speaking peoples, east Africa)

THERE WAS ONCE A MAN, and he lived at Kilwa. And that man married a wife, and built a hut, in which they stayed. Everything that woman asked for he gave her, only that hut he had built without a door.

He himself, when he went abroad and returned, used to climb up a ladder and get in at the window, and when he went away he took away the ladder. So that woman stayed in that hut and was not able to go out, not even for a little, and so she was sick of heart.

Now when her mother heard about this she came and dug a hole under the wall, so that she was able to come and see her daughter whenever the husband had gone out. The mouth of that hole the woman covered over with matting, so that that man, her husband, did not get to see it.

Now that man was a merchant, and used to trade up and down the coast even as far as Maskat.

One day he came home to his wife and said to her, "My wife, it is time that I went up the coast trading, so in a week's time I will start and will go to Zanzibar and Maskat, and then, after the space of one year, I will return again."

So his wife said to him, "It is well, my husband; may you go and return in safety."

When her husband went away again she got out quickly by her tunnel and came to her mother and said, "My mother, my husband is going to travel away for a year and leave me in my hut. Now you must go quickly and get a fast ship ready for me and tell no one."

Then she returned and sat in the hut, and in the evening her husband returned and climbed in by that window of his.

After a week had passed the husband took leave of his wife and went down to the harbour, got on board his ship and set sail for Zanzibar.

After he had gone, the wife came out quickly and went down to the harbour and got on board the vessel her mother had prepared for her and set sail behind him.

In the middle of the ocean that boat of hers passed his. He looked at it and called out, "Who is that in the ship that is passing me?"

She answered, "It is I, my name is Kitangatanga of the sea."

She arrived at Zanzibar, moored her vessel and went ashore, and found that house where he stayed and entered it and sat down. Presently her husband arrived, moored his boat and went up to that house.

When he saw that woman he was surprised and said to her, "How like you are to my wife whom I left in Kilwa!"

So he talked to her for a while and then asked, "Are you married?"

She replied, "No, I am a widow."

Then he said, "If you will marry me I will settle on you a hundred reals."

So that woman agreed, and they were married, and they stayed together. After two weeks he said to her, "My wife, I must continue my journey to Maskat now; but in the space of six months I will return and stay with you."

She said, "It is well, my husband; go, and return in safety."

So he got in his boat and set sail for Maskat. After he had gone she got in her boat and set sail behind him. In the middle of the sea her vessel passed his, and he called out, "Who is that who is passing me?"

She replied, "It is I, Kitangatanga of the sea." She arrived first in Maskat and found that house where he stopped and went and sat in it. Presently her husband arrived, moored his ship and went up to the house.

When he saw that woman sitting there he was very surprised and said, "How like you are to my wife whom I left in Kilwa, and also to that woman I married in Zanzibar."

Then he asked her, "Are you married?"

She replied, "No, I am a widow." So he said, "I will marry you for one hundred reals."

She agreed, and they were married, and he stayed with her six months there in Maskat. At the end of that time he said, "My wife, I must now return home. I will stay a year, and then I will return to you."

She said, "Go, and return in peace, my husband."

So he set sail from Maskat, and that woman set sail after him. In the midst of the ocean she passed him again, and when he asked who it was, she replied, "It is I, Kitangatanga of the sea."

She arrived at Zanzibar and went up to that house.

Presently her husband arrived, and she said, "Welcome, stranger; what is the news?"

He replied, "The news is that I have made a prosperous journey to Maskat, and that there I met a woman just like the wife I left at Kilwa and also like you, and I married her."

She replied, "It is well, my husband."

After he had stopped several weeks he said to her, "My wife, I must now return home. I will stop one year, and then I will return to you."

So she said, "May your journey be prosperous, my husband, and may you return in safety."

So he set sail for Kilwa, and she set sail after him. In the midst of the ocean she passed him again, and when he asked who it was, she replied, "It is I, Kitangatanga of the sea."

When she arrived in Kilwa she moored her vessel and went up to her house. She entered by her underground doorway and sat down. After a while her husband arrived and climbed in by his window. She said, "Welcome, my husband."

Then she cooked food for him, and when he had eaten she asked him, "What is the news of there where you have been?"

He replied, "I made a good voyage to Zanzibar, and there I met a woman just like you. I married her for one hundred reals, and stayed with her for two weeks. Then I went on to Maskat, and there I met a woman exactly like you and like that woman I married in Zanzibar. I married her, too, for a hundred reals, and stopped with her six months.

"Then I returned to Zanzibar and stayed with my wife there a few weeks, then set out for home, and here I am. Now what is the news here of this place whilst I have been away?"

That wife replied, "The news is this, my husband. I was angered because you put me in a hut without a door, so I made this underground door which you see there.

"Then, when you set sail, I set sail after you, and I passed you in the sea; and when you asked who I was, I replied, "Kitangatanga of the sea!"

"I came first to Zanzibar, and it was I whom you married there for a hundred reals.

"When you left for Maskat, I set sail behind you, and arrived there first. It was I also whom you married in Maskat for one hundred reals. That is my news, my husband."

When her husband heard that, he said, "Indeed, this is true. Now I will build you a very fine hut with a door in it, so that you may go out when you please."

So he built her a splendid hut with a door and put her into it, and there they lived happily.

The Story of the Fools

(From the Swahili-speaking peoples, east Africa)

ONCE UPON A TIME there lived a man called Omari and his wife, and they had a very fine fat black ox. So fat was this ox that all the young men in the village wanted to eat it, but Omari would not part with it. Till one day he went away on a journey; then they thought, "Now we will be able to get that ox and have a feast, for his wife is a great fool."

So twenty men set out and came to the house of that woman, Omari's wife, and they knocked on the door.

"Hodi!"

And she replied, "Come near."

So they went in and told that woman, "We have had a vision, and in that vision we saw that you were going to have a child, a beautiful boy, who will be rich and clever, and will marry the daughter of the Wazir."

Now when the woman heard this she was wondrously pleased, for she had no child.

Then these men said, "There was, in our dream, the sacrifice of a black ox, before this came to pass."

So she said, "Take my ox and sacrifice him, that the vision may come true."

They replied, "Shall we kill him, though, while your husband is away?"

She said, "Take him, yes, take him, for my husband will be only too pleased when he knows for what purpose the ox has been slain; and he, too, desires a son."

So the youths took away the ox and killed it and feasted and made merry.

After three days the husband returned, and when he did not see his ox in its stall he asked his wife, "Where is the ox?"

She said to him, "It has been slaughtered."

"Why?"

She replied, "Men came who had dreamed a dream that we should have a beautiful male child of great good fortune, and as the sacrifice of a black ox was necessary to bring it true, I gave ours to them."

Omari then said to his wife, "You are a fool. Now I am going out to search for as great a fool as you are. If I cannot find anyone who is your equal in folly, I shall leave you; you will cease to be my wife."

So Omari took his donkey and rode away till he came to the house of a certain rich man, and this house had a verandah beneath it. Omari got off his donkey, and as he stood there, a woman, one of the slaves of the household, passed in, and said to him, "Master, where do you come from?"

Omari replied, "I come from the next world."

Then was that slave very astonished, and she went upstairs to her mistress and said to her, "There, below in the verandah, is a man who comes from the next world."

"Is that indeed so?" asked the mistress.

"It is indeed true, and if you doubt me ask him yourself, for he is there below," said the slave.

So the mistress sent her slave down to call Omari up into the house, and she came to him and said, "The mistress asks you to come upstairs."

Omari replied, "I cannot come upstairs; I am afraid, because it is a stranger's house."

When the slave brought these words to her mistress, she herself came down and called to Omari, "Do not be afraid; come upstairs; there is no danger."

So Omari went upstairs, and that woman asked him, "Master, where do you come from?"

Omari replied, "I come from the next world."

"See," said the slave; "were not my words true?"

Then was that mistress very amazed, and she asked him, "Why have you left the next world?"

"I have come to see my father," answered Omari.

"My father, who is dead," said the woman; "have you met him there in the next world?"

"What is he called, and what is he like?" said Omari.

"He is called so-and-so, son of so-and-so," said the woman, and she described to him his appearance.

Omari replied, "I have seen him."

"And how is he?"

At that Omari put on an air of grief and shook his head and sighed.

"Oh, tell me, what is the matter with my father?" asked the woman.

Omari replied, "He is in great trouble. He has no money or clothes or food. Oh, his state is very bad!"

When that woman heard these words she wept. Then she asked Omari, "When do you return to the next world?"

"I return tomorrow. First, I must see my father, who is still alive, and then I go back."

"Will you see my father when you return?"

"Most certainly," said Omari. "Do I not live next door to him?"

"Then," said that woman, "you must take him a present from me."

So she went into an inner room and took out a bag of a thousand dollars, and clothes, and a robe, and turbans, and came and gave them to Omari, and said, "Take these and give them to my father, and say that they are from his daughter, Binti Fatima."

Then she went in and brought out another bag and said, "Take these hundred dollars; they are a present for you, as you are taking these things for my father."

So Omari gathered up the bags of money and the clothes and left that woman, and mounted his donkey and rode away.

He had only just left when the husband of that woman in the house returned home. He noticed that his wife was very joyful, so he asked her, "My wife, why are you so glad today?"

She said to him, "A man has just been here who has come from the next world, and he has met my father there in great trouble. So I have given him a thousand dollars and clothes to take to my father. That is why I am so happy; for now the spirit of my father will be very pleased with us, and it will bring us great good fortune."

Now that man saw that his wife had been fooled, but he feared to say so, in case his wife should tell him no more, and he wished to follow that man and get the money back.

So he said to her, "You are not a good wife, for when a man came from the next world to tell you about your father you gave him an offering to take back to him, but you never asked him about my father, or gave him anything to take to him."

Then the wife said, "Oh, forgive me, my husband, but as he has only just left you may overtake him. He was riding a donkey, and he left by that road."

Then she described him. So the husband called for his horse, and the wife ran in and brought out another bag of a thousand dollars, and as he mounted she gave it to him, saying, "Take this, my husband, and give it to him for your father, and if you gallop after him down that road you will surely overtake him."

Now Omari had ridden away on his donkey till he came to a plantation, then he turned his head and saw, in the distance, the dust made by a galloping horse. There was no one on that plantation except one male slave, and so Omari said to him, "Do you see that dust? It is made by a man of great violence. I am going to hide from him, and I advise you to climb up into a coconut tree, lest he do you some harm. If he speaks to you do not answer him, for it will only make him more angry."

So that slave scrambled up a coconut palm as fast as he could, whilst Omari hid himself and his donkey in a thicket close by.

Presently the husband of the woman galloped up, and saw the slave clambering up to the top of a tall coconut tree.

He stopped and called out, "Have you seen a man riding a donkey pass here?"

The slave did not answer, but continued climbing higher and higher. He asked him again and again, and the slave did not reply, but only made more haste to get well out of reach.

Then was that man very angry, and he got down from his horse and divested himself of all his robes, except only an under-garment, and placing them and the money on the ground, started climbing up after the slave.

Omari watched him from behind the thicket, and, when he had got well up the tree, he came out and seized that man's money and clothes, as well as those he already had, and then mounted his horse and galloped off.

When that man came down from the tree he found all his clothes and his money and his horse gone, and he was very ashamed. So he had to return home wearing only a loin-cloth.

When he came in his wife asked him, "My husband, why do you return naked like that?"

He was ashamed to tell her that he also had been fooled by that man, so he said, "I met the man from the next world, who told me that my father was in a very distressed condition, that he had no clothes, and was dressed in rags. So when I heard that, I took off all my clothes and gave them to that man to take to my father."

Now Omari took all that money, and the clothes, and the horse, and came back to his wife and told her, "I said that I would seek for a fool like unto yourself, and if I did not find one that you would cease to be my wife. Well, now I am content, for I have found two fools, each one more foolish than you."

So they lived together, Omari and his wife, and they spent the money and were happy together.

Here ends the story of the fools, the fool-wife, and the husband and wife who were fooled.

The Poor Man and His Wife Of Wood

(From the Swahili-speaking peoples, east Africa)

ONCE UPON A TIME there was a poor man who used to beg. One day he sat thinking to himself, "I am a poor man and have no wife. When I go out begging there is no one to come back to in my house or to cook my food for me whilst I am away."

So he went out to the forest and cut down a tree and carved out of it a woman of wood, and when he had finished he decorated her with jewels and necklaces of wood, and then brought her back to his house.

Then that tree turned into a woman, and he called her Mwanamizi, the child of a root, and he lived with her many days. Till one day, when that poor man had gone forth to beg, a slave girl ran out from the palace of the Sultan in search of a brand with which to light the fire.

She came and knocked at the poor man's door, and when she got no answer she entered and went into the kitchen, and there she saw a lovely woman decked out with pearls and jewels. She went running back to the Sultan and said to him, "I have just seen the most wondrously beautiful woman in the house of that beggar who lives near us."

The Sultan then ordered his soldiers, "Go to fetch the wife of the beggar, that I may see if the words of this slave are true or false."

So they went and took Mwanamizi and brought her to the palace. When the Sultan saw her he thought her very beautiful.

So he said, "This woman is too beautiful for a beggar. I will take her for my wife."

Now when that poor man returned from begging he could not find his wife; then the neighbours told him, "The woman has been taken by the Sultan to his palace."

So he threw down his bag and went round to the palace, and rushed in before the Sultan and asked him, "Where is my wife whom you have taken?"

The Sultan replied, "Get out of my sight, you foolish fellow, or I will order my soldiers to beat you."

Then he said, "If you will not give me back my wife, take off my ornaments which she is wearing and return them to me, that I may go."

At that the Sultan called his soldiers and had him turned out of the palace.

After that the poor man went under the Sultan's window and sang –

"Oh listen, master, unto me:
My wife I carved from yonder tree;
I carved her well, with zeal untold,
And decked her out with fetters gold.
These ornaments and jewels fine,
Oh, give them back, for they are mine;
And, Mwanamizi, let me go."

When the woman heard the poor man's song she was bathed in tears.

The Sultan then said to her, "Take off those silly ornaments and throw them to him, that he may go away. I will give you things tenfold more fine and rare."

The woman did not want to take off those things.

The poor man sang again:

"Oh listen, master, unto me:
I carved my wife from yonder tree."

Then the woman took off her ornaments and threw them down to him, saying –

"The ornaments are thine,
The golden fetters fine;
Take them, oh, take them,
Makami, and go."

She cried then very much, and took off all her things, till there was left a single charm round her neck.

The Sultan said, "Take off all his ornaments quickly and throw them to him, that he may go." But Mwanamizi did not want to take off that charm, for it was her soul. Then the poor man sang again, and Mwanamizi unfastened the charm from her neck and threw it to him, and at that moment she turned into a tree there in the house of the Sultan.

The poor man sighed and went back to his house, but the Sultan in his palace was seized with great fear.

The telling of the story ends here.

The Sultan's Daughter

(From the Swahili-speaking peoples, east Africa)

LONG AGO IN OLDEN TIMES there was a Sultan, and he had a daughter beautiful as the moon at its fulness. This Sultan said that he would only marry his daughter to a man of wisdom. So to all who came to seek his daughter's hand he asked three questions.

The first was, "When famine comes to a place and leaves it again, where does it go?"

The second was, "When sickness comes to a place and leaves it again, where does it go?"

And the third was, "When war comes to a place and leaves it again, where does it go?"

No one was able to answer these questions for many months and many years, till at last there came a man who said, "I will answer your questions, oh Sultan."

The Sultan replied, "Speak on, stranger."

So that man said, "When famine comes to a country and leaves it again it goes to the idle, for they make no profit and sit always with hunger for a cup-fellow.

"When sickness comes to a country and leaves it again it goes to the aged, for they sit always with sickness and death for a companion.

"When war comes to a country and leaves it again it goes to those men who have more than one wife, for in their houses quarrels never cease."

When the Sultan heard these words he was very pleased, and gave his daughter to the stranger.

The Woman with Two Skins
(From southern Nigeria)

EYAMBA I OF CALABAR was a very powerful king. He fought and conquered all the surrounding countries, killing all the old men and women, but the able-bodied men and girls he caught and brought back as slaves, and they worked on the farms until they died.

This king had two hundred wives, but none of them had borne a son to him. His subjects, seeing that he was becoming an old man, begged him to marry one of the spider's daughters, as they always had plenty of children. But when the king saw the spider's daughter he did not like her, as she was ugly, and the people said it was because her mother had had so many children at the same time. However, in order to please his people he married the ugly girl, and placed her among his other wives, but they all complained because she was so ugly, and said she could not live with them. The king, therefore, built her a separate house for herself, where she was given food and drink the same as the other wives. Everyone jeered at her on account of her ugliness; but she was not really ugly, but beautiful, as she was born with two skins, and at her birth her mother was made to promise that she should never remove the ugly skin until a certain time arrived save only during the night, and that she must put it on again before dawn. Now the king's head wife knew this, and was very fearful lest the king should find it out and fall in love with the spider's daughter; so she went to a Ju Ju man and offered him two hundred rods to make a potion that would make the king forget altogether that the spider's daughter was his wife. This the Ju Ju man finally consented to do, after much haggling over the price, for three hundred and fifty rods; and he made up some 'medicine', which the head wife mixed with the king's food.

For some months this had the effect of making the king forget the spider's daughter, and he used to pass quite close to her without recognising her in any way. When four months had elapsed and the king had not once sent for Adiaha (for that was the name of the spider's daughter), she began to get tired, and went back to her parents. Her father, the spider, then took her to another

Ju Ju man, who, by making spells and casting lots, very soon discovered that it was the king's head wife who had made the Ju Ju and had enchanted the king so that he would not look at Adiaha. He therefore told the spider that Adiaha should give the king some medicine which he would prepare, which would make the king remember her. He prepared the medicine, for which the spider had to pay a large sum of money; and that very day Adiaha made a small dish of food, into which she had placed the medicine, and presented it to the king. Directly he had eaten the dish his eyes were opened and he recognised his wife, and told her to come to him that very evening. So in the afternoon, being very joyful, she went down to the river and washed, and when she returned she put on her best cloth and went to the king's palace.

Directly it was dark and all the lights were out she pulled off her ugly skin, and the king saw how beautiful she was, and was very pleased with her; but when the cock crowed Adiaha pulled on her ugly skin again, and went back to her own house.

This she did for four nights running, always taking the ugly skin off in the dark, and leaving before daylight in the morning. In course of time, to the great surprise of all the people, and particularly of the king's two hundred wives, she gave birth to a son; but what surprised them most of all was that only one son was born, whereas her mother had always had a great many children at a time, generally about fifty.

The king's head wife became more jealous than ever when Adiaha had a son; so she went again to the Ju Ju man, and by giving him a large present induced him to give her some medicine which would make the king sick and forget his son. And the medicine would then make the king go to the Ju Ju man, who would tell him that it was his son who had made him sick, as he wanted to reign instead of his father. The Ju Ju man would also tell the king that if he wanted to recover he must throw his son away into the water.

And the king, when he had taken the medicine, went to the Ju Ju man, who told him everything as had been arranged with the head wife. But at first the king did not want to destroy his son. Then his chief subjects begged him to throw his son away, and said that perhaps in a year's time he might get another son. So the king at last agreed, and threw his son into the river, at which the mother grieved and cried bitterly.

Then the head wife went again to the Ju Ju man and got more medicine, which made the king forget Adiaha for three years, during which time she was in mourning for her son. She then returned to her father, and he got some more medicine from his Ju Ju man, which Adiaha gave to the king. And the king knew her and called her to him again, and she lived with him as before. Now the Ju Ju who had helped Adiaha's father, the spider, was a Water Ju Ju, and he was ready when the king threw his son into the water, and saved his life and took him home and kept him alive. And the boy grew up very strong.

After a time Adiaha gave birth to a daughter, and her the jealous wife also persuaded the king to throw away. It took a longer time to persuade him, but at last he agreed, and threw his daughter into the water too, and forgot Adiaha again. But the Water Ju Ju was ready again, and when he had saved the little girl, he thought the time had arrived to punish the action of the jealous wife; so he went about amongst the head young men and persuaded them to hold a wrestling match in the market-place every week. This was done, and the Water Ju Ju told the king's son, who had become very strong, and was very like to his father in appearance, that he should go and wrestle, and that no one would be able to stand up before him. It was then arranged that there should be a grand wrestling match, to which all the strongest men in the country were invited, and the king promised to attend with his head wife.

On the day of the match the Water Ju Ju told the king's son that he need not be in the least afraid, and that his Ju Ju was so powerful, that even the strongest and best wrestlers in the country would not be able to stand up against him for even a few minutes. All the people of the country came to see the great contest, to the winner of which the king had promised to present prizes of cloth and money, and all the strongest men came. When they saw the king's son, whom nobody knew, they laughed and said, "Who is this small boy? He can have no chance against us." But when they came to wrestle, they very soon found that they were no match for him. The boy was very strong indeed, beautifully made and good to look upon, and all the people were surprised to see how like he was to the king.

After wrestling for the greater part of the day the king's son was declared the winner, having thrown everyone who had stood up against him; in fact, some of his opponents had been badly hurt, and had their arms or ribs broken owing to the tremendous strength of the boy. After the match was over the king presented him with cloth and money, and invited him to dine with him in the evening. The boy gladly accepted his father's invitation; and after he had had a good wash in the river, put on his cloth and went up to the palace, where he found the head chiefs of the country and some of the king's most favoured wives. They then sat down to their meal, and the king had his own son, whom he did not know, sitting next to him. On the other side of the boy sat the jealous wife, who had been the cause of all the trouble. All through the dinner this woman did her best to make friends with the boy, with whom she had fallen violently in love on account of his beautiful appearance, his strength, and his being the best wrestler in the country. The woman thought to herself, "I will have this boy as my husband, as my husband is now an old man and will surely soon die." The boy, however, who was as wise as he was strong, was quite aware of everything the jealous woman had done, and although he pretended to be very flattered at the advances of the king's head wife, he did not respond very readily, and went home as soon as he could.

When he returned to the Water Ju Ju's house he told him everything that had happened, and the Water Ju Ju said:

"As you are now in high favour with the king, you must go to him tomorrow and beg a favour from him. The favour you will ask is that all the country shall be called together, and that a certain case shall be tried, and that when the case is finished, the man or woman who is found to be in the wrong shall be killed by the Egbos before all the people."

So the following morning the boy went to the king, who readily granted his request, and at once sent all round the country appointing a day for all the people to come in and hear the case tried. Then the boy went back to the Water Ju Ju, who told him to go to his mother and tell her who he was, and that when the day of the trial arrived, she was to take off her ugly skin and appear in all her beauty, for the time had come when she need no longer wear it. This the son did.

When the day of trial arrived, Adiaha sat in a corner of the square, and nobody recognised the beautiful stranger as the spider's daughter. Her son then sat down next to her, and brought his sister with him. Immediately his mother saw her she said:

"This must be my daughter, whom I have long mourned as dead," and embraced her most affectionately.

The king and his head wife then arrived and sat on their stones in the middle of the square, all the people saluting them with the usual greetings. The king then addressed the people, and said that he had called them together to hear a strong palaver at the request of the young man who had been the victor of the wrestling, and who had promised that if the case went against him he would offer up his life to the Egbo. The king also said that if, on the other hand, the case was decided in the boy's favour, then the other party would be killed, even though it were himself or one of his wives; whoever it was would have to take his or her place on the killing-stone and have their heads cut off by the Egbos. To this all the people agreed, and said they would like to hear what the young man had to say. The young man then walked round the square, and bowed to the king and the people, and asked the question, "Am I not worthy to be the son of any chief in the country?" And all the people answered "Yes!"

The boy then brought his sister out into the middle, leading her by the hand. She was a beautiful girl and well made. When everyone had looked at her he said, "Is not my sister worthy to be any chief's daughter?" And the people replied that she was worthy of being anyone's daughter, even the king's. Then he called his mother Adiaha, and she came out, looking very beautiful with her best cloth and beads on, and all the people cheered, as they had never seen a finer woman. The boy then asked them, "Is this woman worthy of being the king's wife?" And a shout went up from everyone present that she would be a proper wife for the king, and looked as if she would be the mother of plenty of fine healthy sons.

Then the boy pointed out the jealous woman who was sitting next to the king, and told the people his story, how that his mother, who had two skins, was the spider's daughter; how she had married the king, and how the head wife was jealous and had made a bad Ju Ju for the king, which made him forget his wife; how she had persuaded the king to throw himself and his sister into the river, which, as they all knew, had been done, but the Water Ju Ju had saved both of them, and had brought them up.

Then the boy said: "I leave the king and all of you people to judge my case. If I have done wrong, let me be killed on the stone by the Egbos; if, on the other hand, the woman has done evil, then let the Egbos deal with her as you may decide."

When the king knew that the wrestler was his son he was very glad, and told the Egbos to take the jealous woman away, and punish her in accordance with their laws. The Egbos decided that the woman was a witch; so they took her into the forest and tied her up to a stake, and gave her two hundred lashes with a whip made from hippopotamus hide, and then burnt her alive, so that she should not make any more trouble, and her ashes were thrown into the river. The king then embraced his wife and daughter, and told all the people that she, Adiaha, was his proper wife, and would be the queen for the future.

When the palaver was over, Adiaha was dressed in fine clothes and beads, and carried back in state to the palace by the king's servants.

That night the king gave a big feast to all his subjects, and told them how glad he was to get back his beautiful wife whom he had never known properly before, also his son who was stronger than all men, and his fine daughter. The feast continued for a hundred and sixty-six days; and the king made a law that if any woman was found out getting medicine against her husband, she should be killed at once. Then the king built three new compounds, and placed many slaves in them, both men and women. One compound he gave to his wife, another to his son, and the third he gave to his daughter. They all lived together quite happily for some years until the king died, when his son came to the throne and ruled in his stead.

Ituen and the King's Wife

(From southern Nigeria)

ITUEN WAS A YOUNG MAN OF CALABAR. He was the only child of his parents, and they were extremely fond of him, as he was of fine proportions and very good to look upon. They were poor people, and when Ituen grew up and became a man, he had very little money indeed, in fact he had so little food, that every day it was his custom to go to the market carrying an empty bag, into which he used to put anything eatable he could find after the market was over.

At this time Offiong was king. He was an old man, but he had plenty of wives. One of these women, named Attem, was quite young and very good-looking. She did not like her old husband, but wished for a young and handsome husband. She therefore told her servant to go round the town and the market to try and find such a man and to bring him at night by the side door to her house, and she herself would let him in, and would take care that her husband did not discover him.

That day the servant went all round the town, but failed to find any young man good-looking enough. She was just returning to report her ill-success when, on passing through the market-place, she saw Ituen picking up the remains of corn and other things which had been left on the ground. She was immediately struck with his fine appearance and strength, and saw that he was just the man to make a proper lover for her mistress, so she went up to him, and said that the queen had sent for him, as she was so taken with his good looks. At first Ituen was frightened and refused to go, as he knew that if the King discovered him he would be killed. However, after much persuasion he consented, and agreed to go to the queen's side door when it was dark.

When night came he went with great fear and trembling, and knocked very softly at the queen's door. The door was opened at once by the queen herself, who was dressed in all her best clothes, and had many necklaces, beads, and anklets on. Directly she saw Ituen she fell in love with him at once, and praised his good looks and his shapely limbs. She then told her servant to bring water and clothes, and after he had had a good wash and put on a clean cloth, he rejoined the queen. She hid him in her house all the night.

In the morning when he wished to go she would not let him, but, although it was very dangerous, she hid him in the house, and secretly conveyed food and clothes to him. Ituen stayed there for two weeks, and then he said that it was time for him to go and see his mother, but the queen persuaded him to stay another week, much against his will.

When the time came for him to depart, the queen got together fifty carriers with presents for Ituen's mother who, she knew, was a poor woman. Ten slaves carried three hundred rods; the other forty carried yams, pepper, salt, tobacco, and cloth. When all the presents arrived Ituen's mother was very pleased and embraced her son, and noticed with pleasure that he was looking well, and was dressed in much finer clothes than usual; but when she heard that he had attracted the queen's attention she was frightened, as she knew the penalty imposed on anyone who attracted the attention of one of the king's wives.

Ituen stayed for a month in his parents' house and worked on the farm; but the queen could not be without her lover any longer, so she sent for him to go to her at once. Ituen went again, and, as before, arrived at night, when the queen was delighted to see him again.

In the middle of the night some of the king's servants, who had been told the story by the slaves who had carried the presents to Ituen's mother, came into the queen's room and surprised her there with Ituen. They hastened to the king, and told him what they had seen. Ituen was then made a prisoner, and the king sent out to all his people to attend at the palaver house to hear the case tried. He also ordered eight Egbos to attend armed with machetes. When the case was tried Ituen was found guilty, and the king told the eight Egbo men to take him into the bush and deal with him according to native custom. The Egbos then took Ituen into the bush and tied him up to a tree; then with a sharp knife they cut off his lower jaw, and carried it to the king.

When the queen heard the fate of her lover she was very sad, and cried for three days. This made the king angry, so he told the Egbos to deal with his wife and her servant according to their law. They took the queen and the servant into the bush, where Ituen was still tied up to the tree dying and in great pain. Then, as the queen had nothing to say in her defence, they tied her and the girl up to different trees, and cut the queen's lower jaw off in the same way as they had her lover's. The Egbos then put out both the eyes of the servant, and left all three to die of starvation. The king then made an Egbo law that for the future no one belonging to Ituen's family was to go into the market on market day, and that no one was to pick up the rubbish in the market. The king made an exception to the law in favour of the vulture and the dog, who were not considered very fine people, and would not be likely to run off with one of the king's wives, and that is why you still find vultures and dogs doing scavenger in the market-places even at the present time.

Of the Pretty Stranger Who Killed the King
(From southern Nigeria)

MBOTU WAS A VERY FAMOUS KING of Old Town, Calabar. He was frequently at war, and was always successful, as he was a most skilful leader. All the prisoners he took were made slaves. He therefore became very rich, but, on the other hand, he had many enemies. The people of Itu in particular were very angry with him and wanted to kill him, but they were not strong enough to beat Mbotu in a pitched battle, so they had to resort to craft.

The Itu people had an old woman who was a witch and could turn herself into whatever she pleased, and when she offered to kill Mbotu, the people were very glad, and promised her plenty of money and cloth if she succeeded in ridding them of their worst enemy. The witch then turned herself into a young and pretty girl, and having armed herself with a very sharp knife, which she concealed in her bosom, she went to Old Town, Calabar, to seek the king.

It happened that when she arrived there was a big play being held in the town, and all the people from the surrounding country had come in to dance and feast. Oyaikan, the witch, went to the play, and walked about so that everyone could see her. Directly she appeared the people all marvelled at her beauty, and said that she was as beautiful as the setting sun when all the sky was red. Word was quickly brought to king Mbotu, who, it was well known, was fond of pretty girls, and he sent for her at once, all the people agreeing that she was quite worthy of being the king's wife. When she appeared before him he fancied her so much, that he told her he would marry her that very day. Oyaikan was very pleased at this, as she had never expected to get her opportunity so quickly. She therefore prepared a dainty meal for the king, into which she placed a strong medicine to make the king sleep, and then went down to the river to wash.

When she had finished it was getting dark, so she went to the king's compound, carrying her dish on her head, and was at once shown in to the king, who embraced her affectionately. She then offered him the food, which she said, quite truly, she had prepared with her own hands. The king ate the whole dish, and immediately began to feel very sleepy, as the medicine was strong and took effect quickly.

They retired to the king's chamber, and the king went to sleep at once. About midnight, when all the town was quiet, Oyaikan drew her knife from her bosom and cut the king's head off. She put the head in a bag and went out very softly, shutting and barring the door behind her. Then she walked through the town without anyone observing her, and went straight to Itu, where she placed king Mbotu's head before her own king.

When the people heard that the witch had been successful and that their enemy was dead, there was great rejoicing, and the king of Itu at once made up his mind to attack Old Town, Calabar. He therefore got his fighting men together and took them in canoes by the creeks to Old Town, taking care that no one carried word to Calabar that he was coming.

The morning following the murder of Mbotu his people were rather surprised that he did not appear at his usual time, so his head wife knocked at his door. Not receiving any answer, she called the household together, and they broke open the door. When they entered the room, they found the king lying dead on his bed covered in blood, but his head was missing. At this a great shout went up, and the whole town mourned. Although they missed the pretty stranger, they never connected her in their minds with the death of their king, and were quite unsuspicious of any danger, and were unprepared for fighting. In the middle of the mourning, while they were all dancing, crying, and drinking palm wine, the king of Itu with all his soldiers attacked Old Town, taking them quite by surprise, and as their leader was dead, the Calabar people were very soon defeated, and many killed and taken prisoners.

Moral: Never marry a stranger, no matter how pretty she may be.

Of the Fat Woman Who Melted Away
(From southern Nigeria)

THERE WAS ONCE a very fat woman who was made of oil. She was very beautiful, and many young men applied to the parents for permission to marry their daughter, and offered

dowry, but the mother always refused, as she said it was impossible for her daughter to work on a farm, as she would melt in the sun. At last a stranger came from a far-distant country and fell in love with the fat woman, and he promised if her mother would hand her to him that he would keep her in the shade. At last the mother agreed, and he took his wife away.

When he arrived at his house, his other wife immediately became very jealous, because when there was work to be done, firewood to be collected, or water to be carried, the fat woman stayed at home and never helped, as she was frightened of the heat.

One day when the husband was absent, the jealous wife abused the fat woman so much that she finally agreed to go and work on the farm, although her little sister, whom she had brought from home with her, implored her not to go, reminding her that their mother had always told them ever since they were born that she would melt away if she went into the sun. All the way to the farm the fat woman managed to keep in the shade, and when they arrived at the farm the sun was very hot, so the fat woman remained in the shade of a big tree. When the jealous wife saw this she again began abusing her, and asked her why she did not do her share of the work. At last she could stand the nagging no longer, and although her little sister tried very hard to prevent her, the fat woman went out into the sun to work, and immediately began to melt away. There was very soon nothing left of her but one big toe, which had been covered by a leaf. This her little sister observed, and with tears in her eyes she picked up the toe, which was all that remained of the fat woman, and having covered it carefully with leaves, placed it in the bottom of her basket. When she arrived at the house the little sister placed the toe in an earthen pot, filled it with water, and covered the top up with clay.

When the husband returned, he said, "Where is my fat wife?" and the little sister, crying bitterly, told him that the jealous woman had made her go out into the sun, and that she had melted away. She then showed him the pot with the remains of her sister, and told him that her sister would come to life again in three months' time quite complete, but he must send away the jealous wife, so that there should be no more trouble; if he refused to do this, the little girl said she would take the pot back to their mother, and when her sister became complete again they would remain at home.

The husband then took the jealous wife back to her parents, who sold her as a slave and paid the dowry back to the husband, so that he could get another wife. When he received the money, the husband took it home and kept it until the three months had elapsed, when the little sister opened the pot and the fat woman emerged, quite as fat and beautiful as she had been before. The husband was so delighted that he gave a feast to all his friends and neighbours, and told them the whole story of the bad behaviour of his jealous wife.

Ever since that time, whenever a wife behaves very badly the husband returns her to the parents, who sell the woman as a slave, and out of the proceeds of the sale reimburse the husband the amount of dowry which he paid when he married the girl.

The Lucky Fisherman
(From southern Nigeria)

IN THE OLDEN DAYS there were no hooks or casting nets, so that when the natives wanted to catch fish they made baskets and set traps at the river side.

One man named Akon Obo, who was very poor, began to make baskets and traps out of bamboo palm, and then when the river went down he used to take his traps to a pool and set them baited with palm-nuts. In the night the big fish used to smell the palm-nuts and go into the trap, when at once the door would fall down, and in the morning Akon Obo would go and take the fish out. He was very successful in his fishing, and used to sell the fish in the market for plenty of money. When he could afford to pay the dowry he married a woman named Eyong, a native of Okuni, and had three children by her, but he still continued his fishing. The eldest son was called Odey, the second Yambi, and the third Atuk. These three boys, when they grew up, helped their father with his fishing, and he gradually became wealthy and bought plenty of slaves. At last he joined the Egbo society, and became one of the chiefs of the town. Even after he became a chief, he and his sons still continued to fish.

One day, when he was crossing the river in a small dug-out canoe, a tornado came on very suddenly, and the canoe capsized, drowning the chief. When his sons heard of the death of their father, they wanted to go and drown themselves also, but they were persuaded not to by the people. After searching for two days, they found the dead body some distance down the river, and brought it back to the town. They then called their company together to play, dance, and sing for twelve days, in accordance with their native custom, and much palm wine was drunk.

When the play was finished, they took their father's body to a hollowed-out cavern, and placed two live slaves with it, one holding a native lamp of palm-oil, and the other holding a matchet. They were both tied up, so that they could not escape, and were left there to keep watch over the dead chief, until they died of starvation.

When the cave was covered in, the sons called the chiefs together, and they played Egbo for seven days, which used up a lot of their late father's money. When the play was over, the chiefs were surprised at the amount of money which the sons had been able to spend on the funeral of their father, as they knew how poor he had been as a young man. They therefore called him the lucky fisherman.

Goso, the Teacher
(From Zanzibar, Tanzanian coast)

ONCE THERE WAS A MAN named Goso, who taught children to read, not in a schoolhouse, but under a calabash tree. One evening, while Goso was sitting under the tree deep in the study of the next day's lessons, Paa, the gazelle, climbed up the tree very quietly to steal some fruit, and in so doing shook off a calabash, which, in falling, struck the teacher on the head and killed him.

When his scholars came in the morning and found their teacher lying dead, they were filled with grief; so, after giving him a decent burial, they agreed among themselves to find the one who had killed Goso, and put him to death.

After talking the matter over they came to the conclusion that the south wind was the offender.

So they caught the south wind and beat it.

But the south wind cried: "Here! I am Koosee, the south wind. Why are you beating me? What have I done?"

And they said: "Yes, we know you are Koosee; it was you who threw down the calabash that struck our teacher Goso. You should not have done it."

But Koosee said, "If I were so powerful would I be stopped by a mud wall?"

So they went to the mud wall and beat it.

But the mud wall cried: "Here! I am Keeyambaaza, the mud wall. Why are you beating me? What have I done?"

And they said: "Yes, we know you are Keeyambaaza; it was you who stopped Koosee, the south wind; and Koosee, the south wind, threw down the calabash that struck our teacher Goso. You should not have done it."

But Keeyambaaza said, "If I were so powerful would I be bored through by the rat?"

So they went and caught the rat and beat it.

But the rat cried: "Here! I am Paanya, the rat. Why are you beating me? What have I done?"

And they said: "Yes, we know you are Paanya; it was you who bored through Keeyambaaza, the mud wall; which stopped Koosee, the south wind; and Koosee, the south wind, threw down the calabash that struck our teacher Goso. You should not have done it."

But Paanya said, "If I were so powerful would I be eaten by a cat?"

So they hunted for the cat, caught it, and beat it.

But the cat cried: "Here! I am Paaka, the cat. Why do you beat me? What have I done?"

And they said: "Yes, we know you are Paaka; it is you that eats Paanya, the rat; who bores through Keeyambaaza, the mud wall; which stopped Koosee, the south wind; and Koosee, the south wind, threw down the calabash that struck our teacher Goso. You should not have done it."

But Paaka said, "If I were so powerful would I be tied by a rope?"

So they took the rope and beat it.

But the rope cried: "Here! I am Kaamba, the rope. Why do you beat me? What have I done?"

And they said: "Yes, we know you are Kaamba; it is you that ties Paaka, the cat; who eats Paanya, the rat; who bores through Keeyambaaza, the mud wall; which stopped Koosee, the south wind; and Koosee, the south wind, threw down the calabash that struck our teacher Goso. You should not have done it."

But Kaamba said, "If I were so powerful would I be cut by a knife?"

So they took the knife and beat it.

But the knife cried: "Here! I am Keesoo, the knife. Why do you beat me? What have I done?"

And they said: "Yes, we know you are Keesoo; you cut Kaamba, the rope; that ties Paaka, the cat; who eats Paanya, the rat; who bores through Keeyambaaza, the mud wall; which stopped Koosee, the south wind; and Koosee, the south wind, threw down the calabash that struck our teacher Goso. You should not have done it."

But Keesoo said, "If I were so powerful would I be burned by the fire?"

And they went and beat the fire.

But the fire cried: "Here! I am Moto, the fire. Why do you beat me? What have I done?"

And they said: "Yes, we know you are Moto; you burn Keesoo, the knife; that cuts Kaamba, the rope; that ties Paaka, the cat; who eats Paanya, the rat; who bores through Keeyambaaza, the mud wall; which stopped Koosee, the south wind; and Koosee, the south wind, threw down the calabash that struck our teacher Goso. You should not have done it."

But Moto said, "If I were so powerful would I be put out by water?"

And they went to the water and beat it.

But the water cried: "Here! I am Maajee, the water. Why do you beat me? What have I done?"

And they said: "Yes, we know you are Maajee; you put out Moto, the fire; that burns Keesoo, the knife; that cuts Kaamba, the rope; that ties Paaka, the cat; who eats Paanya, the rat; who bores through Keeyambaaza, the mud wall; which stopped Koosee, the south wind; and Koosee, the south wind, threw down the calabash that struck our teacher Goso. You should not have done it."

But Maajee said, "If I were so powerful would I be drunk by the ox?"

And they went to the ox and beat it.

But the ox cried: "Here! I am Ngombay, the ox. Why do you beat me? What have I done?"

And they said: "Yes, we know you are Ngombay; you drink Maajee, the water; that puts out Moto, the fire; that burns Keesoo, the knife; that cuts Kaamba, the rope; that ties Paaka, the cat; who eats Paanya, the rat; who bores through Keeyambaaza, the mud wall; which stopped Koosee, the south wind; and Koosee, the south wind, threw down the calabash that struck our teacher Goso. You should not have done it."

But Ngombay said, "If I were so powerful would I be tormented by the fly?"

And they caught a fly and beat it.

But the fly cried: "Here! I am Eenzee, the fly. Why do you beat me? What have I done?"

And they said: "Yes, we know you are Eenzee; you torment Ngombay, the ox; who drinks Maajee, the water; that puts out Moto, the fire; that burns Keesoo, the knife; that cuts Kaamba, the rope; that ties Paaka, the cat; who eats Paanya, the rat; who bores through Keeyambaaza, the mud wall; which stopped Koosee, the south wind; and Koosee, the south wind, threw down the calabash that struck our teacher Goso. You should not have done it."

But Eenzee said, "If I were so powerful would I be eaten by the gazelle?"

And they searched for the gazelle, and when they found it they beat it.

But the gazelle said: "Here! I am Paa, the gazelle. Why do you beat me? What have I done?"

And they said: "Yes, we know you are Paa; you eat Eenzee, the fly; that torments Ng"ombay, the ox; who drinks Maajee, the water; that puts out Moto, the fire; that burns Keesoo, the knife; that cuts Kaamba, the rope; that ties Paaka, the cat; who eats Paanya, the rat; who bores through Keeyambaaza, the mud wall; which stopped Koosee, the south wind; and Koosee, the south wind, threw down the calabash that struck our teacher Goso. You should not have done it."

The gazelle, through surprise at being found out and fear of the consequences of his accidental killing of the teacher, while engaged in stealing, was struck dumb.

Then the scholars said: "Ah! he hasn't a word to say for himself. This is the fellow who threw down the calabash that struck our teacher Goso. We will kill him."

So they killed Paa, the gazelle, and avenged the death of their teacher.

The Magician and the Sultan's Son
(From Zanzibar, Tanzanian coast)

THERE WAS ONCE a sultan who had three little sons, and no one seemed to be able to teach them anything; which greatly grieved both the sultan and his wife.

One day a magician came to the sultan and said, "If I take your three boys and teach them to read and write, and make great scholars of them, what will you give me?"

And the sultan said, "I will give you half of my property."

"No," said the magician; "that won't do."

"I'll give you half of the towns I own."

"No; that will not satisfy me."

"What do you want, then?"

"When I have made them scholars and bring them back to you, choose two of them for yourself and give me the third; for I want to have a companion of my own."

"Agreed," said the sultan.

So the magician took them away, and in a remarkably short time taught them to read, and to make letters, and made them quite good scholars. Then he took them back to the sultan and said: "Here are the children. They are all equally good scholars. Choose."

So the sultan took the two he preferred, and the magician went away with the third, whose name was Keejaanaa, to his own house, which was a very large one.

When they arrived, Mchaawee, the magician, gave the youth all the keys, saying, "Open whatever you wish to." Then he told him that he was his father, and that he was going away for a month.

When he was gone, Keejaanaa took the keys and went to examine the house. He opened one door, and saw a room full of liquid gold. He put his finger in, and the gold stuck to it, and, wipe and rub as he would, the gold would not come off; so he wrapped a piece of rag around it, and when his supposed father came home and saw the rag, and asked him what he had been doing to his finger, he was afraid to tell him the truth, so he said that he had cut it.

Not very long after, Mchaawee went away again, and the youth took the keys and continued his investigations.

The first room he opened was filled with the bones of goats, the next with sheep's bones, the next with the bones of oxen, the fourth with the bones of donkeys, the fifth with those of horses, the sixth contained men's skulls, and in the seventh was a live horse.

"Hullo!" said the horse; "where do you come from, you son of Adam?"

"This is my father's house," said Keejaanaa.

"Oh, indeed!" was the reply. "Well, you've got a pretty nice parent! Do you know that he occupies himself with eating people, and donkeys, and horses, and oxen and goats and everything he can lay his hands on? You and I are the only living things left."

This scared the youth pretty badly, and he faltered, "What are we to do?"

"What's your name?" said the horse.

"Keejaanaa."

"Well, I'm Faaraasee. Now, Keejaanaa, first of all, come and unfasten me."

The youth did so at once.

"Now, then, open the door of the room with the gold in it, and I will swallow it all; then I'll go and wait for you under the big tree down the road a little way. When the magician comes home, he will say to you, 'Let us go for firewood;' then you answer, 'I don't understand that work;' and he will go by himself. When he comes back, he will put a great big pot on the hook and will tell you to make a fire under it. Tell him you don't know how to make a fire, and he will make it himself.

"Then he will bring a large quantity of butter, and while it is getting hot he will put up a swing and say to you, 'Get up there, and I'll swing you.' But you tell him you never played at that game, and ask him to swing first, that you may see how it is done. Then he will get up to show you; and you must push him into the big pot, and then come to me as quickly as you can."

Then the horse went away.

Now, Mchaawee had invited some of his friends to a feast at his house that evening; so, returning home early, he said to Keejaanaa, "Let us go for firewood;" but the youth answered, "I don't understand that work." So he went by himself and brought the wood.

Then he hung up the big pot and said, "Light the fire;" but the youth said, "I don't know how to do it." So the magician laid the wood under the pot and lighted it himself.

Then he said, "Put all that butter in the pot;" but the youth answered, "I can't lift it; I'm not strong enough." So he put in the butter himself.

Next Mchaawee said, "Have you seen our country game?" And Keejaanaa answered, "I think not."

"Well," said the magician, "let's play at it while the butter is getting hot."

So he tied up the swing and said to Keejaanaa, "Get up here, and learn the game." But the youth said: "You get up first and show me. I'll learn quicker that way."

The magician got into the swing, and just as he got started Keejaanaa gave him a push right into the big pot; and as the butter was by this time boiling, it not only killed him, but cooked him also.

As soon as the youth had pushed the magician into the big pot, he ran as fast as he could to the big tree, where the horse was waiting for him.

"Come on," said Faaraasee; "jump on my back and let's be going."

So he mounted and they started off.

When the magician's guests arrived they looked everywhere for him, but, of course, could not find him. Then, after waiting a while, they began to be very hungry; so, looking around for something to eat, they saw that the stew in the big pot was done, and, saying to each other, "Let's begin, anyway," they started in and ate the entire contents of the pot. After they had finished, they searched for Mchaawee again, and finding lots of provisions in the house, they thought they would stay there until he came; but after they had waited a couple of days and eaten all the food in the place, they gave him up and returned to their homes.

Meanwhile Keejaanaa and the horse continued on their way until they had gone a great distance, and at last they stopped near a large town.

"Let us stay here," said the youth, "and build a house."

As Faaraasee was agreeable, they did so. The horse coughed up all the gold he had swallowed, with which they purchased slaves, and cattle, and everything they needed.

When the people of the town saw the beautiful new house and all the slaves, and cattle, and riches it contained, they went and told their sultan, who at once made up his mind that the owner of such a place must be of sufficient importance to be visited and taken notice of, as an acquisition to the neighbourhood.

So he called on Keejaanaa, and inquired who he was.

"Oh, I'm just an ordinary being, like other people."

"Are you a traveller?"

"Well, I have been; but I like this place, and think I'll settle down here."

"Why don't you come and walk in our town?"

"I should like to very much, but I need someone to show me around."

"Oh, I'll show you around," said the sultan, eagerly, for he was quite taken with the young man.

After this Keejaanaa and the sultan became great friends; and in the course of time the young man married the sultan's daughter, and they had one son.

They lived very happily together, and Keejaanaa loved Faaraasee as his own soul.

King Gumbi and His Lost Daughter

(From the Manyema people of the Congo)

IT WAS BELIEVED IN THE OLDEN TIME that if a king's daughter had the misfortune to be guilty of ten mistakes, she should suffer for half of them, and her father would be punished for the rest. Now, King Gumbi had lately married ten wives, and all at once this old belief of the elders about troubles with daughters came into his head, and he issued a command, which was to be obeyed upon pain of death, that if any female children should be

born to him they should be thrown into the Lualaba, and drowned, for, said he, "the dead are beyond temptation to err, and I shall escape mischief."

To avoid the reproaches of his wives, on account of the cruel order, the king thought he would absent himself, and he took a large following with him and went to visit other towns of his country. Within a few days after his departure there were born to him five sons and five daughters. Four of the female infants were at once disposed of according to the king's command; but when the fifth daughter was born, she was so beautiful, and had such great eyes, and her colour was mellow, so like a ripe banana, that the chief nurse hesitated, and when the mother pleaded so hard for her child's life, she made up her mind that the little infant should be saved. When the mother was able to rise, the nurse hastened her away secretly by night. In the morning the queen found herself in a dark forest, and, being alone, she began to talk to herself, as people generally do, and a grey parrot with a beautiful red tail came flying along, and asked, "What is it you are saying to yourself, O Miami?"

She answered and said, "Ah, beautiful little parrot, I am thinking what I ought to do to save the life of my little child. Tell me how I can save her, for Gumbi wishes to destroy all his female children."

The parrot replied, "I grieve for you greatly, but I do not know. Ask the next parrot you see," and he flew away.

A second parrot still more beautiful came flying towards her, whistling and screeching merrily, and the queen lifted her voice and cried:

"Ah, little parrot, stop a bit, and tell me how I can save my sweet child's life; for cruel Gumbi, her father, wants to kill it."

"Ah, mistress, I may not tell; but there is one comes behind me who knows; ask him," and he also flew to his day's haunts.

Then the third parrot was seen to fly towards her, and he made the forest ring with his happy whistling, and Miami cried out again:

"Oh, stay, little parrot, and tell me in what way I can save my sweet child, for Gumbi, her father, vows he will kill it."

"Deliver it to me," answered the parrot. "But first let me put a small banana stalk and two pieces of sugar-cane with it, and then I shall carry it safely to its grandmamma."

The parrot relieved the queen of her child, and flew through the air, screeching merrier than before, and in a short time had laid the little princess, her banana stalk, and two pieces of sugar-cane in the lap of the grandmamma, who was sitting at the door of her house, and said:

"This bundle contains a gift from your daughter, wife of Gumbi. She bids you be careful of it, and let none out of your own family see it, lest she should be slain by the king. And to remember this day, she requests you to plant the banana stalk in your garden at one end, and at the other end the two pieces of sugar-cane, for you may need both."

"Your words are good and wise," answered granny, as she received the babe.

On opening the bundle the old woman discovered a female child, exceedingly pretty, plump, and yellow as a ripe banana, with large black eyes, and such smiles on its bright face that the grandmother's heart glowed with affection for it.

Many seasons came and went by. No stranger came round to ask questions. The banana flourished and grew into a grove, and each sprout marked the passage of a season, and the sugar-cane likewise throve prodigiously as year after year passed and the infant grew into girlhood. When the princess had bloomed into a beautiful maiden, the grandmother had become so old that the events of long ago appeared to her to be like so many dreams, but she still worshipped her child's child, cooked for her, waited upon her, wove new grass mats for her bed, and fine grass-cloths for her dress, and every night before she retired she washed her dainty feet.

Then one day, before her ears were quite closed by age, and her limbs had become too weak to bear her about, the parrot who brought the child to her, came and rested upon a branch near her door, and after piping and whistling its greeting, cried out, "The time has come. Gumbi's daughter must depart, and seek her father. Furnish her with a little drum, teach her a song to sing while she beats it, and send her forth."

Then granny purchased for her a tiny drum, and taught her a song, and when she had been fully instructed she prepared a new canoe with food – from the bananas in the grove, and the plot of sugar-cane, and she made cushions from grass-cloth bags stuffed with silk-cotton floss for her to rest upon. When all was ready she embraced her grand-daughter, and with many tears sent her away down the river, with four women servants.

Granny stood for a long time by the river bank, watching the little canoe disappear with the current, then she turned and entered the doorway, and sitting down closed her eyes, and began to think of the pleasant life she had enjoyed while serving Miami's child; and while so doing she was so pleased that she smiled, and as she smiled she slept, and never woke again.

But the princess, as she floated down and bathed her eyes, which had smarted with her grief, began to think of all that granny had taught her, and began to sing in a fluty voice, as she beat her tiny drum:

"List, all you men,
To the song I sing.
I am Gumbi's child,
Brought up in the wild;
And home I return,
As you all will learn,
When this my little drum
Tells Gumbi I have come, come, come."

The sound of her drum attracted the attention of the fishermen who were engaged with their nets, and seeing a strange canoe with only five women aboard floating down the river, they drew near to it, and when they saw how beautiful the princess was, and noted her graceful, lithe figure clad in robes of fine grass-cloths, they were inclined to lay their hands upon her. But she sang again:

"I am Gumbi's child,
Make way for me;
I am homeward bound,
Make way for me."

Then the fishermen were afraid and did not molest her. But one desirous of being the first to carry the news to the king, and obtain favour and a reward for it, hastened away to tell him that his daughter was coming to visit him.

The news plunged King Gumbi into a state of wonder, for as he had taken such pains to destroy all female children, he could not imagine how he could be the father of a daughter.

Then he sent a quick-footed and confidential slave to inquire, who soon returned and assured him that the girl who was coming to him was his own true daughter.

Then he sent a man who had grown up with him, who knew all that had happened in his court; and he also returned and confirmed all that the slave had said.

Upon this he resolved to go himself, and when he met her he asked:

"Who art thou, child?"

And she replied, "I am the only daughter of Gumbi."

"And who is Gumbi?"

"He is the king of this country," she replied.

"Well, but I am Gumbi myself, and how canst thou be my daughter?" he asked.

"I am the child of thy wife, Miami, and after I was born she hid me that I might not be cast into the river. I have been living with grandmamma, who nursed me, and by the number of banana-stalks in her garden thou mayest tell the number of the seasons that have passed since my birth. One day she told me the time had come, and she sent me to seek my father; and I embarked in the canoe with four servants, and the river bore me to this land."

"Well," said Gumbi, "when I return home I shall question Miami, and I shall soon discover the truth of thy story; but meantime, what must I do for thee?"

"My grandmamma said that thou must sacrifice a goat to the meeting of the daughter with the father," she replied.

Then the king requested her to step on the shore, and when he saw the flash of her yellow feet, and the gleams of her body, which were like shining bright gum, and gazed on the clear, smooth features, and looked into the wondrous black eyes, Gumbi's heart melted and he was filled with pride that such a surpassingly beautiful creature should be his own daughter.

But she refused to set her feet on the shore until another goat had been sacrificed, for her grandmother had said ill-luck would befall her if these ceremonies were neglected.

Therefore the king commanded that two goats should be slain, one for the meeting with his daughter, and one to drive away ill-luck from before her in the land where she would first rest her feet.

When this had been done, she said, "Now, father, it is not meet that thy recovered daughter should soil her feet on the path to her father's house. Thou must lay a grass-cloth along the ground all the way to my mother's door."

The king thereupon ordered a grass-cloth to be spread along the path towards the women's quarters, but he did not mention to which doorway. His daughter then moved forward, the king by her side, until they came in view of all the king's wives, and then Gumbi cried out to them: "One of you, I am told, is the mother of this girl. Look on her, and be not ashamed to own her, for she is as perfect as the egg. At the first sight of her I felt like a man filled with pleasantness, so let the mother come forward and claim her, and let her not destroy herself with a lie."

Now all the women bent forward and longed to say, "She is mine, she is mine!" but Miami, who was ill and weak, sat at the door, and said:

"Continue the matting to my doorway, for as I feel my heart is connected with her as by a cord, she must be the child whom the parrot carried to my mother with a banana stalk and two pieces of sugar-cane."

"Yes, yes, thou must be my own mother," cried the princess; and when the grass-cloth was laid even to the inside of the house, she ran forward, and folded her arms around her.

When Gumbi saw them together he said, "Truly, equals always come together. I see now by many things that the princess must be right. But she will not long remain with me, I fear, for a king's daughter cannot remain many moons without suitors."

Now though Gumbi considered it a trifle to destroy children whom he had never seen, it never entered into his mind to hurt Miami or the princess. On the contrary, he was filled with a gladness which he was never tired of talking about. He was even prouder of his daughter, whose lovely shape and limpid eyes so charmed him, than of all his tall sons. He proved this by the feasts he caused to be provided for all the people. Goats were roasted and stewed, the fishermen brought fish without number, the peasants came loaded with weighty bunches of bananas, and baskets of yams, and manioc, and pots full of beans, and vetches, and millet and corn, and honey and palm-oil, and as for the fowls – who could count them? The people also had plenty to drink of the juice of the palm, and thus they were made to rejoice with the king in the return of the princess.

It was soon spread throughout Manyema that no woman was like unto Gumbi's daughter for beauty. Some said that she was of the colour of a ripe banana, others that she was like fossil gum, others like a reddish oil-nut, and others again that her face was more like the colour of the moon than anything else. The effect of this reputation was to bring nearly all the young chiefs in the land as suitors for her hand. Many of them would have been pleasing to the king, but the princess was averse to them, and she caused it to be made known that she would marry none save the young chief who could produce matako (brass rods) by polishing his teeth. The king was very much amused at this, but the chiefs stared in surprise as they heard it.

The king mustered the choicest young men of the land, and he told them it was useless for anyone to hope to be married to the princess unless he could drop brass rods by rubbing his teeth. Though they held it to be impossible that anyone could do such a thing, yet every one of them began to rub his teeth hard, and as they did so, lo! brass rods were seen to drop on the ground from the mouth of one of them, and the people gave a great shout for wonder at it.

The princess was then brought forward, and as the young chief rose to his feet he continued to rub his teeth, and the brass rods were heard to tinkle as they fell to the ground. The marriage was therefore duly proceeded with, and another round of feasts followed, for the king was rich in flocks of goats, and sheep, and in well-tilled fields and slaves.

But after the first moon had waned and gone, the husband said, "Come, now, let us depart, for Gumbi's land is no home for me."

And unknown to Gumbi they prepared for flight, and stowed their canoe with all things needful for a long journey, and one night soon after dark they embarked, and paddled down the river. One day the princess, while she was seated on her cushions, saw a curious nut floating near the canoe, upon which she sprang into the river to obtain it. It eluded her grasp. She swam after it, and the chief followed her as well as he was able, crying out to her to return to the canoe, as there were dangerous animals in the water. But she paid no heed to him, and continued to swim after the nut, until, when she had arrived opposite a village, the princess was hailed by an old woman, who cried, "Ho, princess, I have got what thou seekest. See." And she held the nut up in her hand. Then the princess stepped on shore, and her husband made fast his canoe to the bank.

"Give it to me," demanded the princess, holding out her hand.

"There is one thing thou must do for me before thou canst obtain it."

"What is that?" she asked.

"Thou must lay thy hands upon my bosom to cure me of my disease. Only thus canst thou have it," the old woman said.

The princess laid her hands upon her bosom, and as she did so the old woman was cured of her illness.

"Now thou mayest depart on thy journey, but remember what I tell thee. Thou and thy husband must cling close to this side of the river until thou comest abreast of an island which is in the middle of the entrance to a great lake. For the shore thou seekest is on this side. Once there thou wilt find peace and rest for many years. But if thou goest to the other side of the river thou wilt be lost, thou and thy husband."

Then they re-embarked, and the river ran straight and smooth before them. After some days they discovered that the side they were on was uninhabited, and that their provisions were exhausted, but the other side was cultivated, and possessed many villages and plantations. Forgetting the advice of the old woman, they crossed the river to the opposite shore, and they admired the beauty of the land, and joyed in the odours that came from the gardens and the plantations, and they dreamily listened to the winds that crumpled and tossed the great fronds of banana, and fancied that they had seen no sky so blue. And while they thus dreamed, lo! the river current was bearing them both swiftly along, and they saw the island which was at the entrance to the great lake, and in an instant the beauty of the land which had charmed them had died away, and they now heard the thunderous booming of waters, and saw them surging upward in great sweeps, and one great wave curved underneath them, and they were lifted up, up, up, and dropped down into the roaring abyss, and neither chief nor princess was ever seen again. They were both swallowed up in the deep.

What is the object of such a story? Why, to warn people from following their inclinations. Did not the girl find her father? Did not her father welcome her, and pardon the mother for very joy? Was not her own choice of a husband found for her? Was not the young chief fortunate in possessing such a beautiful wife? Why should they have become discontented? Why not have stayed at home instead of wandering into strange lands of which they knew nothing? Did not the old woman warn them of what would happen, and point to them how they might live in peace once again? But it was all to no purpose. We never know the value of anything until we have lost it. Ruin follows the wilful always. They left their home and took to the river, the river was not still, but moved on, and as their heads were already full of their own thoughts, they could not keep advice.

Out of the Mouths of Babes

(From the Bantu-speaking peoples of the Zambezi region, central-southeast Africa)

ONCE UPON A TIME there was a married couple who had two children. Not long after the birth of the second, the wife said she wanted to go and see her mother. The husband agreed, and they set out. It happened to be a time of famine, and they had little or nothing to eat, so when they came to a wild fig-tree by the wayside the man climbed it and began to shake down the fruit.

The wife and the elder child picked up the figs and ate them as fast as they fell. Presently there fell, among the rest, a particularly large and fine one. The husband called out: "My wife, do not eat that fig! If you do I will kill you." The wife, not without spirit, answered, "Hunger has no law. And, really, would you kill me, your wife, for a fig? I am eating it; let us see whether you dare kill me!"

She ate the fig, and her husband came down from the tree and picked up his spear.

"My fig! Where has it gone?" he said, pointing the weapon at her.

She answered, "I have eaten it."

He said not another word, but stabbed her. As she fell forward on her knees the baby she was carrying on her back stared at him over her shoulder. He took no notice, only saying, "My children, let us go now, as I have killed your mother."

The elder boy picked up his little brother and put him on his back. The baby, Katubi, looked behind him at the dead woman and began to cry. His brother sang:

"How can I silence Katubi?
Oh, my dear Katubi!
How can I silence Katubi?"

The father asked him what he was saying, but he said, "I am not speaking; it is only baby crying." The father said, "Let us go on. You shall eat when you get there." They went on and on, and at last the baby himself began to sing:

"Silence Katubi!
My brother has become my mother!"

That is, he is carrying him on his back, as his mother had been doing.

The father heard it, and, thinking it was the elder boy who sang, said, "What are you talking about, you little wretch? I am going to kill you. What, are you going to tell tales when we get to your grandmother's?" The child, terrified, said, "No! I won't say anything!"

Still they went on, and the baby kept looking behind him, and after a while began again:

"What a lot of vultures
Over the fig-tree at Maya's!
What a lot of vultures!"

And he cried again. The father asked, "What are you crying for?" and the boy said that he was not crying; he was only trying to quiet the baby. The man, looking back, saw a number of vultures hovering over the place he had left, and as he did so he heard the song again:

"What a lot of vultures!"

The boy, when asked once more why the baby was crying, answered, "He is crying for Mother!" And the father said, "Nonsense! Let us get on. You're going to see your grandmother!"

The same incident was repeated, till the father, in a rage, turned back and began beating both the children. The boy asked, "Are you going to kill me, as you killed Mother?" The furious man shouted, "I do mean to kill you!" However, he held his hand for the moment, and the boy slipped past him and went on in front, and presently the baby's voice was heard again:

"What a lot of vultures!"

They reached the village at last, and the man exchanged greetings with his mother-in-law. He seems to have failed to satisfy her when she inquired after his wife, for, on the first opportunity, she questioned the little boy: "Now where has your mother been left?" The child shook his head, and did not speak for a while. Then he said, "Do you expect to see Mother? She has been killed by Father – all for the sake of a wild fruit!"

At the same moment the baby began to sing:

"What a lot of vultures!"

The grandmother must have been convinced by this portent, for she questioned the boy no further, but only said, "Stop, Baby! We are just going to kill your father also!" She set some men to dig a deep, narrow hole inside the hut, while she prepared the porridge. When the hole was ready she had a mat spread over it, and then brought in the porridge and sent the boy to call his father to supper. The guilty man came in, saw the mat spread in what appeared to be the best place, and immediately sat down on it. The grandmother had large pots of boiling water ready, and as soon as he had fallen into the hole they poured it over him and killed him.